The

Pre-Nup

PRENUPTIAL AGREEME

Beth Kendrick

A Bantam Discovery

THE PRE-NUP
A Bantam Discovery Book / December 2008

Published by Bantam Dell
A Division of Random House, Inc.
New York, New York

This is a work of fiction. Names, characters, places, and incidents either are the product of the author's imagination or are used fictitiously. Any resemblance to actual persons, living or dead, events, or locales is entirely coincidental.

Library of Congress Catalog Card Number: 2008034916

Bantam Books and the rooster colophon are registered trademarks and Bantam Discovery is a trademark of Random House, Inc.

ISBN 978-0-553-59150-7

Printed in the United States of America

www.bantamdell.com

OPM 10 9 8 7 6 5 4 3 2 1

Praise for
BETH KENDRICK'S NOVELS

Nearlyweds

"A fun and funny look at marriage, commitment, and figuring out what your next best step is ... whether it be down the aisle or not."

—Alison Pace, author of *Through Thick and Thin* and *Pug Hill*

"Very funny."

—Carole Matthews, author of *The Chocolate Lovers' Club*

Fashionably Late

"Wickedly clever." —*Booklist*

"Kendrick gives chick lit clichés an adroit turn."
—*Publishers Weekly*

"Kendrick's keen sense of humor and pitch-perfect gift for dialogue are excellent accessories to this fun and frothy tale."
—*Chicago Tribune*

Exes and Ohs

"Breaking up is hard to do, but *Exes and Ohs* is hilarious! You won't be able to put this book down."

—Cara Lockwood, author of *I Did (But I Wouldn't Now)*

My Favorite Mistake

"Absolutely fabulous! Beth Kendrick is a major new talent."
—Melissa Senate, author of *Love You to Death* and *See Jane Date*

"A laugh-out-loud treat as frothy and appealing as a raspberry sorbet." —*BookPage*

This one's for my dad, who's given me lots of good advice over the years:

"Bridge freezes first,"
"The more you do, the more you do,"
and, of course,
"Always get it in writing."

Many thanks to . . .

Estate attorney Dick Bredemann, who talked me
through the whys and wherefores of pre-nups and
suggested some truly diabolical ways to leave your
lover.

Joe "Sucks!" Lavin, who was equally adept at answering
my legal questions and getting annoying songs stuck
in my head.

Danielle Perez, editor extraordinaire, whose insight and
finesse brought out the best in this book.

Meg Ruley and Christina Hogrebe, who agent with
grace, charm, and ninjalike skill.

Lynn Andreozzi and the art department at Bantam, who
created the kind of cover every author hopes for.

Barbara Ankrum and Kresley Cole, who cheered me on
and talked me down and always picked up the
phone, even when they knew it was me calling. *Again.*

And my eternally supportive husband, who came up
with the name "Noda" during an eleven P.M. dog
walk. Honey, you're a genius.

Ellie

Chapter 1

"Another exciting, exhilarating extravaganza. And I am *exhausted*." Ellie Barton rubbed her eyes and smiled up at her husband as he held open the door between the garage and the house. "Smudged mascara never felt so good."

"You know you love organizing these black-tie shindigs." Michael smiled back and dropped a kiss onto her forehead. "Admit it."

"It is nice to get out of jeans and sneakers," Ellie admitted. "See a bit of the world beyond Gymboree and Tumbling Tots. Talk about something besides Curious George and imaginary friends named Moodle."

"And you're a natural at it. My mom says you're turning into quite the society queen."

"I don't know about that," Ellie demurred. Her voice was still hoarse from straining to be heard over the brass band. "But I'm learning from the master. Fund-raising is the toughest committee, but your mother can get blood from a stone and not spill a single drop on her Escada. I just scurry around and do her bidding and everything magically falls into place."

"Any excuse to buy more Escada," Michael translated.

"Be nice. It's all for a good cause." Ellie furrowed her brow. "Wait. What was tonight?"

"Heart disease." Michael loosened his bow tie and reached under his tuxedo sleeves to unfasten his cuff links. "Next week is domestic violence, and next month is cancer."

"Right." She paused to clear her throat. "You know, I was thinking, it's great that we organize these galas to raise money and awareness and all, but I'm sure the women's shelter could use some hands-on volunteers, too. Once Hannah starts preschool five days a week, I could commit to that."

Her husband dropped back a step and asked, "Commit to what?"

"Whatever they need. Administrative stuff, sorting out donations, childcare... I'd like to really get involved."

Michael picked up the pace as they rounded the corner from the side hallway to their home's foyer. "Sweetheart, believe me, getting the Mayfair Estates crowd sloshed enough to write a big stack of checks is by far the best way to help that shelter. Besides, you know how much business I get through these committee connections." He threw her a wink. "The mortgage's not going to pay itself."

Ellie glanced up at the massive, custom-made crystal chandelier Michael's mother had commissioned from an artisan in France. "Right. We're one step away from living in a refrigerator carton under the freeway." She extracted a small tube of hand sanitizer from her evening bag. "Could you pay the baby-sitter? I'm going to go check on Hannah."

"I'll check on Hannah. You relax." Michael steered her into the master suite. "And lay off the Purell, woman, before we have to sign you up for a twelve-step program."

"Go ahead, mock me. But it's the height of flu season, and some of those city councilmen we shook hands with? Not exactly the picture of personal hygiene."

He grinned and kissed her freshly disinfected fingertips. "Howard Hughes in high heels."

"Speaking of high heels..." Ellie made her way across the bedroom and into the huge, mirrored bathroom, where she collapsed onto a carved antique rosewood stool and kicked off her strappy stilettos. She curled her toes against the cool travertine floor. "Ahh. Sweet relief."

Michael met her gaze in the mirror and shook his head. "I will never understand why you insist on wearing those things to events where you're expected to be on your feet for five hours. Aren't you in pain?"

"A little," she admitted. "But they look good. And I need all the help I can get these days."

"You look beautiful," he said immediately, and, Ellie noticed, a bit absently.

Not that she blamed him. She knew she was guilty of the cardinal sin of their exclusive gated community: she'd let herself go. Not entirely, not all at once, but since giving birth to their daughter three years ago, she'd abandoned the strict exercise, makeup, and moisturizer regimen of her early twenties. She was just too busy to devote all day, every day to the pursuit of personal perfection. The first crinkles of crow's feet were encroaching at the corners of her eyes. Breast-feeding had taken an undeniable toll on her figure. And sometimes she would spend an entire morning running errands and shuttling her daughter between play groups before noticing a coffee stain on her cardigan.

Michael caught her frown in the mirror. "What's wrong?"

"Nothing." She stifled a small sigh. "Do you ever wish I'd get a little, you know, work done? Botox? Tummy tuck?"

"Don't start with that again." He rested his warm hands on her shoulders, then tugged at her zipper to peek at the label of her dress. "Size ten? Someone call Jenny Craig, stat!"

Her cheeks flushed. "Don't make fun of me! I'm the only double-digit-wearing woman under sixty in this whole neighborhood. Compared to all the second and third wives at the country club, I'm a——"

"You're a hell of a lot more interesting than the Stepford sorority," Michael assured her. "You're an original. First edition!"

"I don't want to be interesting. I want to be sexy and beguiling, and . . . God." She folded her arms on the bathroom counter and rested her chin on her hands. "I'm just so *tired.*"

"Sweetheart, come on, you know you—— Hang on." Michael broke off as a loud buzzing noise emanated from his tuxedo pants pocket. He extracted a small silver

PDA, squinted down at the screen, then tapped at the keyboard. "Work. Hang on."

Ellie scrunched up her nose. "Again? How can anyone be thinking about real estate at this hour on a Friday night?"

"No one's thinking about real estate right now; they're thinking about the golf course where we're going to discuss the development deal tomorrow morning. We have to change our tee time." He placed the PDA on the bathroom counter next to her evening bag and returned his attention to her. "Now. Back to you. Where were we?"

She glowered at her own reflection. "I was bemoaning my lack of Stepford sultriness."

"Listen to me. You're the perfect wife. Especially when you're all charming like tonight, making small talk with the new investor about—who's that writer? Henry James?"

"Henry Fielding," Ellie corrected.

"See? Brilliant to boot. I rest my case." He emptied his pants pockets and peeled a pair of twenties from his engraved money clip. With his broad shoulders and dimpled smile, he was the epitome of tall, dark, and debonair.

Her scowl melted into a smile. "Did I ever tell you that you look like James Bond when you go black-tie?"

"Every time I break out this monkey suit. And that is why I married you. Sit tight, relax, and I'll drive Shannon home. Oh, as long as I'm out, I better fill up your car. Don't want you running out of gas tomorrow while you and Hannah hit the birthday party circuit."

Emboldened by his praise and loath to let a new dress and a professional hair-and-makeup job go to waste, Ellie sat up and blew him a kiss. "Maybe I'll take a nice hot bath and get warmed up for when you come home?"

His eyebrows shot up a fraction of an inch. "That's quite an offer. But I thought you were sleep-deprived?"

"Sleep is for the weak and the childless. That's why God invented caffeine. Besides, it's not every day a girl gets her chance with James Bond."

They heard footsteps in the hall, and Michael glanced down at his watch. "I should really get Shannon home. I promised her mom she'd be back by eleven. And listen, about the bath...hold that thought. Next weekend we'll leave Hannah with my mom and get a suite at the Fairmont. Order room service, get a massage..."

"It's a date." She quashed a twinge of disappointment.

"Baby, just wait 'til I get you alone. We are going to sleep *all night long* 'til we can't sleep no more." He jingled his car keys as he headed down the hall.

Ellie waited until she heard the door close, then shimmied out of her sequined black silk gown and turned on the faucet of the enormous jetted bathtub in the center of the room. She poured in some vanilla-scented bath oil, stripped off her bra and panties, and had one foot in the tub when Michael's PDA vibrated off the edge of the counter and onto the floor.

She was shocked he'd left it there. He prided himself on being accessible to his clients at all times. The tiny red light on the top of the screen was blinking insistently, so Ellie pulled her foot back out of the bathwater and minced across the room, hoping that the plastic casing hadn't cracked from the fall.

"You have one message waiting," the screen announced. Then an ominous exclamation point appeared. "URGENT!"

Her eyes widened. What if this was an emergency? A lot of Michael's clients had attended tonight's bash and most of them were as impatient as they were wealthy. She'd have to figure out how to get in touch with him right away. She clicked the scroll wheel.

To: mbarton007
From: Vixen_MD
Mick—
You KNOW I'm always up for that. I'm wearing the red thong you gave me. Get over here and rip it off. Meet you in 5 minutes. Make me moan.

Ellie stood motionless for a full minute, blinking down at the screen until the letters blurred together into one mottled gray blob.

Make me moan.

This had to be a mistake. First of all, no one ever called Michael "Mick." He hated nicknames of any kind; even "Mike" was verboten.

Secondly...no. Just no. There was no way. Not Michael. Not her. System failure. Syntax error. Please reboot and download program again.

There were plenty of philandering husbands in Mayfair Estates, but Michael was the exception. Not that he'd never had the opportunity to cheat—she wasn't *that* naïve—but he just wasn't that kind of guy. He loved his family, his work, and his golf clubs, in that order. He looked forward to their regular Sunday dinners with his parents and he called Ellie twice daily when he was out of town on business. Just last week, when he'd been in California on Valentine's Day, he'd had lilies delivered for her and a big stuffed penguin for Hannah.

But had he really been in California?

Ellie slowly raised her gaze to the mirror. She hardly recognized herself, trembling and naked, clutching the little silver square with both hands. Steam from the hot bathwater started to fog the reflection, but she could see angry pink lines lingering on her skin where her strapless bra and long, body-shaping underpants had cut into her flesh.

The words "red thong" flashed through her mind. Red thongs were for women totally devoid of insecurities and C-section scars. A red thong wouldn't hold in your stomach—it would emphasize your curves. Red thongs were for, well, vixens.

Vixen_MD. What the hell did that even mean, anyway?

And mbarton007? James Bond was *Ellie's* thing, a silly private joke they'd bandied about their marriage for years.

This was insane. Things like this only happened in movies and sudsy TV dramas. Vixens and red thongs were sordid subplots from someone else's life.

She took a deep breath and scrolled back through the message file to search for previous conversations between mbarton007 and Vixen_MD:

I'm so hot... Want you in the shower... I think I pulled something last night...

Finally, she couldn't bear to read any more. She placed the PDA back on the countertop where she'd found it. When she turned back to the mirror, she realized she'd forgotten to take off her diamond and emerald earrings.

Michael's mother had given Ellie the emeralds—the proverbial family jewels—on the night before her wedding, to welcome her to the Barton family. Her in-laws had treated her like a daughter since the moment she promised to love, cherish, and honor their son. Even though she was an Army brat with fashion sense that ran more toward secondhand stores than Saks, Michael's parents had never once insinuated that Ellie was anything less than their equal. They had opened the doors to Scottsdale society and made her feel secure in the cultured, cutthroat world in which Michael had grown up.

Ellie unclipped her earrings, stowed them carefully in their velvet box, and hurried toward the wall safe in the huge walk-in closet. Sealed inside these cold metal walls lay irrefutable proof that she and Michael and Hannah were a family: wills, passports, a copy of the lengthy prenuptial agreement she'd signed when she and Michael got engaged.

She spun the combination lock, opened the safe, and put the emerald earrings next to the rectangular cases that contained the matching necklace and bracelet. Her pinky finger brushed the pre-nup and she snatched her hand away as if burned. Then she slammed the safe shut, turned off all the lights, and climbed into the bathtub, which by now was full to the brim. Vanilla-scented water sloshed over onto the slick marble tiles as she submerged herself up to her chin and listened to the overflow drain's steady, slurping gurgle.

She soaked for what felt like hours, staring into the dark, waiting for the familiar whirr of the garage door opening.

Jen

Chapter 2

So? What did he have to say for himself?" Jen Finnerty demanded the next morning as she, Ellie, and Mara Stroebel power-walked the three-mile circuit around the Mayfair Estates golf course. The rising sun was still cresting over the mountains, and the women had bundled up in windbreakers and sweatpants against the cool Arizona winter morning.

"Nothing." Ellie faltered in her stride and took off her baseball cap, revealing bloodshot eyes ringed with faint purple half-moons. Her thick brown hair was gathered into a sloppy ponytail and her cheeks were sunken and pale despite the chilly breeze. Jen had always considered Ellie the optimist among them—she exuded a wholesome, girl-next-door sweetness—but today she looked utterly defeated. "I didn't know what to do. I stayed in the tub until the water got cold, and then I got into bed. He came in an hour later, and I just lay there, pretending to be asleep. Then this morning...I think I'm in shock."

"That would explain why your shoes don't match," Mara agreed.

Ellie stared down at her feet. Her left foot sported a white Nike, while her right was laced into a red Saucony. "Oh. Oops."

Jen shot Mara a filthy look, then squeezed Ellie's elbow. "Of course you're in shock, honey. Of course. Hell, *I'm* in shock. You and Michael are—"

"The perfect couple," Ellie finished dully. "A match made in heaven."

Jen winced. "You guys did seem happy together."

"Oh, we're ecstatic. Except for when he sneaks out at eleven o'clock at night to rip a red thong off some cyberslut." Ellie shook her head and lifted her chin. "Look, we don't have to talk about this now. I know you guys are busy and I'm supposed to be hitting you up for help with the cancer benefit."

"Screw the benefit. We'll get to that later." Mara pulled her long, shiny platinum blond hair back into a ballerina's knot. Despite what she often described as her "stultifying" job as a trust and estate attorney, she always looked like she could be starring in a prime-time courtroom drama. Even in their college days, Mara had had an air of total certainty and self-possession—except when it came to men—and while Jen refused to be bossed around, Ellie wasn't always so resolute.

"This is a code red, all-hands-on-deck emergency," Mara declared. "So let's get down to business. What are you going to do?"

Ellie waved her hands in vague loops. "I'm not sure yet."

Mara was having none of this. "Well, he doesn't know that you know yet, right?"

"*I* don't even know exactly what I know," Ellie said. "I mean, yes, obviously he's up to something, but I don't know with who or for how long or why—"

"The important thing is that you've busted him and he doesn't know it yet. You've got the upper hand!" Mara's blue eyes gleamed. "Now you can get all your ducks in a row before you make your move. You're going to take him for everything he's got. He'll end up penniless and alone, begging you to take him back, but you'll spit on—"

"Excuse me," Jen finally broke in. "When did this turn into a bad honky-tonk song?"

"If it were a honky-tonk song, she'd just grab his shotgun off the front porch and blow him away," Mara said. "Listen, El, here's what you do: First, install a keystroke logger on his computer, get all his passwords, and keep track of the messages going to and from this Vixen_MD harlot. Second, call your cell provider and get copies of his phone records for the last six months. In the meantime, I'll help you find a positively rabid divorce attorney. Oh, and don't forget to make photocopies of all your tax returns and investment portfolio and put them in a safe place. And you might want to make an appointment with your doctor for STD testing, just to be on the safe side."

"Mara! A little tact, please!" Jen admonished.

"I'm giving her good advice, free of charge. Tact is your department."

"Shut up before she passes out." Jen regarded her friend with growing concern. "Ellie? Honey? Are you okay?"

Ellie was still staring down at her shoes. Her complexion had taken on an alarming green undertone.

Jen shucked off her sweatshirt and spread it on the dewy grass next to the asphalt path. "Here, sit down. Put your head between your knees. Do you want me to get you some water?"

Ellie sank to the ground, swallowed hard, and said, "No, I'm okay. But Mara's right. I have to get it together and figure out what I'm going to do."

Jen shook her head. "You don't have to decide anything right now. Take all the time you need. We're here. We'll support you, no matter what."

"Yeah, we're here for you." Mara flashed Jen a discreet thumbs-up and mouthed, "Tact!"

Ellie emitted a strangled bleat that was half laugh, half sob. "Well, I have to leave him. Right? He cheated on me. An affair is a deal breaker; everyone knows that."

"Calm down." Jen squeezed Ellie's shoulder. "Breathe."

Ellie gulped for air. "If you had asked me twenty-four hours ago what I'd do if I found that text message, I'd have said 'Drop him flat.' Wouldn't hesitate. But now . . . it's not that simple. I mean, what about Hannah? She's only three! What's the good-mother thing to do here? Stay, so she has an intact family, or leave, so she sees me as a strong, independent role model?"

"You have to do what's right for you," Jen said. "No one else can make this decision for you."

Ellie turned to her with wide, wild eyes. "What would you do?"

Jen coughed to stall for time. "If I found out Eric was having an affair?"

"Apples and oranges," Mara objected. "Jen wouldn't care if Eric were having an affair."

"Don't say that! Of course she would!" But Ellie looked a bit dubious when she whispered to Jen, "You would, wouldn't you?"

Jen knelt down to retie her shoelace. "I, um...Look, we're not talking about me."

They heard the distant thwack of a golf club, and Mara threw her arms up to shield her face.

"Relax." Jen laughed and pointed out the foursome across the fairway. "They're not even aiming in our direction."

"I can't even tell you how many times I've almost been clocked in the head out here," Mara said. "And I'm sure I'm not the only one. This golf course is a personal-injury lawsuit in the making, I tell you."

"I have to confront him." Ellie dusted off her palms and got back on her feet. "It's the only way. I'll tell him exactly what I found and demand that he—"

"No!" Mara shook her head so fast, her hair came free and whapped her cheeks. "Do not give him a heads-up. You want the element of surprise on your side."

"Screw the element of surprise." Ellie squared her shoulders. "I just want answers. I want brutal honesty."

"Then hire a private investigator! Get dates, names, photos, whatever you need. But don't confront him until you have enough evidence to nail his balls to the wall."

"You are crazy hard-core," Jen marveled. "Remind me never to cross you."

"I'm just getting started," Mara shot back. "Ellie can't

think rationally right now, so someone has to look out for her best interests. I.e., me."

"No. I can do this by myself." Ellie started walking again, gathering speed and indignation with every step. "He's my husband and I will handle him." She was practically running now. "I'm smart, I'm strong, I—I'll unleash the bitch within!"

Jen and Mara exchanged dismayed looks as they hurried after her.

"Maybe you're right," Jen murmured. "She's too emotional right now."

"Well, she's madly in love with her husband." Mara said this with genuine sympathy and then added, with even greater sympathy, "It's not like with you and Eric."

Mara was wrong, Jen chanted over and over in her head as she headed home after the walk. *Mara was wrong.*

She did love Eric; she had for years. Was it a storybook romance bursting at the seams with fate and soulmates and all that Cinderella crap? Of course not. But what they had was better in the long run: a rock-solid relationship that could go the distance. No drama. No surprises.

No one home. Jen twisted her key in the lock and dashed over the threshold to punch in the code on the alarm panel. Bright golden sunlight poured into the foyer through the skylight above the glass tile mosaic inlaid on the floor.

"Hello?" she called down the hall. "Lotus? Here, kitty, kitty."

But the plump black cat didn't appear. Lotus was a former stray, now spoiled rotten and selectively deaf (though he could hear the metal scrape of a can opener from a hundred yards).

Jen kicked off her damp sneakers, padded into the kitchen, and pried open the massive stainless-steel refrigerator doors. The muted hum of the appliance motor was the only sound in the house. Four bedrooms, an office, a living room, a dining room, a family room, a three-car garage, and a huge in-ground pool all to herself, plus a master bathroom big enough to play racquetball in. (The Mayfair Estates crowd was very big on status bathrooms.)

She grabbed the remote control on the countertop and clicked on the small television next to the microwave. The chirpy patter of a morning talk show kept her company as she spooned some cottage cheese into a bowl, then added plain yogurt and a sprinkling of whole-grain oat cereal for texture. High protein, high calcium, and lots of complex carbohydrates. She curled up in one of the wrought-iron kitchen chairs and gazed through the French doors toward the golf course. This was shaping up to be a perfect Scottsdale Saturday: sunny and mellow with a hint of early spring warmth. Other women in the neighborhood were probably getting ready to play tennis or go shopping or... do whatever it was normal suburban wives did with their husbands on the weekends.

Jen ate slowly, gazed out at a pair of golfers trying to pitch their way out of a sand trap, and tried to figure out why she wasn't looking forward to an afternoon of solid, uninterrupted work time. It wasn't as if she had no other options. If she wanted to, she could give herself the afternoon off to go to the movie theater or the spa. She could get her short, wavy blond hair dyed auburn or buy a whole new wardrobe. She could do something wild and spur-of-the-moment.

And yet.

Five minutes later, she rinsed out her dish, trudged into her cluttered home office, and fired up the PC. She opened a series of data files and glanced at the latest sales reports for Noda, the health drink she'd spent the better part of a decade creating and marketing. She'd just hired a new sales rep and a publicist, and wanted to make sure the expenditure was paying off. Her company was her passion—her *obsession*, according to Ellie and Mara. But no matter how Jen tried to focus on the numbers, she couldn't keep herself on-task today. Finally, she turned away from the screen and dialed the cordless phone.

"Hey, honey," she said when Eric picked up. "How's New York?"

"Frigid and claustrophobic. How's the weather there?" Her husband sounded distant and distracted, but business travel exhausted him, so Jen chalked it up to the strain of too many time zone changes and room service meals.

Jen sighed. "Gorgeous. As usual. Do you have a minute to chat?"

"I think I can pull myself away from the division account books." His tone was wry. The year after Jen founded Noda, Eric had passed the CPA exam and worked his way up to head auditor for a telecommunications firm headquartered in Phoenix. As the company expanded, so had his responsibilities, and he spent an increasing amount of time out of town, meeting with regional accounting staffs. Eric's job was definitely *not* his passion (he often joked that his response to "And what do you do?" would kill any cocktail party conversation in under sixty seconds), but so far he'd resisted looking for other positions.

"What's up with you?" he asked. "Let me take a wild guess: you're working?"

She paused, making a concerted effort not to tense up. "Just going over the new sales reports."

"It's like I'm psychic."

"Either that or I'm incredibly boring and predictable." She summoned all her nerve, and forged ahead. "But listen, I have an idea. Do you want me to fly out there?"

"Where, New York?"

"Well, yeah." She laughed, suddenly girlish and flustered. "I could go on-line right now and book a flight. Be there by midnight."

"Tonight? Really?"

He didn't have to sound *so* startled. "Why not? Surely they don't expect you to work all weekend?"

"Well, no, but I figured since it's such a long flight back and I have so much left to do out here, I'd just stay at the hotel until—"

"Perfect timing, then," she said. "We're always saying we should go somewhere together, take a real vacation."

Eric cleared his throat.

"Oh, forget it," she said. "That's stupid, right? I know. You're reading reports and overseeing things and, uh . . . auditing. You don't have time for—"

"No, no," he stammered. "Come on out. It'll be great. We'll go see a show or something. Be total tourists. Take a carriage ride in Central Park."

"Never mind. I don't know what got into me." Jen gnawed the inside of her cheek. "I have a lot going on out here. And besides, someone has to feed the cat."

"Right, the cat." Another long pause. "Well. I know you're working."

"I am, indeed," she said brightly. "And so are you. We'll do it some other time. Plan something really special."

"Absolutely. Go someplace exotic."

"Tahiti, maybe. Or the Canary Islands."

"Whatever you want." His voice was flat.

"I'll look up resorts on-line," she promised, but she knew—and so did Eric—that this mythical vacation was never going to materialize.

Another agonizing silence ensued. Jen squirmed in her cushy leather desk chair.

"Okay. Well, you're busy," he said. "I'll let you go."

"Stay warm!" She flinched at her own forced joviality. "Have a fresh bagel with lox for me."

"Will do. Love you."

"Love you, too."

And that, she told herself sternly as she hung up the phone, would have to be enough. Eric was a good husband, and Jen tried hard to be a good wife, but the truth loomed between them, unspoken but undeniable: They loved each other, but they weren't in love.

She clicked back to her data files, but couldn't process

the information splashed across the computer screen. The burn of shame and failure spread through her body. No way could she sit still. She snatched the phone back up and paced back and forth across the study. First she dialed Ellie's number, but her call went straight to voice mail. Presumably, Ellie was too embroiled in an epic marital showdown to answer right now.

Then she tried Mara, who picked up on the second ring.

"Hey, babe, shouldn't you be working?"

Jen stopped in her tracks. "Hey! I don't work *all* the time, you know."

"Just when you're awake," Mara amended. "My mistake."

"How can you say that? I just saw you a few hours ago. And did I say one word about Noda? No, I did not. I have a life, okay? I have—"

"All right, all right, simmer down there. You don't have to justify yourself to me. Nothing wrong with getting out there and making a little cheddar."

"That's right," Jen huffed. "Damn straight."

"I'm so glad you're not defensive. Jeez."

"I'm not defensive; I'm merely pointing out—"

"Oh, let's not argue, little worker bee. What's up? How may I help you on this fine, sunny afternoon?"

"Well, actually, I'm a little..." Jen stopped before she had to spit out the word *lonely*. "Do you want to get together later? Catch a movie or something?"

"Sounds great, but I'll have to take a rain check. Josh and I are picking out wedding bands as we speak."

Jen automatically glanced down at the diamond sparkling away on her left hand, a reminder of the promise
she and Eric had made to always stay hopeful and happy.
"Aw. Are you having fun?"

"Jewelry shopping is my personal definition of fun.
And, hey, while we're on the subject of fun, want me to
schedule an appointment with the bridal salon to finalize
the bridesmaids' dress selection next weekend?"

"Ooh, be still my heart. I'll be counting the minutes."

"You just earned yourself an extra-poufy butt bow,
missy." Mara suddenly sounded louder, as if she'd cupped
her hand over the phone's mouthpiece. "Oh, and I didn't
want to say anything in front of Ellie this morning, but
rumor has it that a certain tall, dark, and handsome doctor without borders has been spotted back in town."

Jen stopped breathing.

"Hello? Jennifer? Is this thing on?"

Jen clenched her fingers around the smooth alder
planks of her desktop. "I'm here."

"No confirmed sightings, but I figured I should warn
you before you ran into him in a restaurant or something
and had an aneurysm and died before your time."

"I appreciate that," Jen said stiffly, "but I couldn't care
less. That whole fiasco is ancient history, and we will
never speak of it again."

"Okay, but if you do happen to cross paths with
him—"

"I won't."

"Right, but if you ever want to talk—"

"What part of 'we will never speak of it again' is not
clear?" Jen flinched at the sharp serration in her tone.

"And don't mention any of this to Eric. We're working through some stuff right now, and if he hears Patrick's back..."

"Have no fear," Mara assured her. "My lips are sealed."

Mara *Chapter* 3

*W*e'd like to see something with diamonds. Lots of diamonds," Josh told the bespectacled salesman at Paradise Valley Fine Jewelry. "Think P. Diddy."

Mara choked on the breath mint she'd popped in her mouth just before entering the store. "But tasteful."

"Taste, schmaste. Bring on the bling. Only the best for my bride." Josh beamed. So did the sharp-featured salesman with the terrible brown toupee.

"Please, have a seat." He introduced himself as Roger and ushered them over to the matching beige settees in the back corner of the shop. "May I get you something to drink? Water? Coffee? Champagne?"

"Booze and diamonds," Mara mused. "Could be a dangerous combination."

"I like the way you think," Josh said. "Two glasses of champagne, please." Roger rushed off, all but rubbing his hands together in anticipation of the drunken shopping spree about to ensue.

Mara collapsed on the love seat and pressed Josh's

hand between both of hers. "I appreciate the sentiment, I do, but you already bought me the world's most gorgeous engagement ring. We don't have to go crazy with the wedding rings. I'm fine with a simple gold band."

Josh sat down next to her. "Let me ask you a question: How many of the lawyers at your firm have plain gold bands?"

"Well." She shrugged. "All the men do."

"And the women?"

Mara couldn't deny that the ladies at Johnson, Lavin & Hein, LLP, liked their luxe. Everyone from the office assistants to the equity partners was relegated to subdued dark suits, and engagement rings were one of the few acceptable vestiges of conspicuous consumption. So skating rinks in six-prong settings had become de rigueur around the conference table.

"Uh…"

He extricated his fingers from her grasp and squeezed her knee. "Don't you deserve the best?"

NO was Mara's immediate response to this question. But she knew better than to dredge up the past, so she simply smiled and cooed, "I already have the best: you."

They were midway through a leisurely kiss when Roger *ahem*ed behind them. Mara pulled away from Josh and accepted the plastic flute of sparkling wine the salesman proffered. She and Josh touched their glasses together with a dull thunk.

Roger allotted them half a second to savor the romance of the moment, then whipped out a tray full of rings and got right down to business. "These are our eternity bands; diamonds all the way around. We just got this one in last week. The stones are Asscher-cut. Excellent color and clarity. It would complement your engagement ring perfectly."

It would also cost a fortune. Mara didn't know exactly how much Josh had spent on her engagement ring, but she recognized quality when she saw it. His salary as a nonprofit advisor only stretched so far. And when she thought about all their financial goals for the future: travel, having children and putting them through college, retirement...

"Very nice." She glanced at the ring, but didn't pick it up. "But do you have anything a little less, uh, flashy?"

Roger's ingratiating simper wilted. "What did you have in mind?"

She stood up and started scanning the display cases. "I want something understated but chic." She paused and tapped the polished glass. "Something like that."

Roger sighed. "The tiny sapphires?"

"I like the blue." Mara nodded. "Gives the whole thing a little kick."

"Matches your eyes," Josh said.

She and Josh indulged in another totally shameless public display of affection while the salesman grudgingly unlocked the display case and pulled out the sapphire-studded band. "I'll give you two a moment," he said, then escaped to find more commission-worthy prey.

"You realize, of course, that we're making people physically ill," Mara murmured.

"Uh-huh." Josh's lips smiled against hers.

"We're the couple that everyone hates."

He started kissing his way down toward her neck. "They're just jealous."

"I told you booze and jewelry was a dangerous combo." She slid her hand underneath his dark green wool jacket, where her fingers encountered a bulky lump in the lining's inner pocket. "What's this?"

"Oh." He ran his hands through his hair as she extracted a thick sheaf of folded papers. "That's just the new draft of the pre-nup. I was going to give it back to you earlier, but this didn't really seem to be the right time. Kind of kills the mood, you know?"

"Don't be like that." Mara kept her smile flirty and her tone light. "There's no need to feel weird about it. I know it's annoying and uptight and all, but—"

"Yeah, yeah. You attorneys. Always with the worst-case scenarios." Josh's smile faded. "Doesn't it seem a little defeatist to be talking about divorce before we're even married?"

"No," she said firmly. "It's not defeatist at all. It's just common sense. A mere formality." Mara had always believed that couples like Josh and herself—couples who were going to make it to their golden anniversary and beyond—had nothing to fear from a fair and sensible contract protecting the assets they'd accumulated before they said "I do."

"Yeah, well." He scuffed at the carpet with the toe of his black leather Rockports. "I got a lawyer to look over the PDF file you sent, and he basically said the same thing you did: standard stuff, very straightforward."

"So we're all set? Then let's move on to more pressing

matters. Like our honeymoon." She put her hand back on his chest.

"Well ..." Josh still wouldn't meet her eyes. "We're almost all set. My guy reworded a few sentences for clarification, added a short clause or two, nothing major."

"Nothing major?" Mara narrowed her eyes as her bullshit detector kicked into high gear. "Like what, exactly?"

"All his changes are in red ink. Look, let's do this later. Right now, we'll get back to picking out rings and—"

She skimmed through the dense legalese with practiced efficiency. "Okay ... fine ... okay ... Hold up." Her eyes widened as she spied a brand-new clause inserted at the end of the pre-nup's third page. "What the *hell* is this?"

Mara had never had a panic attack—she always preferred fight over flight—but for a few paralyzing seconds, she honestly thought she might pass out right there on the plush green carpet. Her palms started to sweat, her heart raced, and the only thing that kept her on her feet was the thought of Roger's big furry head looming over her to administer CPR.

Josh's voice sounded distant. "Sweetie, are you okay?"

She staggered backward, swaying on her high-heeled boots.

"Don't get upset, I can explain."

"You don't have to explain anything!" Her hip slammed into the glass counter and she knew she'd develop a bruise later, but right now, the pain didn't even register. "I can read it for myself in black and white. Jesus. Josh, this is really what you think of me?"

"Wait, you're missing the point here." He reached out for her hands, but she balled her fingers into fists.

"No, I get the point. Right through the heart. I—" She swiped at her eyes, horrified to realize that she was about to tear up. She hadn't cried in years, hadn't even come close since her first semester of law school, when her voice had cracked at the end of a blistering Socratic cross-examination during Civil Procedure. "Why did you even propose to me? Honestly?"

"Mara, come on..."

She pivoted, stalked past the trays of glittering jewels, shoved her way out through the glass doors, and whipped out her cell phone as she hit the sidewalk.

"Hey," she said when Jen answered. "Remember how I said I was booked solid this afternoon? Change of plans. I'm coming over right now, and I'm going to need about three bottles of wine when I get there. Brace yourself. You are not going to *believe* what just happened."

Ellie

Chapter
4

"Where's Daddy? I want Daddy," Hannah whined from the backseat of Ellie's BMW.

Ellie exhaled slowly and white-knuckled the SUV's steering wheel. "Daddy's working, baby. You know that. He'll be home for dinner."

At least, she hoped he would. "I'm playing nine holes with the guys from the Oro Vista Center deal," he'd announced in the kitchen that morning after she returned from her walk with Mara and Jen. "Maybe eighteen if we have time. See you around six-thirty?"

And then he'd poured some of her freshly brewed coffee into an insulated travel mug and breezed out the door. She'd stared after him, contemplating Mara's advice about tax returns and keystroke loggers, until Hannah tugged on her hand and demanded waffles for breakfast. Then she'd gotten them both dressed and plodded with her daughter through the Saturday crowds at the grocery store and the post office. She had one last stop to make on today's suburbanista tour of duty: the bank. There was certainly no harm in making a list of the contents of all the accounts and the safety deposit box before ... well, before things got even more out of hand.

It's just a little preemptive photocopying, she told herself. *And they're my accounts, too. He's the one who should feel guilty, not me.*

For once, she was going to let her head overrule her heart. Then tonight, after she'd tucked Hannah into bed, she'd confront Michael and they could discuss this like rational adults. Well, "rational adults" might be a bit overambitious. Even *semi*rational was a stretch. She'd try her best to refrain from strangling him to death with a lacy red thong. And ramming his beloved little PDA right up his—

One thing at a time. Breathe in. Breathe out. She braked for a red light and forced her body to relax, starting with her shoulder muscles and working her way down to her toes.

"Mommy, I'm hungry." Hannah kicked at the back of the driver's seat. "I want juice. And a cookie."

"I just gave you a snack, honey."

"Don't like carrot sticks," Hannah whined. "I'm still hungry." She pronounced this word with plaintive desperation: *hon-gry.*

"Hang on, we're almost home. I bought some grapes at the store and we can—"

She broke off in mid-sentence as she noticed a familiar silver Mercedes parked in front of the cozy little bistro across the street.

And there, right next to Michael's car, was a sleek red convertible with a vanity license plate: VIX MD.

"It's your lucky day, little girl," Ellie announced as she executed an illegal U-turn directly over the road's landscaped median. "Mommy's going to give you a snack right now!"

"Not carrots?" Hannah asked suspiciously.

Ellie kept her gaze trained on the restaurant's front door while she waited for a hulking white Cadillac to inch out of the parking lot's only available space. "No, something much better than carrots." She tried to remember the contents of the grocery sacks piled in the cargo area. "Cheerios."

"Don't want Cheerios," Hannah said.

"How about a granola bar?" Ellie offered as she piloted the SUV into the now-vacant parking spot.

"No." Hannah's little feet thrummed against the back of the driver's seat again. "I hate granola."

Ordinarily, Ellie would have quelled this brattiness with a firm hand and a lecture series on good manners. But right now...

"Hey, what about chocolate chips? I know you like chocolate chips."

Hannah squealed at her incredible good fortune. Ellie rolled down the back windows a few inches and turned off the ignition, then raced around to unearth the bright yellow bag of chocolate and a juice box.

"Here you go, honey." She ripped open the plastic with her teeth and thrust the bag at her daughter. "Mommy will be right back. Just stay put for a minute."

Hannah glanced down at the web of car seat straps rendering her immobile and nodded. " 'Kay." She plunged her hand into the chocolate chips and crammed a fistful into her mouth.

Ellie hit the "lock" button on her automated key fob and raced over to peer through the café's plate-glass window. She cupped her hands above her eyes and squinted to see past the glare of the afternoon sun.

Busted.

Her perfect, polished husband sat in the back corner booth. As she watched, he flashed his dimpled grin and reached across the table to refill the wineglass of a woman whose face Ellie couldn't see.

But still. A quick glimpse of silhouette was sufficient to ascertain that his companion had the body of a lingerie model and long, dark hair straight out of a shampoo commercial.

Michael tilted his head and nodded as he hung on to his dining companion's every word. That focus, that intensity, had always been his forte. He had the power to block out the rest of the world and make you feel like you were the only person who mattered. He used to do that with Ellie, back when they were first dating.

Ellie had thought that she could never feel any more heartbroken and alone than she had last night in the tub. But as she watched her husband in the act of betrayal, she realized that last night had provided only a tiny taste of the bitterness churning up inside her.

"Mommy?" Hannah called from inside the car. "Whatcha doin'?"

"I'm..." Her hands dropped to her side and she realized she was still clutching the juice box. "I'm just looking, baby."

"At what? I wanna see."

"Eat your snack, Hannah." This was real. This was

happening. Her family was imploding right before her eyes.

And she was just standing here. Gaping. Accepting it like the good little girl she'd always been. Surely these circumstances called for extreme measures: yelling, smashing things, throwing one's wedding band through the sewer grates. Jen would march right in and slap the cheating weasel. Mara probably would have set the red convertible on fire by now. She had to shake off this paralysis and *take action*.

Slowly and deliberately, Ellie punctured the juice box's foil seal with the thin green straw and drizzled apple juice all over VIX MD's buttery black leather car interior.

"That's what you get for leaving the top down," she murmured as the car alarm started shrieking.

"Mommy! Make it stop!" Hannah covered her ears with chocolate-smeared fingers.

"It's all right, sweetie, we're leaving now." Ellie climbed back into the car with a savage little smile. She'd finally gotten Michael's full attention. He stood frozen in the restaurant's doorway, staring out at her with a mixture of shock and horror.

Then Ellie got a good look at Vixen_MD and stopped smiling. The willowy brunette standing next to Michael could only be described as stunning. She had long, shapely legs and full, pouty lips and she didn't look the least bit alarmed at the thought of what apple juice would do to her upholstery. She met Ellie's gaze with an air of frank assessment, then arched one tapered black eyebrow.

Really? that eyebrow said. *That's all you've got?*

The stitching on the steering wheel dug into Ellie's fingers as she backed out of the parking space and merged into traffic. Her breath came in quick, shallow gasps. To hell with that husband-poaching harpy and her condescending smirks. Ellie had won. She'd made her rage known and unleashed her inner bitch. With organic apple juice. Which, admittedly, might not be the most formidable instrument of revenge, but she awarded herself points for creativity.

In the backseat, Hannah flung aside the bag of chocolate and announced, "I don't feel good."

Pity. That was the emotion flickering in the brunette's eyes. She hadn't seemed threatened because, to her, Ellie was nothing more than a vapid suburban housewife who lounged around eating bonbons all day. Organic apple juice would only add to her derision. She was probably throwing her head back formidable, laughing about the sad little soccer mom's fit of pique.

Sweat poured down Ellie's forehead. Apple juice! What had she been thinking? She should have stormed into the café and grabbed a fistful of steak knives! She should have—

"Mommy, I don't...uh-oh." Hannah gagged, then vomited all over her car seat.

"Oh, sweetheart." Ellie jabbed at her hazard lights and pulled over to the side of the road. "It's okay. You just ate too much chocolate. Hang on. We'll get you cleaned up."

My fault, she admonished herself as she rummaged through the glove compartment for a package of wet wipes. *Bad mother, bad wife, bad person.*

Hannah threw up again as soon as Ellie finished wiping up the first round, then announced, "All better."

"Good." Ellie smoothed her daughter's silky blond curls. "We'll go home now. You can watch a movie and sip some ginger ale."

" 'Kay." Hannah smiled up angelically.

Ellie set her jaw and flicked on her right blinker. "Mommy just has to do one more thing real fast."

The red convertible's alarm had stopped blaring but Ellie triggered it again when she pulled up behind the car and lobbed the vomit-soaked wipes into the driver's seat.

Michael sprinted out to the parking lot, his face red and his eyes wide.

"Holy shit, Ellie! What are you—"

"Watch your mouth." Ellie slammed out of the SUV and strode over to confront him.

"Hi, Daddy!" Hannah chirped from the backseat.

Michael's face changed from crimson to chalk white in the space of two seconds. "Hi, sweet pea." He lowered his voice and hissed, "I mean it, Ellie. I demand to know what you think you're doing."

"Oh, really, you demand?" She brandished her car keys like a weapon. "Well, I have a few demands of my own."

"You . . . ?" He blinked a few times. "What is going *on* with you?"

She widened her stance. "I know, Michael."

He regarded her with what appeared to be genuine confusion. "About . . . ?"

"Don't play dumb." She jabbed her index finger toward the restaurant. "You. Her. I know. So give it up."

He opened his hands and turned both palms toward her. "What are you talking about? That's one of my new clients. Dr. Victoria Locane. She's looking for new office space out by the Biltmore."

Ellie let out a harsh bark of laughter. "Michael, honestly. How stupid do you think I am?"

"I don't—"

"Stop, okay? Stop talking before you make this worse for everybody. Including Hannah."

Michael's voice eased into a low, gentle cadence. "You're not making any sense, honey. Take a deep breath and calm down—"

"You're supposed to be golfing," she reminded him. "Nine holes? The Oro Vista deal? Ring any bells?"

He shrugged one shoulder. "Those guys got stuck in traffic coming across from the west valley. The Fifty-one freeway's under construction, so I pushed the tee time back to two-thirty. Since I had a few free hours, I offered to take Dr. Locane to look at some potential office sites. I tried to call you, but you didn't answer your cell." He reached into his jacket pocket and withdrew a sheaf of real estate listings. "This is just business. So whatever it is that you're accusing me of—"

"I'm accusing you of Vixen_MD and the red thong."

His jaw slackened and his eyes went wide with panic.

"Uh-huh." She crossed her arms tightly and nodded. "Well, I guess that settles that."

"Ellie, listen," he croaked. "You don't understand."

Something inside her snapped as he collapsed into

contrition. She dug the jagged tip of her key into the convertible's shiny red paint and knew she should stop— this was so adolescent, so undignified—but she couldn't. Rage completely engulfed her restraint. She gouged metal against metal all the way from hood to trunk.

Michael looked horrified. "What are you *doing*?"

She lifted her chin. "I'm going home, I'm putting Hannah down for a nap, and then I'm hiring an attorney. As of this moment, we are no longer married."

Jen  *Chapter* 5

Clause 7: Obligation of Fidelity
It is further acknowledged that the parties' marriage is intended to be an exclusive relationship between Husband and Wife that is premised upon the values of emotional and sexual fidelity, and mutual trust. The parties hereto are subject to a legal obligation of emotional and sexual fidelity to the other.

In the event it is shown by a preponderance of the evidence in a court that either party has engaged in any breach of the obligation of sexual fidelity as defined hereinabove, the following terms and conditions shall become effective...

*W*ow." Jen scanned the text, shook her head, and then read it again. "That is..."

"I know." Mara reached across Jen's kitchen table for the bottle of Shiraz and topped off her glass again.

"Why didn't he just break out some brass knuckles and punch me in the face?"

"Does this really mean what I think it means?" Jen squinted down at the tiny font.

"Basically, it means I'm a filthy whore who needs to be threatened with legal retribution to make sure she keeps her legs closed." Mara swilled her wine. "Mmm. This is pretty good stuff."

Jen rolled the wine cork between her thumb and index finger and chose her words carefully. "Let's not over-react. I have excellent reading comprehension skills, and nowhere do I see the words 'filthy whore.'"

"Oh, it's there," Mara assured her. "Between the lines."

"Hmm." Jen kept her expression neutral.

"Don't give me that prim little 'hmm.' Just come out and be scathing and judgmental. Why hold back? Go ahead, you can say it: Mara is a total slut."

"Aaand we're cutting you off." Jen made a grab for the wine bottle, but Mara clutched it to her chest.

"Hands off my vino." Mara abandoned her delicate stemmed glass and started swigging straight from the bottle. "Your friend Mara is a total slut *and* a drunk."

Jen rolled her eyes. "Why am I even trying to have a rational discussion with you right now?"

"I'm drunk, not irrational. Don't patronize me."

Jen had to admit that, even into her fourth serving of wine, Mara's sensibilities were holding up quite well. Mara had always claimed that law firm happy hours were akin to frat parties with forty-year-old Scotch instead of kegs, and her tolerance was impressive.

"If I drank as much as you have in the last hour, I'd be passed out under the table," Jen marveled.

"That's because your poor liver is utterly defenseless. Too many smoothies and sunrise yoga sessions." Mara paused to stifle a tiny belch with the back of her hand. " 'Scuse me. Anyway, the man is clearly sick and depraved. He sprung this on me while we were shopping for *wedding bands.* That's, like, the mark of a sociopath. I'm not marrying a sociopath."

"Then I guess this isn't really an issue anymore." Jen folded the pre-nup draft in half and passed it back to Mara.

"I guess not. Let's open another bottle to celebrate. Got any champagne?"

"How about a gallon of water and a hearty bowl of quinoa with fruit instead?"

"You suggest quinoa at a time like this? Really? Remind me again why we're friends?"

Jen grinned. "Because some admissions staffers at ASU had a warped sense of humor when they assigned freshmen roommates."

Mara grinned back. "Talk about sick and depraved. Anyway, health food would just work against me right now. I have a wedding cake tasting appointment in an hour, and I need to be good and blotto."

"But you just said that you're not going to marry Josh."

"Of course I'm not. The man called me a filthy whore." Mara waved the pre-nup. "But the baker's expecting me and it'd be tacky not to show. Besides, I would kill for a slice of chocolate cake right now, and I know I'm not going to find it in your pantry."

"I have carob chips," Jen offered.

"You're killing me. Come on, let's go gorge ourselves on refined sugar and trans fats. And, hey, we should pick up Ellie on the way. She needs a therapeutic dose of chocolate even more than I do."

As they stood under the vast, arched stone portico of the Barton house, they could hear crashes emanating from within: sharp, staccato shatterings punctuated by muffled slams and thumps.

Jen's eyes widened. "Wow. Do you think she's beating him to death in there?"

"With his golf clubs, sounds like. We got here just in time to save her from a homicide charge." Mara rang the bell and yelled, "Ellie! Put down the weapon! You have potential witnesses out here!"

No response, but Mara wasn't easily deterred. She hammered away on the heavy brass door knocker until Ellie finally opened up.

"Ladies. How lovely to see you both." Ellie's pink polo shirt and fitted dark jeans were splotched with patches of fine white dust, and her right hand was bleeding. She smoothed wisps of dark brown hair back from her face. "What can I do for you?"

Jen tried not to gawk. "Are you okay in there?"

"Yeah, the jig is up." Mara craned her neck to peer down the hallway. "We know you're sending Michael to the great nineteenth hole in the sky."

"Oh, Michael's not here right now. He's having a leisurely lunch with his mistress, and Hannah's at a play date, and I am systematically smashing all of our wedding china." Ellie glanced down at her right palm as if surprised to see the thin ribbon of blood. "So I'm a bit busy at the moment. Come back later?"

"You shouldn't be alone right now." Jen braced her hand against the open door. "Why don't you come with us and—"

"Can't." Ellie shook her head. "I still have the soup tureen, the teacups, and the serving platters to take care of."

"We're going to get cake," Mara coaxed.

"Sounds lovely, but . . ." Ellie's vacant smile was both disturbing and serene. "The soup tureen. Duty calls."

Mara threw Jen a look, then patted Ellie on the shoulder. "You want the soup tureen destroyed? Show me the way. Turns out, I'm having kind of a crockery-smashing day myself."

Ellie ushered them into the elegant dining room done up in warm, red-toned wood and accented with cream and green silks. The doors to the sideboard were flung open and shards of porcelain littered the floor, where the plush green patterned rug had been rolled back to expose the varnished hardwood.

"Jeez." Mara whistled. "You've got quite the pitching arm."

"Remember my wedding day? It was perfect. Perfect weather, perfect dress, perfect couple. And now he's cheating and lying and I'm keying cars and vandalizing with vomit." Ellie rummaged through the sideboard and pulled out a huge oval serving platter, which she lifted high above her head. "Watch out for shrapnel."

Jen flinched as the platter slammed into the floor.

"Okay." Mara seized Ellie's shoulders and spun her toward the doorway. "Time out. Go wash your hands and get a box of Band-Aids. Jen, start the car. We're going—*all* of us—to have cake and regroup."

Ellie resisted for a moment, then relaxed and nodded.

Jen had to ask. "How exactly does one vandalize with vomit?"

"Never mind the vomit—you actually keyed Michael's car?" Mara regarded Ellie with newfound respect.

Ellie hung her head. "I don't know what came over me. Hannah got carsick and Michael was standing there giving me the puppy-dog eyes and denying everything, and I just lost control. And it wasn't Michael's car, it was hers. Her cheesy, cliché red convertible with vanity plates that actually said, swear to God, VIX MD."

"No way." Jen started to laugh. "You're making this up."

"I wish I were." Ellie covered her face with her hands. "I was so angry, I scared myself. The whole thing was, well...it was very unladylike. I'm turning into the kind of woman they gossip about at Pampered Chef parties."

Mara slung one arm around her and gave her a squeeze. "Welcome to the other side, babe. We've been waiting for you."

"So we're here to taste wedding cakes but we're not allowed to talk about the wedding?" Ellie clarified as the three women trooped into the Golden Tulip Bakery in an upscale shopping plaza in North Scottsdale.

"Correct." Mara opened the door, letting the mouth-watering aroma of vanilla and cinnamon waft out. "Sugar good, men bad."

"But…" Ellie glanced to Jen for guidance, but Jen just shook her head and muttered, "Leave it. Trust me."

Mara waved to the white-aproned pastry chef behind the counter and announced, "I have a three-thirty appointment for cake-tasting. Last name Stroebel."

The baker ducked into the back room and emerged with a silver serving plate adorned with paper lace doilies and an assortment of cake slices.

Jen's salivary glands kicked into overtime as she eyed a thin wedge of what the chef described as Bavarian lemon with raspberry filling. "I can feel my thighs expanding already."

"Me, too." Ellie threw up her hands. "And I was so good this week. I did three days of cardio and two days of circuit training, and now it's all going to be erased with two bites of… Oh, dear lord, what is that pink one with the white frosting?"

"That's the strawberry champagne cake. Our specialty," the baker said proudly.

Jen winced. "Dare I ask how many calories?"

"Don't ruin this with calorie talk." Mara seized a fork and dug in. "We may live in Mayfair Estates, but we don't have to drink the sugar-free Kool-Aid and give ourselves eating disorders."

"Just because I eat healthfully doesn't mean I have an eating disorder," Jen protested. "I happen to like quinoa and carob chips. There's nothing pathological about that."

Mara snorted. "I beg to differ."

"I don't have an eating disorder, either," Ellie muttered. "Unfortunately."

"Well, you better keep your guard up," Mara said. "That fundraising lunch you dragged me to last month? I've never heard such hullabaloo about carbs in my life. One chick spent literally ten minutes—I checked my watch—agonizing about whether the fructose in grapes would blow her diet. Panic in the produce aisle!"

Ellie wrinkled her nose and sniffed. "Is that wine on your breath? At three in the afternoon?"

"An entire bottle's worth." Jen tsk-tsked.

They lapsed into a chocolate-fueled feeding frenzy for a few minutes, then Ellie put down her fork and slumped back in her chair. "You should have seen her at the café today. Vixen_MD. Whose real name is Victoria, by the way. She actually is a physician, did I tell you that?" Her big brown eyes shimmered with tears. "Why couldn't Michael have the decency to cheat on me with some brainless bimbo? How am I supposed to compete with a doctor?"

"Oh, honey"—Jen hunted through her bag for a tissue—"it's not a competition."

"Yeah, 'cause she already won! She has the body, the degrees, the career, the car..." Ellie dabbed at her eyes with the Kleenex. "You know who Vixen_MD is? She's the woman I could have become if I hadn't gotten married so young and drunk the sugar-free Kool-Aid. I was accepted to law school two years after we graduated college, did you know that?"

Mara's jaw dropped. "No."

"I didn't even know you applied," Jen said. "Why didn't you tell us?"

"Because I didn't want to have to be embarrassed if I didn't get in." Ellie blew her nose. "And then, when I did get in, Michael's family was so insistent that I needed to help him get his career off the ground, and then, you know, it was one thing after another and then I got pregnant with Hannah..."

"Which law school? When did you take the LSAT?" Mara pressed. "We could've been study buddies."

Jen elbowed her. "That's not the point."

"The point is," Ellie continued, "that Vixen_MD has an important job and a real life, and what do I have?"

"The world's cutest kid," Jen said.

"Kick-ass friends," Mara added.

But Ellie wasn't listening. "A ginormous house and a sterling reputation as the belle of the benefit ball. And you know what the worst part is? I was happy. Blind and in denial and stupid, but happy. We were going to try to get pregnant again this summer. That's what we wanted, both of us." She drummed her short, varnished fingernails on the tabletop. "Well, that's what he said he wanted. Apparently, what he actually wants is hot sex and red thongs. What am I going to do, you guys? I'm serious. What am I supposed to tell Hannah tonight when she asks why Daddy isn't home for dinner?"

Jen and Mara fumbled helplessly.

"Well, you say, uh..."

"Yeah, you could always, um..."

"Exactly." Ellie pushed back her chair and stood up.

"There are no answers. Nothing I do or say is going to make any difference. He's ripping our lives apart, and I have to sit back and take it." She hoisted her brown suede bag onto her shoulder. "I'm going to use the ladies' room."

Jen surveyed the balled-up tissues scattered among the ravaged smears of fondant and cake crumbs. "I'll get the car."

Mara complimented the baker as he passed. "Superb. Love the strawberry champagne cake. I'll get back to you with a final decision next week."

Jen's eyebrows snapped together. "I thought you weren't getting married?"

"Please. Let's be real here. What are the odds that I'm ever going to be attracted to another cute, smart, decent guy who's not a total scumbag?"

Jen did a quick mental inventory of Mara's many ex-boyfriends. "Well," she admitted, "that would appear to be a long shot. But maybe—"

"Maybe nothing. I argued him into this stupid pre-nup, now I'll just have to argue him out of it." Mara looked grim and resigned.

"Ah, true love."

Mara scraped back her chair. "You bring the car around. I'm off to the restroom to check on our girl."

Jen felt an unexpected rush of relief as she headed back out into the afternoon sun. Everyone had marriage problems. Everyone. And she and Eric would never have to endure such heart-wrenching doubt and betrayal. They'd never wavered in the promises they'd made the night before their wedding.

I'll never hurt you and I'll never ask for more than you can give, he had vowed. *I'll love you enough for both of us.*

She squeezed her eyes shut and shook her head. She didn't want to remember the resolve in her husband's voice when he swore eternal devotion, the desperate determination in his eyes.

This was what came of abandoning her work plans on a Saturday afternoon. Drinking, carousing, and wanton cake consumption. Plus guilt, lots of guilt. She should have stayed at home with her spreadsheets and marketing plans and—

"Jen?" A man across the street called her name, then raised his hand in greeting. "Jen Finnerty?"

The smooth, deep voice stopped her in her tracks. She struggled to arrange her face in a smile.

Oh, dear God, no. No, no, no. I'm wearing ratty old yoga pants and no makeup. I can't face him like this.

"You chopped off all your hair." Patrick Spillane loped across the concrete, rapidly closing the distance between them. "I love it."

Jen had spent a lot of time over the last six years mentally composing a cutting little speech to deliver at precisely this moment. Too bad she couldn't remember a word of it.

"What are you doing here?" she blurted out. She couldn't bring herself to look him in the face.

He didn't seem to notice on her discomfort. "Just got back into town last week. I'm looking to join a practice out here. Thinking about buying a place in Fountain Hills."

"You're so . . . tan." Strike two.

Patrick threw back his head and laughed. "That's what a few years in sub-Saharan Africa without sunscreen will do to you. So really, how are you, Jen?"

She stared up at the sky and said loudly, "I got married."

"I heard. Eric's a lucky guy."

She couldn't detect any trace of mockery in his tone.

"Look at you. All grown up. It's been a long time." He leaned in and brushed his lips across the thick waves of hair above her temple. "Let's get together soon and catch up. You, me, and Eric. I'll be in touch." Then he walked away without a backward glance.

Jen remained rooted to the ground for a few minutes, watching him go. Her face burned against the brisk winter wind. Who the hell did he think he was? How dare he kiss her after all that had happened? How dare he have an opinion about her hair, her life, her marriage?

But that was the thing about Patrick Spillane: He always dared.

She whipped out her phone and speed-dialed Eric. Talking to him would bring her back to herself; besides, he deserved to know that she was thinking of him while he was away.

But Eric didn't pick up. And as Jen pressed the phone to her ear, listening to the mechanical ringing and reeling from the sensation of Patrick's lips so close to her face, she had to admit she felt relieved that her husband wasn't available.

Ellie

Chapter 6

Ellie, darling, I just heard and it's dreadful; no way around it." Michael's mother looked simultaneously apprehensive and relieved when Ellie opened the front door. "I had to come over to see how you're holding up."

Patrice Barton exuded an air of effortless chic and endless hospitality. A fixture on the Scottsdale social circuit, she was sweet, petite, and always perfectly put together. This Saturday afternoon was no exception. Her thick blond hair (shot through with just the right amount of silver) was freshly blown out, her blue blazer was classic silk tweed, but her smile couldn't quite disguise the anguish in her eyes.

"Patrice!" Ellie sloshed a bit of lukewarm coffee from her mug onto the floor as she took a step back. "What a surprise!"

"Good surprise or bad surprise?"

"Well, good, of course. I wasn't sure when I'd hear from you, given the, uh, circumstances."

Patrice nodded. "May I come in? I know I should have called first, but ..."

"Don't be silly. You know you're welcome anytime." Ellie beckoned her inside. "This coffee is cold and vile, but if you wait ten minutes, I'll brew a fresh pot." She called into the kitchen. "Hannah! Look who's here!"

"Gramma!" Hannah scampered in and threw her arms around Patrice's knees.

Patrice scooped up the little girl and twirled around the foyer. "Hello there, kitty cat! Goodness, you're getting big."

"Did you bring me a prezzie?"

Ellie gasped and put her hand on her hip. "Hannah Rose Barton! That is rude. You do not ask your grandma—or *anyone* who comes to this house—to give you—"

Patrice waved this away and glanced conspiratorially at Hannah. "Of course I brought you a prezzie. That's what grammas are for. Go peek in the front seat of my car."

Hannah dashed out to the green Jaguar parked in the driveway, jerked open the passenger side door, and seized a large paper bag overflowing with white tissue paper.

"Ooh!" She dug through the wrapping to reveal a large box labeled "Fine English China." "A teapot!"

"That's right." Patrice's smile widened. "A real tea set with blue flowers, just like in *A Bargain for Frances*."

"And a doll!" Hannah glanced sidelong at Ellie, then folded her hands and cooed sweetly, "Thank you, Gramma."

"You're very welcome. Now listen, kitty cat, your

grandma and mommy are going to catch up for a few minutes. Go start a tea party with your dolls in your playhouse in the backyard, and we'll be out to join you in a few minutes."

" 'Kay!" Hannah gathered up her loot and sped off.

When they heard the sliding glass door in the kitchen slam shut, the two women looked at each other and sighed.

"People were whispering at the art gallery opening this afternoon," Patrice said. "It's true, then?"

Ellie knew the expression on her face was confirmation enough. "Oh God. We're the talk of the country club already?"

"You know how fast word travels around this neighborhood."

"What exactly are people saying?" Ellie pressed. "They didn't mention anything about apple juice, did they?"

"Don't worry," Patrice said firmly. "I'll handle the gossip. You have more important matters to think about." She nodded toward the living room. "Let's sit down."

"Give me a minute to start some coffee."

"Please don't trouble yourself. I'm fine. Sit down and we'll . . ." Patrice trailed off as she glanced toward the dining room and noticed the traces of pulverized porcelain still scattered across the floor. "Oh dear. Apparently, I should have bought *you* a new tea set, as well."

"I'm still cleaning up," Ellie stammered. "I wasn't expecting company."

"I completely understand. Sit." Patrice led the way into the living room and perched on the rose-and-cream-striped sofa. "I know that your marriage is none of my business. I've tried very hard not to be one of those burdensome, meddling mothers-in-law—"

"Don't even say that!" Ellie broke in. "You've been wonderful. No one ever could take the place of my mom, of course, but since she passed away, in some ways it's like..."

Patrice pressed her lips together and covered Ellie's hand with her own. "I'm glad to hear you say that, because I've always thought of you as my daughter. I loved raising my boys, of course, but I always wondered if Heath and I had tried again if we would have had a girl."

Ellie swallowed hard. "I'm so grateful for everything you've done for me and Hannah. She adores you. And I want you to know that whatever happens in the future, I hope we can remain close."

"So you haven't made any definite decisions?" Patrice looked hopeful. "About you and Michael?"

"I'm calling a lawyer on Monday."

"What have you told Hannah?"

"Nothing yet, but I'm going to have to come up with something."

"Oh darling, this is so hard." Patrice's voice was strained. "I know how you must be feeling right now."

"No offense, Patrice, but no, you don't."

Her mother-in-law lifted her eyebrows and gave her a meaningful look. "I assure you, I do."

"What?" Ellie couldn't contain her shock. "You mean Heath...?"

Patrice inclined her head slightly in affirmation.

"Are you kidding me? But you guys seem so happy!" Ellie winced as the words left her mouth. Everyone down at the country club was probably saying the same thing about her and Michael.

But then Patrice smiled. "We are happy. Very happy. But thirty years ago, when Michael and Daniel were little and we were just starting out ... things happen."

"They do," Ellie allowed. "But there's a difference between things happening and people *making* them happen."

Patrice continued as if Ellie hadn't spoken. "I swore I'd never get over it. I was furious and humiliated, but most of all, I was devastated because my heart was broken and I thought I could never trust my husband again."

"Check." Ellie nodded. "Check, check, and check."

"But a lot of time has passed since then. Births and deaths and triumphs and tragedies. And do you know what? Somewhere along the way, Heath and I fell back in love. The heart is very resilient. I healed. Our marriage healed."

"Okay," Ellie said slowly. "I don't know all the specifics of your situation with Heath, but—"

"I don't know all the specifics of your situation with Michael. But I do know that he loves you very much."

"You don't treat people you love the way he's treating me."

"Oh, I'm not defending his behavior," Patrice assured her. "He's debased himself and this family and I'm going to express that to him in the strongest possible terms."

"Then what exactly are you saying?"

"When Heath and I reached our crisis point, I learned a lot about compromise." The older woman smiled wryly. "You know me, I'm not one to be led around by the nose. But I refused to give up on my marriage until I was absolutely sure it was beyond salvation. There are very few things in life worth that kind of struggle, but family is one of them. At first, I stayed with Heath not because I loved him, but because I loved my children. I wanted my sons to have a father. Ultimately, keeping the family intact was more important to me than my pride."

Ellie didn't respond, but she considered how alone she would be without Michael and Patrice and Heath in her life. How alone in the world she had felt before she married Michael. She never, ever wanted her daughter to experience that kind of isolation.

"And slowly, Heath and I came back to each other. We're more in love now than we were when we got married." Patrice held up her index finger to hold off Ellie's protests. "I'm not telling you what to do. I'm just giving you a perspective from the other side. You can make it through this together if you both commit to doing the work. Heath and I will help in any way we can. We'll pay for counseling, we'll give you the house in Sedona for the summer so you can spend some quality time together, reconnect."

"I think we're past the point of quality time."

"And if that's really the way you feel, there's nothing more to be said. But if there's even the slightest chance you'd be willing to try again, you need to consider what's at stake. It's a question of compromise." She glanced up at the framed family photograph resting on the mantel. Ellie, Michael, and Hannah beamed out at the photographer. The three of them looked so comfortable and carefree. Hannah's smile still gapped where her baby teeth hadn't come in yet.

She's growing up so fast, Ellie realized. *We'll have to schedule another family portrait soon.*

Except that the next portrait would only show two of them.

"Let's have brunch at the club tomorrow morning. Just the two of us." Patrice winked. "A show of solidarity."

"Thank you," Ellie said softly. "That would mean a lot to me."

The sliding glass door in the kitchen squeaked open. "Gramma, read me *A Bargain for Frances*."

"Coming, kitty cat." Patrice leaned in to kiss Ellie's cheek. "Keep your chin up, darling. And try not to worry about Michael. I'll deal with him."

The doorbell rang again at six-thirty, just as Ellie and Hannah were finishing a makeshift "breakfast for dinner" consisting of fruit salad, pancakes, and crisp veggie bacon (Jen's influence at work).

Ellie tucked her daughter safely away in the family room and turned on a Disney DVD. Then she marched into the foyer and made her stand beneath that huge chandelier, peering out through the thick beveled panes of glass framing the door.

Michael stood on the welcome mat with his head hung low. His hands were jammed into his jacket pockets; his shirt collar was rumpled and unbuttoned. And still he managed to radiate confidence and capability. The all-American husband and father with thick hair and perfect teeth, straight out of central casting. And with acting skills worthy of an Oscar.

The two of them stood there for a few long minutes, separated by slabs of wood and glass, and waited. He didn't raise his face or try the lock. She didn't reach for the knob.

Finally, he lifted his head and mouthed, "I'm sorry."

All of Ellie's rage and resentment evaporated into an almost comical sense of defeat. He was *sorry*?

She cracked open the door a fraction of an inch. "It's a little late for sorry. I have absolutely nothing to say to you."

"Well, I have a lot to say to you." Michael wedged the door open with his foot and hurried over the threshold.

Ellie crossed her arms and rocked back on her heels. "Did your mother send you?"

"No, my mother did not send me." Michael rankled. "I'm here because I need to talk. *We* need to talk."

"Michael . . ." Ellie paused, trying to figure out how to make him understand. "Are you planning to castrate yourself with a rusty spoon in the front yard?"

Michael frowned. "What?"

"Because, honestly, that would be the only thing you could do right now to make me feel better."

He flinched but stood his ground. "I deserve that."

"And so much more."

"I know you hate me right now. I know I screwed up. But here's the thing—"

"No, Michael." The rage and resentment made a surprise comeback. "There is no thing. Nothing you can say or do can make this better. Ever."

"Ellie, I love you."

She recoiled as if he had slapped her. "Fuck you."

She had never dropped the f-bomb in seven years of blissful marriage and motherhood, but now seemed like the appropriate moment.

Michael didn't look so calm and confident anymore. He blanched and wobbled a bit on his feet.

"I don't care what your excuse is or how sorry you are," Ellie spat. "Pack your bags. Everything you leave behind is going to Goodwill. You have two minutes. The clock starts now."

He refused to retreat. "I'm not here for my clothes. Give them to Goodwill; I don't care. All I care about are you and Hannah."

"Oh really?" Her laugh was bitter. "Then why are you having an affair? Or is it *affairs*—plural? How many women have you slept with since we got married?"

"Only one." He maintained eye contact as she glared at him. "I know that doesn't make anything any better, but it's the truth. And I broke up with her this afternoon. That's why we were at lunch, actually. I was ending it with her before you even showed up."

"Bullshit!" (Hey, as long as she was cursing, she might as well go for broke.) "How stupid do you think I am?"

He raised his hand like a Boy Scout about to recite his oath. "Swear to God. I knew I'd made a mistake and I was trying to rectify things before—"

"Oh please. You were trying to ply her with red wine and squeeze in a quickie before you hit the golf course."

"I never meant to hurt you."

"You were out with her in public on a Saturday afternoon!"

"Ellie, I know you're pissed and you have every right to be, but I love you. Always have, always will. What can I do to prove that to you?"

"Nothing! Your two minutes are up and you have now officially forfeited the entire contents of your closet. Get out."

"I'll do anything you say. You name it, I'll do it."

Ellie thought this over for a moment. "Okay. Turn back time and keep your putter in your pants!"

"Sweetheart—"

"You 'sweetheart' me again, I'm getting the rusty spoon," she warned. "Now get out of my house."

Michael shook his head. "Not until you hear me out. All I'm asking for is a chance to show you—"

"Fine, if you're going to stay, then tell me why. Why would you do this to our family? What does she have that I don't?"

He looked sad and defeated but didn't answer so she upped the volume of her voice. *"Why?"*

"I don't know," he muttered, then cleared his throat. "But I am deeply, truly sorry and I don't want you and Hannah to be punished for the stupid mistake I made."

Ellie kept seething, but let him talk.

"I'll sleep in the guest room. I'll let you have at me with the rusty spoon, if that's what you need," he vowed. "All I'm asking is that you hold off on making any huge decisions for a few weeks. Think about the future, El. Think about Hannah."

She stared down at the floor.

He took her silence as an invitation to forge ahead. "I called a couples therapist and left a message requesting an emergency appointment first thing Monday morning. I hope you'll go with me, but if you won't, I'll go alone."

"I *hate* you," she finally said.

"I mean it, Ellie. I will do whatever it takes. Anything. Just tell me what you want."

She gave up trying not to cry. "I don't want to have to make this choice."

"I know. I'm sorry. But you're the only one who can."

She flung the door open wide, letting in gusts of cold, damp wind.

He nodded slowly and turned to leave. "Take as much time as you need. I'll wait."

"Stop making this harder than it already is. Just..." Her whole body went limp and shaky. "Go."

He stepped outside but hunkered down on the front step and stayed there, weathering the wind and falling darkness with only a thin jacket and no further protest. Ellie closed the door and busied herself with cleaning up the kitchen. When Hannah's movie ended, Michael was still sitting out there, silent and motionless.

"Mommy," Hannah called from the foyer. "Daddy's outside and he won't come in."

"I know, honey. Come on, it's bath time," Ellie called back.

Hannah was full of questions through the bath/ teeth brushing/storytime routine:

"Is Daddy camping out there?"

"When is he coming inside?"

"Can I get my blankets and go camping with him?"

"No, baby." Ellie smoothed back her daughter's silky curls, then folded back the bubble-gum pink blankets on the canopied bed. "You have to sleep inside. You had a very busy day."

"But why—"

Ellie gathered her close. She could feel Hannah's quick, steady heartbeat thudding against her own. "Mommy and Daddy both love you so much. We'll talk about this tomorrow, okay? All three of us together."

She read and sang and rubbed Hannah's back until, finally, the little girl drifted off to sleep. As she headed back into the hall, she forced herself to stare straight ahead and not sneak a glance toward the front door to see if Michael was still there.

Let him freeze. Let him suffer. Let him go see the therapist by himself to figure out why he's a duplicitous, scum-sucking cheater. He's not my problem anymore.

By midnight, she had slugged back two cups of warm milk and a glass of wine, but despite her exhaustion, she couldn't fall asleep. She curled up in a corner of the king-size bed and listened to the wind howling down from the mountains.

Michael was still out on the doorstep. She could feel his presence permeating her house, her mind, her heart. He might as well be in bed next to her. Damn him to hell. She threw aside the comforter and stalked toward the linen closet.

"Here." Without bothering to turn on the porch light, Ellie yanked open the front door and hurled a pillow and rolled-up sleeping bag at Michael.

"Oof." The sleeping bag connected with his head. "Thank you. Does this mean . . . ?"

She slammed and locked the door, stalked back to bed, and burrowed under the covers.

Hannah's thin, high-pitched voice woke her at dawn. "Daddy's still camping on the porch, Mommy! I'm gonna get my sleeping bag!"

Ellie rolled over in bed and squinted at the digital clock on the nightstand. Six-thirteen A.M. Hannah was going to freeze out there in her pink flannel pajamas.

Hopefully, Michael had already lost a few extremities to frostbite.

She wrapped the comforter around her like a cape, then padded out to the foyer and opened the door.

"Fine," she said dully without looking down. "You can come in."

Ellie | *Chapter* 7

I'm a size *what?*" Ellie clapped her hands over her mouth as the bridal salon owner tightened a tape measure around her hips and rattled off numbers to the assistant holding a clipboard. "Are you kidding me? How could I have gone up two whole dress sizes in under a week? I mean, I grant you I've been a little depressed and the gym has slipped down on my priority list and I may have had a few late-night indiscretions with both Ben and Jerry, but two sizes in a week?"

"Chill." Mara glanced up from the legal documents she was perusing in the overstuffed pink chair outside the dressing rooms. "It's couture sizing. Totally different from street clothes."

"She's right." Jen's voice drifted over the flimsy white partition separating the two dressing rooms.

"So I haven't gained twenty pounds since Saturday?" Ellie breathed a sigh of relief.

"Nope," Jen said. "But you really shouldn't be gorging on ice cream—it's nothing but empty calories and processed sugars. You need to keep up your strength and endurance right now. Try snacking on walnuts. They're chock-full of omega-three fats and magnesium, which should help with the depression."

"Walnuts? Seriously? That's your big mental-health tip?" Mara shook her head in disgust. "Remind me not to call you when my marriage falls apart."

"Your marriage isn't going to fall apart," Jen said.

"Josh and I may not even make it down the aisle in the first place." Mara's ice blue eyes took on a steely glint. "Pre-nup negotiations are at a standstill."

"Then why, may I ask, am I being forced to spend a Friday night trying on twee bridesmaid dresses?"

"Don't complain. You're getting off easy," Mara said. "No tulle, no petticoats, no beribboned hats. Lucky for you, I have excellent taste."

Ellie glanced down at the clingy, off-the-shoulder cocktail dress that barely covered her bosom. "But black satin? For a June wedding?"

"She's just doing it to annoy her mother." Jen emerged from the dressing room. The sample size absolutely swam on her petite, muscular frame, and the salesclerk abandoned Ellie to pin in the waist, hips, and chest on Jen.

Mara grinned. "Oh, how well you know me."

"Wow." Ellie's shoulders slumped. "You look gorgeous."

Jen wrinkled up her nose. "Such sincerity."

"No, I mean it." Ellie plucked at the fabric draped across her breasts. "You look all thin and effervescent and I just . . . don't."

Mara stashed her paperwork back in her briefcase and focused on her friends. "Ellie, hon, what's going on?"

"Nothing." Ellie rubbed the back of her neck. "Everything."

"This is about Michael," Jen predicted.

"Of course it's about Michael. I just keep asking myself why he did it. Why why *why*?"

"I have a theory about that," Mara said. "It has to do with the fact that he's a complete tool."

"Repeat after me." Jen hiked up her hemline and crossed over to Ellie. "This is not your fault. Nothing you did or didn't do made him cheat. You're an excellent wife. An excellent mom."

"Well, if I had nothing to do with anything, that leaves me completely powerless, doesn't it?" Ellie dropped her arms in frustration. "We went to our first couples' counseling session this week."

Mara leaned forward. "And? How was it?"

"Well." Ellie chose her words carefully. "It was interesting. The therapist asked why we were there, and Michael basically threw himself under the bus. He said he'd do anything to earn back my trust. You know, give me all his e-mail passwords, et cetera."

"Well, what do you think?" Jen asked. "Do you believe him?"

"I don't know," Ellie mused. "I *want* to believe him, but I'm afraid to. He sleeps in the guest room; he acts totally attentive and remorseful. At least I'm not homicidal with rage anymore. I feel . . . frozen. Empty. But I guess we have to start somewhere if we're going to rebuild." She clapped her hands together and smoothed out the satin puckering around her hips. "I shouldn't be talking like this in front of the blushing bride-to-be."

"Oh yeah, that's me." Mara rolled her eyes. "All lace and lily of the valley."

"You and Josh are both being ridiculous," Jen admonished. "Why don't you just sit down together and talk it out?"

"Talk it out? Sure. Look what happened the last time we had problems and decided to 'talk things out': I ended up with some skeevy guy at a bar and a lifetime of guilt."

"Wait, what?" Ellie stopped fussing with her gown and whipped around to face Mara. "What are you talking about?"

Mara's eyes widened to cartoonish proportions. "Oops. Forget I said anything."

"About a skeevy guy at a bar and a lifetime of guilt? I don't think so. Spill."

Mara turned on Jen. "Look what you made me do!"

"You brought it up, not me," Jen pointed out.

"Since when do you two keep secrets from me?" Ellie couldn't keep the hurt out of her voice.

"We all have secrets," Mara said. "You got into law school, I had a one-night stand."

Ellie was torn between feeling offended and ravenous for details. Curiosity quickly won out. "When?"

Mara glanced helplessly at the bridal magazines and gown catalogs stacked on the coffee table next to her chair. "Do we really have to get into this right now?"

"*Yes!*"

The sales assistant backed out of the dressing room with a vague, polite smile. "I'll put a rush on the order for the black satin. Let us know if you need anything else."

When the three friends had the dressing room to themselves, Mara huffed and harrumphed and finally confessed. "It was a while ago. Josh and I were starting to get serious and I freaked out and pulled away, so then *he* freaked out and started making impossible demands."

"What kind of impossible demands?"

"Oh, crazy stuff like he wanted to adopt a dog and buy a house together. And the more I told him I wasn't ready for that, the harder he pushed. He would leave my Internet browser open to Petfinder.com, stuff like that."

"Diabolical," Jen teased.

"I know! He knew I couldn't even keep a houseplant alive, let alone a four-legged mammal. As for cohabitation, I think you will have to agree that has not worked out well for me in the past."

Ellie did agree. However, she attributed Mara's dismal romantic track record more to the character of the men involved than to specific living arrangements.

"I told him all that right from our first date. Which, come to think of it, was all your fault." She looked accusingly at Ellie.

"My fault?"

"Yeah. You strong-armed me into going to that food bank fund-raiser where I met him and now look at my life: a shambles! I should have stayed off the charity circuit and stuck to the martini bars in Old Town. I'm way too dysfunctional to make it work with a do-gooder."

Mara grimaced. "*Anyway*, we'd only been seeing each other for like six months and one Sunday, he talked me into hitting an open house in Fountain Hills and he told the Realtor we were in the market for a three-bedroom and I said no we weren't and we got into a huge blowout in some stranger's kitchen. I left for a firm retreat the next day and . . ." She gritted her teeth. "Mistakes were made. You had just had Hannah and you were overwhelmed and sleep-deprived and—"

Ellie lifted her chin. "Oh, I see how it is. I get a touch of postpartum depression, and my best friends go AWOL on me."

"I didn't want to stress you out more!" Mara cried.

"This was right at the height of Hannah's colic," Jen said. "Don't you remember how frazzled you were?"

"I've blocked it out," Ellie said. "Nature's way of tricking you into considering a second child."

"Well, *I* remember," Mara declared. "You were hanging on by one bloody fingernail. And then, by the time you got your head above water, I just wanted to forget the whole thing ever happened."

Ellie searched for a glimmer of hope here, and she found it in the engagement ring on Mara's left hand. "But you and Josh managed to work it out, right?"

"Um, have you noticed that he and I aren't speaking to each other?" Mara said. "We analyzed the whole thing to death for over two years, and what good did it do us? He still doesn't trust me." She turned to Jen. "I should have just taken your advice and never told him."

Ellie turned to Jen. "You told her not to tell Josh she slept with someone else?"

"Well, yeah." Jen started to squirm. "I mean, if he was never going to find out otherwise, and she was truly sorry and would never, ever do it again, what was the point of tormenting him by telling him?"

"How about honesty?" Ellie bristled.

"She would have to be honest with herself about what she did. Living with the guilt and remorse would be her punishment." Jen fluffed up her short blond waves.

"Guilt and remorse? Give me a break." Ellie rolled her eyes. "That sounds like something Michael would say."

"Whoa." Mara motioned for a time-out. "Let's not turn this into a personal—"

"Cheating is personal!" Ellie clenched her fists.

"Okay, well, point taken," Mara conceded. "But in retrospect, I do think Jen's argument has merit. If I had never told Josh about what happened in San Diego—"

"You'd still be a cheater," Ellie finished. "But you'd be a liar, too, on top of that. Let's not sugarcoat the truth." She knew she should shut up, but she couldn't stop herself. "*You're* the one who told me to file for divorce the day after I found out," she reminded Mara. "*You're* the one who said I should get the upper hand and screw him over."

"I was trying to protect you, El."

"You're a hypocrite," Ellie said. "And you know what? I don't blame Josh for making you sign a cheating clause. He should be able to protect himself, too." She yanked the black bridesmaid dress over her head in a rage. The zipper caught on the clasp of her necklace and ripped out a chunk of her silky brown hair. "*Ow.*"

A deathly hush fell over the dressing room. Only the faint strains of piped-in classical music and the rustling of stiff taffeta broke the silence.

Mara snatched up her handbag and coat and stormed out of the salon. Ellie retreated into her dressing room. She hung her head and waited for Jen to break the silence.

Finally, her shame overcame her anger. "Well? Aren't you going to say anything?"

Jen cleared her throat. "I think we've all said enough."

Ellie dug her fingernails into the fleshy pad of her palm. "I shouldn't have..." She sighed. "That wasn't fair."

"Nooo," Jen agreed. "No, it was not."

"Should I go after her?"

"I'd leave her alone right now. She's tough, but she's not *that* tough, and you know she hates to show weakness."

"No wonder she didn't tell me." Ellie sighed again. "I'm turning into a shrill, self-righteous bitch."

The thin partition between the two dressing rooms shuddered slightly as Jen changed out of her gown. "You're not a bitch. You're just hurting right now. And angry. But get angry at the person who really deserves it: Michael. Don't take it out on Mara."

Ellie didn't say anything.

"Hello?" Jen prompted.

"You're right," Ellie said. "But I can't say to Michael what I just said to Mara."

"Why not?"

"Because." She thought about that framed family

photo resting on the mantel. "Sometimes we have to make compromises."

"Meaning what?" Jen sounded confused.

"I don't know." Ellie pressed her lips together. "I'm sure we'll get it all worked out in therapy."

"You need to start taking better care of yourself." Jen's shadowy form appeared on the other side of the slatted white door to Ellie's dressing room. "A salad and a morning walk here and there isn't going to cut it. Tell you what: Call me tomorrow afternoon when Hannah goes down for her nap, and I'll come over and go through some yoga poses with you. Work up a detailed exercise and nutrition plan."

"Once a personal trainer, always a personal trainer." Ellie pulled on her green cashmere hoodie and jeans and emerged from her fitting room.

"I'll swing by around three-thirty. You know you can't wait." Jen closed her eyes and pretended to meditate. "Ommm…"

Ellie laughed and surrendered to the inevitable. "Bring on the walnuts and the downward-facing dog. Are you sure you'll have time, though? I know you have to work, and with the new P.R. push—"

Jen stopped smiling. "I can take some time off."

"So you keep telling us."

"No, I mean it." Jen's voice rose. "I know everyone likes to tease me, but it's not funny anymore. I'm not just some soulless workaholic. I have needs, I have feelings—"

Ellie squinted at her. "What's going on with you?"

Jen hesitated, then whispered, "Can you keep a secret?"

"Oh, please, no more secrets." Ellie recoiled in horror.

"Well then, can you do me a favor?"

"That I can do. Anything. You name it."

"I need the number for your marriage therapist," Jen said. "Or I'm going to have a few pre-nup problems of my own."

Mara  *Chapter* 8

"Don't freak out," said a familiar voice when Mara opened the front door to her town house.

She jumped and dropped her keys with a clatter. "Holy crap, Josh, don't *do* that!"

"Sorry. I was trying not to startle you."

"Too late." She clutched her chest. "You didn't happen to bring a defibrillator, did you?"

He was standing in front of the glass doors that overlooked the golf course, which was dark and empty at this hour. "We need to talk."

"I'm all talked out." She deposited her handbag on the chair next to the door and tossed her keys into the little silver bowl on the hall table. "And I've had more than enough drama for one night. How'd you get in here, anyway?"

"You gave me a set of keys," Josh reminded her. "When you moved in."

"Well, how'd you get past the guard at the front gate?"

"I waved and said hi. They recognize me."

"I told the home-owners' association president that security in this community was a joke." Mara strode toward the breakfast bar that separated the kitchen from the living room. "I'll take my keys back now, thank you very much."

Josh shifted his weight and ignored her demand. "Look. I didn't mean to spring the new version of the pre-nup on you at the jewelers'. If you hadn't found it in my pocket—"

She rounded on her heel and started pacing a tight, straight line between the kitchen sink and the refrigerator. "Don't give me that. Why would you carry it around in your pocket if you didn't want me to find it?"

"How was I supposed to know you'd pat me down like a customs officer looking for contraband?"

"You *wanted* me to find it," Mara accused, her boot heels clicking on the Saltillo tiles. "You *wanted* to hurt me."

Josh studied her face. "And did I? Hurt you?"

"Aha!" Mara jabbed her index finger toward him. "So you admit it."

"We're not in court, Mara. And we're supposed to be on the same team. You shouldn't be trying to win."

"Bullshit," she retorted. "One party always wins when it comes to legal contracts."

Josh made himself comfortable on her cushy leather club chair and stretched his long, thin legs out in front of him. "I know you're still angry. But I'm pretty mad myself."

"Well, I guess that leaves us at an impasse," she replied

with a flippancy she didn't really feel. "And what on earth do you have to be mad about? You're the one who started this! All I asked for was a bare-bones, cut-and-dried, totally fair pre-nup."

"There's no such thing as a totally fair pre-nup." He switched on the lamp next to his chair. "You just said so yourself. One party always wins, which by definition means the other party loses."

"Well..." She sputtered for a few seconds, then yanked open the fridge and scanned the shelves as if the answer to this dilemma could be found in the crisper. "Perhaps I overstated the case."

"No, I think you summed it up perfectly." Josh waited until she turned toward him, then looked her in the eyes. "I love you. I want to marry you and spend the rest of my life with you. But you have to trust me."

Mara slouched over the breakfast bar and braced her hands on the counter. "I do trust you. Or, at least, I did."

"Then act like it," he said softly. "Give me a sign of good faith."

"Says the man who insisted on a snarkily worded clause about how much joint property I have to forfeit if I start dallying with the pool boy."

"No, I'm the man who didn't want a pre-nup in the first place," Josh corrected her.

"Which I still don't get. Honestly, what's the big deal?" She pounded the counter in frustration. "It's just a minor legal formality."

"In case we get divorced."

Mara recommenced pacing. "Having a pre-nup does not mean we're going to get divorced."

"It means you've thought about it, though. Extensively."

She shook her head. "I've just seen too many cases where people didn't bother to communicate about what they wanted and what they deserved until it was too late. And then things get messy, Josh. And vicious. And litigious."

"And this is what you're focusing on while we're planning our wedding," Josh said dryly. "Our messy, vicious, litigious divorce."

"You know what I think?" she challenged. "This pre-nup isn't what you're really upset about."

"Uh, yeah, it is."

"No, this is about what happened in San Diego. Still. You say you've forgiven me, but you haven't. You say you trust me, but you don't."

"*You* don't trust *me*," he countered.

"How can I?" She leaned back against the cold refrigerator door. "When you want to litigate my loyalty?"

"You're right." He gave a quick nod. "We've reached an impasse."

Mara was terrified that she knew what he was going to say next, but she didn't interject. He was going to leave her and she wasn't going to stop him, because what rational argument could she make in her own defense?

He took a deep, purposeful breath and she steeled herself for the worst. But then he said, "Let's scrap the pre-nup, get married like normal people, and just take our chances. What do you say?"

The nape of her neck beaded with sweat until a veritable tributary river system of perspiration soaked her back.

He sat up straighter, looking energized. "We don't need a legal contract to keep us together."

"No," she said slowly. "We don't."

"What? What is that look about?"

"It's just..." She laced her fingers together. "Why bother with a marriage license at all, then?"

His whole body went rigid. "Do you really think a marriage license is the same as a pre-nup? Or is this your way of telling me you don't want to get married anymore?"

"I do want to get married. But I need a safety net."

"Marriage doesn't come with a safety net. Sorry. I stand by my offer: I'll scrap the cheating clause if you scrap the rest of the pre-nup."

She wrapped her arms around herself. "I can't. I'm sorry. I wish it were that simple, but..."

"But what?" Josh crossed his arms, mirroring her defensive posture.

"But things happen. I mean, look at Ellie. She thought she and Michael would be together forever."

"You're not Ellie. I'm not Michael."

"I realize that, but do you see where I'm going with this?"

"All I see is that you sabotage us every chance you get."

She gasped. "How can you say that? I have never—"

"Let me finish." He set his jaw. "Whenever I try to take things to the next level, you kick and scream and do something guaranteed to push me away. You were sabotaging us in San Diego, and you're sabotaging us now with this pre-nup."

Mara didn't say anything.

"I don't know what you expect me to do," Josh said. "I'm not a masochist. I'm not a doormat."

She reached out for him and murmured, "I love you."

He didn't take her hand. "It's decision time, Mara. Say what you mean and mean what you say. Do you really want our marriage to be based on a bunch of conditions starting with 'hereto' and 'whereas'?"

Her hands remained outstretched. "I will never, ever cheat on you again. You have to believe that by now."

"According to you, it doesn't matter what I believe." He fished her house keys out of his pocket and plunked them down on the counter. "It's about what we put in writing. If you get to protect yourself, so do I."

Jen

Chapter 9

"So tell us." Chelsea Kincaid, the perky, Permatanned host of *Up with the Sun, Phoenix!* flashed her dazzling white smile and settled back into her interview chair. "How does a local woman like you build her own nutrition empire before the age of…how old *are* you, if you don't mind my asking?"

Jen tried to laugh this off. "A lady never reveals her weight or age."

"But you look so young," Chelsea exclaimed. "You look like you're barely out of college. And certainly, you've got nothing to play coy about in the weight department. Come on, let us in on some of your secrets."

Jen smiled, took a deep breath, and reminded herself to speak clearly and slowly, just like she'd practiced with Deb, the publicist she'd hired to help springboard her company's profile from local to national. "Balance and variety," she said into the TV camera. "That's the key to health, inside and outside. Eat a variety of whole, unprocessed foods and challenge your body by changing up your workouts. Don't be afraid to try something new." Deb had coached her to turn all her interview responses into a pitch for her product. "In fact, I came up with the idea for Noda one day while I was rock climbing in Sedona."

Chelsea played along with the segue and held up a bottle of Jen's energy drink. "Noda: the antisoda. Love it! So you came up with the idea on a cliff?"

Jen forced herself to relax and let her guard down a bit. "Well, I wasn't always so health-conscious. Back in college, I developed what would probably qualify as a clinical dependency on diet cola."

"A caffeine junkie!" Chelsea bobbed her head. "I can relate!"

"I knew all the chemicals were bad for me, but I just couldn't kick the habit. I swear, diet cola is more addictive than nicotine! And I had lots of friends in the same boat. We drank six cans a day, some of us, and every time we tried to quit, we'd get horrific withdrawal symptoms: headaches, irritability, the shakes."

"That's what I'm like when I don't get my morning coffee!" Chelsea laughed.

"I majored in nutrition, and I spent a few years working as a personal trainer. I would tell my clients to cut the caffeine and preservatives out of their diets, but I wasn't practicing what I preached." She leaned in, as if confiding in Chelsea. "I'd exercise and eat tofu 'til the cows came home, but soda was my dirty little secret."

"So what finally pushed you over the edge?"

"Well..." Jen waited a beat, trying to decide if she should continue with this story. "I was camping in Sedona with an old boyfriend, and he bet me that I couldn't make it through the weekend without diet soda. We were out in the middle of nowhere, so I couldn't cheat. After about thirty-six hours, I freaked out—I was in serious withdrawal but I refused to let him win the bet. So I dragged him back down the mountain to a health food store and started messing around with seltzer water and all kinds of roots and herbs." She grinned. "The early versions of Noda tasted, to put it mildly, not good."

"But the finished product is delish!" Chelsea hoisted up the bottle again for the camera. "I tried it before the show and I have to tell you, I am amazed! It really does taste like cola. You'd never guess it's good for you!"

"Thank you." Jen felt her cheeks flush. "It took me about two years to get the formula just right."

"And did your boyfriend help you test all the failed prototypes?"

"No; he broke up with me. But it all worked out for the best," she said quickly, "because it freed up lots of time for me to work. I tinkered with the recipe on my own for a while, then finally brought in a pair of food chemists to help me refine the flavor and make sure it could withstand packaging and shipping."

"Well, you did an excellent job," Chelsea gushed. "This caffeine addict gives you two thumbs up! And Noda is currently available at health food stores all over Phoenix."

"Right now, we only distribute locally, but we're hoping to take Noda nationwide in the next few years." Jen tried to convey both ambition and modesty. "It's definitely a product whose time has come."

"A real lifesaver for those of us who are getting off-track with our New Year's resolutions," Chelsea said.

The producer started making "wrap-it-up" gestures behind the cameras, but Chelsea wasn't quite ready to cut to commercial. She consulted her interview note cards and said, "Now, your husband is also your business partner, correct?"

"Um," Jen hedged, "he was one of my first major supporters, both financially and emotionally. Chelsea, thank you so much for having me—"

Chelsea leaned into Jen's personal space. "How does he feel about representing a product that you and an ex-boyfriend came up with?"

Jen glanced desperately at the producer, who indicated with a curt nod that she should answer the question. "Well, he...My husband doesn't actually *represent* Noda. He's more of a silent partner."

"So your ex-boyfriend's loss was his gain?"

"Um." *Shouldn't we have cut to a word from our freaking sponsor like thirty seconds ago?* "I suppose you could say that."

"Wow, he must be really secure." Chelsea laughed. "My husband would flip out if I built an empire from a bet with one of my exes."

Jen didn't know where to look. "He's always been very supportive."

"A match made in health food heaven!" Chelsea exclaimed. "Noda, people! It's going to be the next huge thing. Look for it at your local supermarket."

"Oh!" Jen popped her head back up. "And we have a website: www dot No—"

"Too late," the producer announced. "We've already gone to break."

"Oh." She reminded herself to stay positive, focused, and low-maintenance. *Be a delight to work with,* her publicist had instructed. *Always leave the door open for them to invite you back.*

"It was a pleasure to meet you," Jen called to Chelsea, who had whipped out a compact mirror and was touching up her lipstick. "I really appreciate the opportunity to come on the show."

"Mm-hmm." Chelsea finished up with the lipstick and bared her teeth to check for smudges. "Good luck with everything, Jess."

"Thanks. But actually, my name's—"

"Next guest!" the producer bellowed, and a skinny, wild-eyed woman dressed in head-to-toe sequins and carrying a Chihuahua swept in from the green room. "Ninety seconds!"

"Follow me," ordered a production assistant with headphones and a clipboard. "You did great. Here's the exit. Bye, Jess."

Fifteen minutes later, Jen was still wandering around the TV station parking lot in a daze, clutching her keys in one hand and her cell phone in the other.

Wait. What kind of car do I drive, again?

There was a reason why she'd majored in nutrition instead of communications. One unexpected interview question and she'd completely lost her composure. And *Up with the Sun, Phoenix!* wasn't exactly hard-hitting investigative journalism. If she couldn't even hack the local morning shows, how did she expect to land a spot on *Today* or *Good Morning America?*

She probably should not have recounted the details of the Sedona bet on live television. She *definitely* shouldn't have implied that Eric was anything less than a full partner in Noda. Deb insisted that a happily married, health-conscious couple made for a better marketing image than an "obsessive" single woman.

Her marriage had become a marketing tool. And Jen was increasingly terrified that image was all that remained of the relationship.

When she and Eric had first announced their engagement almost six years ago, one of Jen's aunts had sidled up to her at a family dinner and whispered that sometimes being married was lonelier than being single. At the time, Jen dismissed this as sour grapes from a disenchanted divorcee, but lately, she had started to understand what her aunt had meant.

Eric had been her best friend when she walked down the aisle. Emphasis on *friend.* The grand passion and raging chemistry she'd experienced with Patrick wasn't there, but grand passion had broken her heart and raging chemistry had left her with third-degree burns. Eric had been there for her when her spirit bottomed out, and she concluded that the steady, subdued love she shared with him was a healthier alternative to all the Sturm und Drang with Patrick.

Except now she and Eric weren't best friends anymore. They were kind of like roommates. Cordial, considerate, painstakingly polite roommates who hadn't had sex in... God, how long *had* it been?

Jen wandered up and down the aisles of cars until she located her black sedan. She slid into the driver's seat, flipped open her phone, and dialed Eric. This time she'd get it right. This time she'd find a way to share all the fear and hope ricocheting around in her heart and—

"Hello?" Her husband sounded completely unenthused to hear from her.

"Hi, hon." She tried to compensate for him by oozing positivity. "I just finished with *Up with the Sun, Phoenix!* and I wanted to check in."

"Mmm." He stifled a yawn. "How'd that go?"

She frowned. He could at least pretend to care. "It started off okay, but I definitely need more media training."

"I'm sure you were fine."

She tapped her fingers on the steering wheel. "Don't you want to know what went wrong? The interviewer started asking all these personal questions about you and how our partnership works."

"Into the minefield," he deadpanned.

"I told her that you're totally supportive and secure and my dream man."

"So basically, you lied?"

"Oh, that's nice." She gave up on positivity. "You know what? I have to go. Enjoy the rest of your trip."

"Wait, wait. Don't hang up. I'm sorry." He sounded gruff and uncertain. "And I appreciate your saying that I'm your dream man."

"I wasn't just saying it," she insisted.

He paused, then changed the subject. "Hey, did you get the package I sent?"

And that's when she realized the date: Next week would be their fifth anniversary. She had completely forgotten. But she knew that when she returned to the house, something truly spectacular awaited her. Eric outdid himself every year with extravagant gifts of jewelry. He didn't believe in practical gifts like vacuum cleaners or new tires. "Weddings are romantic, and anniversaries should be, too," he'd announced after their first year together. "You'll always be my bride."

From *you'll always be my bride* to *basically, you lied* in just under five years. Jen shuddered to imagine what he might come up with by their tenth anniversary.

"Check the front porch when you get home," Eric continued. "I overnighted a box from the hotel yesterday. Call me when you open it, okay? It's valuable and I want to make sure it didn't get damaged during shipping."

"I will. Honey, you're always so sweet."

"What?" His voice faded into a cacophony of blaring horns and rumbling bus engines. "I just stepped out of the cab and I'm on my way into a meeting, so—"

"I'll call you when I get home," Jen yelled into her phone. "And, hey! Happy early anniv—"

Click. His end of the connection went dead.

Okay. So maybe they had a little work to do in the

communication department. But Jen was nothing if not focused. She would redirect some of her energy and drive toward resurrecting her marriage. By this time next year, they'd be past this rough patch and happier than ever. And in the meantime, she had a lavish gift waiting for her at home. What a guy.

"What the hell?" she muttered as she dug a plastic-encased baseball out of the express delivery box. Jen squinted at the signature scribbled under the ball's red stitching.

Then she spied the note nestled underneath a layer of white packing peanuts:

J—
Finally found a genuine Reggie Jackson for my collection. Please put in my office. See you soon.
—E

And that was it. She sifted through the layers of packaging at the bottom of the box, but there was no anniversary card, and definitely no jewelry.

No "love" on the note, even.

She warned herself not to jump to conclusions. Maybe a little blue box would be arriving tomorrow. Maybe Eric didn't want to ruin the surprise.

Or maybe your marriage just went from life support to flatline.

As she stood motionless in her big, empty kitchen, staring down at the grimy old baseball, she'd never felt more alone. Talking about this with anyone, even Ellie or Mara, would make it too real. She wouldn't be able to stave off the fear and the failure anymore.

So she let the silence linger. This was what her life would be without the constant distraction of work: nothing. She and Eric had nothing left.

Then her cell phone rang, jolting her back into action, and she snatched it up without even checking caller ID.

"This is Jen."

"I can't believe you're still talking about that camping trip to Sedona," teased a low, sexy voice.

Her breath caught. "How did you get this number?"

Patrick ignored the question. "And on TV, no less. For commercial gain. I can't believe you'd exploit me like that." He laughed. "I feel so cheap and dirty."

Jen dissolved into a flurry of inarticulate denials.

"But you left out all the best parts. If I'm remembering correctly, caffeine withdrawal made you do some crazy things. Ah, the good old days."

Jen tried to block out the memories, but it was too late. Hearing Patrick talk like this was opening doors in her psyche that she had slammed shut and locked.

And Eric was on the other side of the country.

"I'm married," she blurted out.

"So I hear."

"I have to go."

"Then I won't keep you." He sounded drolly amused. Damn him. "Good talking to you, kid."

He hung up before she did. *Damn* him!

She pulled her frequent flier card out of her wallet and scanned the fine print on the back for a customer service number. "Hello?" she said briskly when the airlines representative picked up. "I'd like to book a flight from Phoenix to JFK, please. As soon as possible. Tonight, if you have anything available."

Ellie | Chapter 10

"Sweetheart, I promise: This is just a boring, run-of-the-mill business trip." Michael reached across the BMW's front seat and cupped Ellie's cheek in his hand. "Bunch of potential investors abusing my expense account at a steakhouse. Maybe a few cigars if things get really wild. Nothing to worry about. Okay?"

Ellie tucked her chin down and watched the traffic speeding by their car at the departures curb at the airport. "I'm not worried. Well, maybe just a little."

"I can't blame you for that." He sounded sad, but not sullen. "Re-earning your trust is going to be a long process. But I can handle it; I thrive on challenge."

She finally cracked a smile. "Spoken like a man who just left a therapist's office."

"Hey, nothing wrong with that. I think Dr. Kline is really helping, don't you?"

Ellie mulled this over for a moment. "I guess. But, I mean, she's just so ... At the end of every session, no matter what, she always says we're making excellent progress."

"Give the good doctor a chance," he said. "We've only had two sessions."

"That's my point. We barely got the backstory out. How can we already be making excellent progress? She probably says the same thing to everybody who comes through her office. Even the no-hopers."

"Well, for what she charges per hour, she better suck up to her patients," Michael said, and they both laughed. "And FYI, we are not no-hopers. We are going to come back from this thing stronger than ever."

This thing. Like they'd survived a natural disaster or a life-threatening disease. Her distaste must have shown on her face because Michael immediately sobered into sincerity.

"I know this is hard for you, El. I know I deserve to be drop-kicked from here to Shanghai. And I appreciate your trying."

"I *am* trying," she said. "But it's hard. I can't just erase—"

"I know." He gathered her up in his arms and squeezed. "I know. And I appreciate it. Even if you're only hanging in there for Hannah's sake."

She let his crisp white shirtfront absorb her tears and thanked the Lord she hadn't put on mascara that morning.

"I'm not just doing this for Hannah's sake." She wavered for a moment, then remembered what Dr. Kline had said about owing each other total honesty. "I still … love you. Even though I don't actually *like* you right now."

"I love you, too."

"I want our family to work again."

"It will," he swore. "Track all my text messages and e-mails, cell phone records, credit card statements, you name it. Stalk my every move, because this really is going to be the world's most tedious business trip."

"And having a stalker will make it more interesting?"

"Sure. Makes me feel important," he teased. "And when I get back on Monday, we'll continue with our excellent progress with Dr. Kline."

"I can hardly wait. Have a safe flight." Ellie let him kiss her lightly on the forehead. "Call me when you land."

"Will do." He flashed his rakish dimpled grin. "And, hey, check the glove compartment."

"Right now?" She pushed the silver latch beneath the dashboard. "Why?"

"Just a little something to keep you sane while I'm gone," he said as she pulled out a creamy white envelope tied with a green ribbon.

"What did you do?" She made every effort to appear delighted, even though part of her—the part that was not making excellent progress, apparently—was screaming *guilt gift, guilt gift!*

"Well, you always have to take care of everything with Hannah and the house and even my parents while I'm away," he said. "You deserve a little pampering."

Guilt gift, guilt gift!

She opened the envelope and pulled out a gift certificate to her favorite day spa.

"You're going to spend the whole day there tomorrow. Starting at nine A.M." He looked inordinately proud of himself. "Facial, pedicure, massage, the works. Even a mud bath."

"A mud bath? Sounds intense."

"The girl on the phone said it was all the rage and, I quote, 'very centering.' She was quite the sales shark, now that I think about it," Michael mused. "I should hire her."

"Do you think there'll be seaweed and salt scrubs along with the mud?"

"You're the spa expert; you'll have to report back to me."

They shared a smile and, just for a moment, Ellie's anger and despair subsided to the point that she could glimpse the possibility of a future with him. For a split second, she felt back at home in her marriage. Maybe Patrice was right. Maybe time could heal the rift between them. "I wish you didn't have to go out of town right now."

"Me, too. God." He raked his hands through his dark brown hair. "Believe me, El, if there were any way I could skip this trip...But we've got a major potential investment on the line here, big money, and my dad really wants me to handle it myself."

She nodded. "Well, that's why the company's called Barton Properties, right?"

"Maybe I can come home a day early." He opened the driver's-side door and walked around to let her out of the passenger side. "See you in seventy-two hours, okay?"

"Seventy-two hours," she echoed softly. The air was cold and filled with stale diesel fumes and shrill security guard whistles.

"Have a good time at the spa." Michael touched her

cheek again and gazed at her with an expression she didn't recognize. "I already checked with my mom—she'll watch Hannah tomorrow while you're getting centered in the mud."

"Wow. You thought of everything. I'm impressed."

"I better go," he said as the sliding doors to the terminals opened and a garbled voice on the loudspeaker announced an impending departure. "Security line's a mile long these days."

"Okay." She brushed her thumb against his. "I'll, you know. Miss you. Hannah, too. She's already informed me she'll be dictating an e-mail to you after dinner. I'm to act as her secretary."

He nodded distractedly as his brain shifted into work mode. "Don't worry about picking me up on Thursday; it'll be right in the middle of rush hour, so I'll have the office send a car." Then he hurried through the sliding doors, his stride purposeful and commanding.

Ellie watched him disappear into the crowd and tucked the beribboned envelope into her purse. She merged into outbound traffic and headed for the freeway, then picked up her cell and dialed the one person she knew who needed a spa day even more than she did.

"Hey, Mara, it's me. Wait, wait, don't hang up. I know you're still upset about last Friday and I deserve it. But maybe I can make it up to you tomorrow with a ninety-minute shiatsu followed by ten minutes of intensive groveling?"

Jen *Chapter* 11

Keep the change." Jen thrust a fistful of bills at the cab driver who had ferried her from the airport to the posh Manhattan hotel where Eric was staying. She wrapped her thin wool coat tighter around her torso while she waited for the driver to unload her hastily packed suitcase from the taxi's trunk. As a lifelong resident of the Southwest, Jen usually avoided traveling to the Northeast between November and April. She couldn't bear the snow, slush, and gloomy gray skies that dominated New York on February mornings like this one. The rows of skyscrapers created giant wind tunnels, channeling blasts of frigid air across the city. Less than sixty seconds outside, and she was already losing feeling in her cheeks and nose.

The first pale streaks of dawn feathered across the horizon as she slung her bag over her shoulder and hustled through the hotel's revolving doors. She'd managed to catch the red-eye from Phoenix last night (also anathema in her personal travel philosophy, but desperate times called for desperate measures) and after a cramped five-hour flight she'd arrived in Midtown exhausted but utterly determined.

The lobby was deserted at this hour on a Sunday morning, save a uniformed housekeeper polishing the mirrored wall by the elevators. An abandoned newspaper lay strewn across the cluster of maroon upholstered chairs.

She approached the registration desk, her steps buoyed by optimism. The time had come to take action and she had a plan. She *always* had a plan.

The stoop-shouldered clerk greeted her with a rather weary "Good morning. Welcome to the Hotel McMillan. Checking in?"

"Actually, I'm joining my husband. He's already a guest here—Eric Kessler." She spelled out the surname and stifled a yawn while the clerk checked the computer records.

"Very good." The clerk picked up the desk phone. "Shall I call him and let him know you're here?"

"No, no, it's kind of a surprise visit. Just give me his room number, and I'll be on my way."

The clerk's forehead creased. "I'm not authorized to do that, ma'am. We're supposed to clear all visitors with our guests."

"But I'm not a visitor; I'm his wife."

"Yes, well, nevertheless..." The clerk shifted his weight from foot to foot.

"Oh." Jen suddenly got it. "*Oh.* You're afraid I'll catch him with another woman?"

The clerk's face reddened. "Of course not, ma'am. But it's strict hotel policy. I'm sure your husband isn't— I mean, the Hotel McMillan doesn't—"

Jen had to laugh. "Have no fear, my husband's definitely not up there canoodling with some chippy. Trust me."

The clerk hesitated. "Even so..."

Jen glanced left, then right to make sure that the coast was clear before peeling a fresh fifty out of her wallet and sliding it across the counter. "Tell you what. You don't have to say anything. Just write down the room number. Come on, I flew all the way across the country for this. Help a girl out."

The clerk stopped dithering and fixated on the cash. "This is highly irregular."

"Well, love makes us all do crazy things. Here's a pen."

"I have principles, you know."

"So do I; I'm not coughing up another fifty. My final offer's on the table," she bluffed. "Take it or leave it."

The clerk cleared his throat and reached for the money. "If my manager finds out about this..."

"Finds out about what? I'm not allowed to tip a helpful hotel employee?"

The clerk seized the pen and scribbled down a number on a piece of hotel stationery. "Have a nice day."

"Thanks." She snatched up the slip of paper and hurried toward the elevator. "I fully intend to."

Jen announced her arrival at room 3316 with three quick knocks. She leaned forward, tense with anticipation, and waited.

And waited. And waited.

She knocked again, louder this time. Still no response.

"Eric?" *Rap, rap, rap.* "Honey?"

Finally, she heard something on the other side of the door: a long, rumbling snore.

She had often envied her husband's ability to fall into an almost impenetrable slumber at the drop of a hat. Even on airplanes, he could sleep peacefully through turbulence, loudspeaker announcements, and squalling infants. She should have thrown that front desk clerk an extra ten-spot for a copy of the room key.

So much for taking him totally by surprise. She set down her bag, dug out her cell phone, and dialed Eric's number. She heard his phone ringing on the other side of the door, the chirpy ringtone alternating with his snores.

When she got bounced to voice mail, she hung up and dialed again, then pounded on the door with the heel of her hand.

The snore sputtered into a cough as Eric stirred and answered his phone. "'Lo?"

She stopped knocking and lowered her voice to a breathy, teasing lilt. "Hey, honey, it's me. Guess where I'm standing right now?"

He mumbled something unintelligible.

"Honey?" she cooed.

"Jen?" He sounded bewildered. "What's going on? Is everything okay?"

She sighed. "Everything's fine. Open the door."

Muffled rustling on the other end of the line. "What door? I'm in New York, Jen."

"So am I." She struck a pose and rubbed her lips together to freshen the gloss she'd applied in the elevator. "Go open your hotel room door. It'll be worth it, I promise."

"Can I call you back in the morning?" His words slurred together.

"Hey. Don't fall asleep on me," she barked. "Just get up for two seconds and open your hotel room door. Humor me."

"But I—"

"Please."

The door swung inward and her husband's sleep-lined, unshaven face peered out at her. His sandy blond hair stuck out from his head at odd angles and he was clad in plain white briefs and a white undershirt, but he'd never looked better to her.

"Surprise." She hugged him, tucking her head under his chin. His body felt warm and solid against hers, and she inhaled deeply to savor his clean, soapy scent.

He didn't say anything for a minute, just absorbed the impact of her embrace. Then he put both arms around her waist and squeezed.

"Hi," she whispered.

"What on earth are you doing here?" he murmured.

"I missed you." She clung to him and said a silent

prayer of thanks for her steady, solid husband. He would always be her anchor. He would never let her down.

He was, in short, the polar opposite of Patrick Spillane.

She tilted back her head. "Did you miss me? I know you said not to bother coming all this way, but I just couldn't wait." She faltered for a moment before purring, "I need you."

His eyes snapped wide open.

"Well, look who's awake." She pressed the full length of her body against his.

His arousal stirred and hardened against her side, but the rest of him remained absolutely still. He seemed to be holding himself in check, afraid of scaring her off.

She pulled away long enough to unbutton her jacket, then glanced around to make sure the hallway was empty before peeling off her sweater. Underneath, she wore a skimpy black lace demibra she'd bought right after their honeymoon. The bra had been buried at the bottom of her sock drawer, tags still attached, for five years. She and Eric had never been a sexy-lingerie kind of couple. Until now.

Eric's eyes got even bigger, as did the bulge in his shorts.

She lowered her eyelashes and threw him a sultry half-smile. "Aren't you going to ask me to come in so I can show you what I've got on under my jeans?"

Eric yanked her inside, hung the "Do Not Disturb" sign over the knob, and slammed the door shut. His fingers fumbled with the zipper on her jeans as they stumbled toward the bed.

She let herself fall back against the crisp cotton sheets that were still warm from her husband's body. She closed her eyes and cleared her mind and made love to her husband with a focused, ferocious energy that she hoped would bridge the gulf widening between them.

Jen listened to the slow, steady rasp of Eric's breathing and repositioned her pillow. She'd been lying here for the last half hour, her agitation mounting as the minutes ticked by on the luminous digital clock on the night-stand. His warm, solid body curled around hers and she couldn't bear to be so close to anyone right now. Not while the scent of sex still clung to the sheets and all of her emotions were roiling so close to the surface.

Carefully, inch by inch, Jen pulled away from her husband and tiptoed across the bedroom, nearly stumbling as her feet got tangled in a comforter that had been tossed to the floor. She needed to staunch all the hope and fear and pain coursing through her heart. She needed to go numb.

She retrieved her laptop computer from her suitcase, retreated to the alcove between the bedroom and the bathroom, and clicked the cursor to open up some marketing reports. The light emanating from the screen bathed the dark walls in a pale blue glow. She stared at the data, refusing to think about anything except the numbers directly in front of her.

She heard rustling behind her, then Eric's voice, thick with sleep. "Jen? What are you doing?"

"I thought you were asleep."

"I was. But I'm freezing in there by myself now that we kicked all the blankets onto the floor. What's wrong?"

"Nothing."

He came closer. "Was I snoring?"

"No. I'm just too wired to sleep right now. I can't relax."

"Well, if you need to work off some excess energy, I'm up for round two." He placed his palms on her shoulders and gently kneaded the muscles at the base of her neck.

She pulled away from his touch. "Sorry. I'm a little jittery. Travel."

"I'll stay up with you," he offered. "Want me to make coffee?"

"No, I'm okay."

"Or, I know, there's a twenty-four-hour diner around the corner. We could grab something to eat and read the Sunday paper. You must be starving." He sounded so happy and confident.

"Not really."

"What can I do to help you?"

This was her chance to talk to him about everything. She could smash through the barriers of silence between them and use last night's lovemaking as the first step in establishing a marriage worthy of the title. She could finally let him in.

"Nothing." She squeezed her hands together until her knuckles hurt and the edges of her wedding ring bit into her fingers. "I need a little time alone, that's all."

He hesitated. "But you just got here. And we haven't seen each other in almost two weeks."

"I know, but..."

"Staring at your laptop in the dark isn't going to help you. A little fresh air and some food will do you good. Come on, I'll get your coat."

"No!" she said, her voice louder than she'd intended. "I can't do this right now."

"Do what? You flew across the country and showed up at my hotel room in the middle of the night and ripped off my clothes and now you're telling me you can't stand to look at me?"

"I know it doesn't make sense, but..." She drew up her knees and covered her face. "It's not you. This has nothing to do with you."

"Then what does it have to do with?" The confusion and anxiety in his voice vanished. "*Oh.*"

"What?" She twisted around to look at him, but he'd already turned his back to her.

"You can have the bed. I'll sleep on the couch in the other room. Have your alone time. Have as much as you want. See you in the morning."

Jen startled awake to find bright afternoon sunlight filtering through the hotel curtains and onto her face. She could hear muffled traffic noises in the distance—horns honking, doors slamming. Her neck ached from hunching over her computer and her throat was parched. It took her a moment to remember where she was.

She'd been too distracted to appreciate it last night, but the McMillan Hotel offered quite the cushy digs. Lustrous ice blue wallpaper offset the heavy, dark wood four-poster bed and armoire. The linens were high-thread-count and a pristine white duvet enveloped the fluffy down comforter. The pillow next to hers still bore the concave impression of Eric's head. As the memories of their conversation came rushing back, she swung her feet down to the carpet.

She heard faint clinks and clatters from the other side of the door next to the armoire. "Honey?" she called.

The clinking ceased. "In here."

She arranged herself into what she hoped was an irresistible picture of morning-after dishabille and waited for him to come to her, but the door remained closed.

Not a good sign. She clambered out of bed, slipped on an embroidered white robe she found hanging in the bathroom, tugged a damp comb through her hair, and prepared to face the consequences of last night's amorous ambush.

Eric sat reading the newspaper in a gray wingback chair in the corner of a small sitting room. His stocking-feet were propped up on a glass coffee table, but the rest of him was decked out in full office regalia: starched shirt, striped power tie, pressed black pants. Jen noticed the remains of a room service meal on the side table next to him: buttery crumbs and smudges of jam on an elegant silver-rimmed plate.

She sidled up to the coffee table and waited for him to acknowledge her.

He didn't look up from the paper.

She rubbed her ankle with the instep of her other foot. "Um, hi. Good morning."

He very slowly and deliberately folded up the newspaper. "Good morning to you. Did you sleep well?"

She sank down on the ottoman next to his chair. "I guess so. I missed you, though. You didn't have to move to the sofa out here." The lapels of her robe gaped forward as she leaned toward him. He didn't appear to notice.

"So last night was pretty incredible, huh?" she prompted.

"Mmm. I ordered you some egg whites and fresh grapefruit. Over there on the wet bar." He nodded toward a tray covered with a metal dome, then returned his attention to the business section.

She cleared her throat. "I'm sorry about...everything. I don't know what was going on in my head."

He didn't lift his gaze. "Apology accepted."

"So we're okay?" She nibbled her lower lip. "I had a great time last night. You were amazing. I mean, we were just out of control! I'm surprised no one called security."

He set aside the newspaper.

She tucked her feet under her and smiled. "It's been a while, hasn't it? A really long while. In fact, now that I'm thinking about it, I can't even remember the last time we—"

"Enough," he snapped. "I get it. We've had a long, agonizing, sexless marriage."

She flinched at the rancor in his voice. "Don't say that. I flew all the way out here to show you how much I love you."

"Give me a break." He turned his face toward the wall. "You didn't fly out here because you love me. You flew out here to make yourself feel better about the fact that you *don't* love me and you never have. Don't deny it.

We both know the bottom line: we never should have gotten married. This whole thing was a huge mistake."

At first, she was too shocked to be hurt. Eric had never spoken to her this way. Ever. He was the sweetest, mildest, most considerate man she'd ever met. "Where is this coming from?"

He didn't respond.

"Stop ignoring me!" She shook off her confusion and leapt to her feet. "I want to talk about this!"

He spread out his arms in a gesture of surrender. "I'm done talking. It's over. I give up."

"You give up? Right after we have the best sex of our lives? What the hell is going on?"

"You know exactly what's going on." His expression hardened. "Patrick Spillane is back. And whatever was going on between you two never really ended."

Jen's throat closed up. "You heard about Patrick?"

"About a week ago." He watched her face for any flicker of emotion. "I was wondering when you'd find out, and last night, I got my answer."

"Last night had nothing to do with Patrick," she insisted. "You're being ridiculous. And paranoid. And… and…"

Eric smoothed out his tie. "So you haven't seen him or spoken to him since he came back to town?"

She sidestepped the question and tried to focus on what mattered most. "Patrick has nothing to do with us, Eric. He's history, and you're my future. That's what I was trying to show you last night. I love you. You're my best friend."

"That's the problem right there. I'm the best friend, and I'll never be able to compete with the guy you really loved."

"There's no competition!"

"I'll say. You can't even stand to sleep in the same bed with me."

She leaned toward him, beseeching him with both her eyes and words. "I am so, so sorry. I was just...I promise you, Eric, that wasn't about you."

"It's never about me. Always *him*." He got to his feet and gathered up his jacket and briefcase. "I'm leaving."

"Well, when will you be back? We need to—"

"No, I mean I'm leaving this. Us. I can't do this anymore." He looked both resigned and resolute. "We wasted five years already. Let's not waste another five."

"Our marriage is not a waste!" she cried.

He turned his back to her and reached for the door handle.

"Don't you love me?" She winced at the note of desperation in her voice.

He already had one foot in the hallway.

She panicked and fell back on the only remaining tactic she could think of to stall him: "Wait! Wait. You can't leave me. We're partners, Eric. What about the company?"

She knew it was the wrong thing to say as soon as the words left her mouth. The heavy metal door slammed behind him, and he was gone.

Ellie

Chapter 12

*Y*ou're lucky I'm easily bought off," Mara huffed as she changed into a terry-cloth robe at the spa locker next to Ellie's. "*Some* people would hold a grudge forever. *Some* people would never be able to forget the hurtful and slanderous things you said at the bridal salon last week."

"Thank God you're not one of those people." Ellie grinned.

"Yes, well, my motto has always been, hate the sin and love the sinner." Mara pulled her hair up into a ponytail. "Particularly if she's footing the bill for a massage."

"And a mud bath. Don't forget the mud bath."

"The jury's still out on the mud bath. Exactly what kind of mud are we talking here—Dead Sea silt or sewage waste?"

"Your guess is as good as mine." Ellie sipped the chilled, lemon-scented water she'd been instructed to imbibe before meeting up with the masseuse. "But Michael says it's supposed to be luxurious and centering."

"Hmm."

"Aren't you going to ask how everything's going with the reconciliation and the STD testing and the fifty-minute therapy hours?"

Mara shook her head. "I thought the point of today was to de-stress and enjoy ourselves."

"Well, am I allowed to ask if you and Josh made up?"

Mara chugged half of her water in one gulp. "Let's not ruin this with talk, darling. Serenity in silence and all that crap."

"Serenity in silence," Ellie agreed, and the next few hours blurred into a blissful haze of relaxation. She even lapsed into a catnap during her rubdown in the candlelit, lavender-scented massage chamber.

At noon, Ellie and Mara met up for a healthful lunch of salad and grilled fish in the lobby. Then it was back to the capable hands of the staff for facials, eyebrow shaping, and the much-ballyhooed mud bath.

"Considering I just spent the last hour wallowing in filth, I feel surprisingly refreshed," Mara admitted at five o'clock, when both women had showered and changed back into their street clothes. "That was some very chichi mud."

"Probably imported," Ellie said. "From Paris or Milan."

"Hey, my stylist said that this brow shape takes five years off my face." Mara preened in one of the gilt-framed mirrors lining the lobby. "Do I look five years younger to you?"

"You look about fourteen," Ellie assured her. She handed her gift certificate to the petite redhead working the cash register. "That's for me. And I'll be paying for her, too."

The employee ran the card through the machine, then frowned. "Oops. Let me try that again." She swiped the card twice more, concluded that there might be a problem with the magnetized strip, and manually entered the account number into the computer.

She tapped a corner of the plastic card against the granite counter, then glanced up with obvious distress. "I apologize, Mrs. Barton, but this card doesn't seem to be going through. I'm sure it's just a glitch in our system..."

"No problem." Ellie opened her wallet. "Just put it on this one instead."

The employee nodded and exchanged cards. Thirty seconds later, the pained expression returned. "Um..."

"That one's not going through, either?" Ellie frowned. "Are you sure?"

"Actually, it wants me to call the credit card company." The cashier pointed out a blinking message on the screen. "I'm sure it's my mistake, though. Let me get my manager, and—"

"Try this one." Ellie whipped out another card. "Or this one. Or this one."

Declined. Declined. Declined. The redhead looked ready to commit hara-kiri.

"How bizarre." Ellie pursed her lips, more perplexed than upset. "Maybe I put my bag down on a magnetized counter and screwed up all my cards without knowing it."

"Maybe," Mara muttered darkly.

"What's that supposed to mean?"

"Please," begged the cashier. "Let me get my manager."

"You do that." Mara adopted her most authoritative attorney-at-law tone and took charge of the situation. "In the meantime, we need to use your phone." She grabbed Ellie's Visa and dialed the toll-free number printed on the back. "Hello? Yes, this is Elinor Barton."

"Hey," Ellie protested.

Mara shushed her and continued, "My card was just rejected at a local spa, and I'm hoping you can help me." She rattled off the account number, expiration date, and, with whispered assistance from Ellie, the last four digits of Michael's social security number. "Uh-huh...I see..."

"What?" Ellie asked.

Mara's eyes got narrower and narrower as she continued to grill the credit card rep. "Oh really? And when exactly did that take effect?"

"What?" Ellie demanded.

Mara slammed down the phone. "You're fucked, that's what. I'm going to ask you a question, and I want you to think very carefully before you answer."

"Don't be so dramatic." Ellie managed a shaky laugh. "You're freaking me out."

Mara cocked her head. "Do you have a credit card that's in your name only?"

"Of course. They're all in my name." Ellie pointed to the embossed printing on each card.

"No, I mean, do you have any accounts that you don't share with Michael? That you applied for all by yourself?"

Ellie's alarm intensified. "Why?"

"Just think about it. Any active accounts that you opened by yourself? Maybe from back in college? Department store cards?"

"I don't think so. Michael took over the finances after we got married. He didn't want too many revolving lines of credit; he said it would hurt our FICO scores. Why? What's going on?"

Mara exhaled loudly. "Michael—a.k.a. the primary account holder on presumably all of your credit cards— has officially revoked your authorized user privileges as of this morning."

"But that's ridiculous," Ellie sputtered. "Why would he do that?"

Mara just looked at her.

"There must be some mistake!" She could hear the roar of blood pounding in her ears.

"Not according to the good people at Visa."

"I'm calling him right now." Ellie dialed Michael's number, but got shunted immediately to voice mail. "Crap."

"Ellie. Please. Tell me you took my advice and made copies of all your financial records."

Ellie stared back, her eyes huge. "I was going to. I was on my way to the bank. But then...Oh no. Oh my God."

Mara waved off the approaching spa manager. "Ladies, this whole thing has just been an unfortunate misunderstanding. Put everything on my card and we'll call it a day." She settled up the bill and hustled Ellie out to the parking lot, where the brisk evening wind provided a jarring contrast to the aromatherapized spa humidity. "All right, El. Good air in, bad air out. Let's get you home."

Ellie wanted to protest that this was all a mistake, that Michael would fix everything and they'd all laugh about this later. But her last reserves of denial had evaporated when the cashier had given her that condolatory look. She had seen herself through a stranger's eyes, and the view was not pretty.

"What am I going to do?" she whispered. "What am I going to *do*?"

"We're going straight to your house to start damage control." Mara dragged her toward the black BMW. "You can't afford to have a nervous breakdown right now. Keep moving."

"You don't have to do this." Ellie slid into the driver's seat. "It's not your job to save my marriage."

"I'm not saving your marriage, I'm saving your credit rating, which I think you'll find to be worth a lot more in the long run. Hop to, babe. Time is of the essence."

Just setting eyes on her home comforted Ellie. Every detail, from the brick pavers lining the driveway to the weathered bronze mailbox to the motion-activated light on the garage, had been carefully selected to suit her family's needs. She could handle anything as long as she was safely ensconced within those walls.

"All right, here we go," Mara said with the air of a military general assuming command of a disaster area.

"You collect all the paperwork you can find and I'll man the phones."

"Yoo-hoo!" a high, quavery voice called from across the street.

Ellie stifled a groan and waved to Gertie Hadwick, their elderly neighbor whose primary joys in life were her pair of miniature poodles and fresh gossip. "Hello, Mrs. Hadwick." She turned to Mara and muttered, "Inside. Quick."

Mara wiped her black boots on the welcome mat and hurried inside as soon as Ellie unlocked the front door. She hit the light switch, illuminating the foyer and living room.

Ellie froze in the doorway, one foot over the threshold, and gasped.

"What?" Mara demanded. "God, what now?"

All Ellie could do was point at the vast expanse of empty carpet on the living room floor.

"It's gone," she choked out.

Mara glanced around the hall. "And when you say gone, you're referring to . . . ?"

"The piano. The baby grand."

Mara's jaw dropped. "Are you kidding me? Someone broke into your house and stole a freaking *piano*?"

"Oh, you poor thing." Gertie Hadwick materialized behind Ellie on the front stoop. "How are you holding up?"

Mara yanked Ellie inside the house and started to shut the door in the neighbor's face. "You'll have to excuse us; we're right in the middle of something."

"Oh, I *heard*." Mrs. Hadwick wedged her green rubber gardening clog in between the closing door and the jamb. "Michael told me all about it this afternoon while the movers were here." She elbowed her way inside and enfolded Ellie in a talcum-scented hug. "Poor dear. And poor little Hannah. Divorce is always hardest on the children."

"Michael was here today?" Mara asked.

"He's supposed to be in Dallas!" Ellie exclaimed.

"Oh"—Mrs. Hadwick patted the back of Ellie's head—"I had no idea you two were having such problems. Now, I know it's none of my business, but you should really try counseling before you give up. Marriage is a sacred vow not meant to be—"

"What exactly were these movers moving?" Mara wanted to know.

Mrs. Hadwick readjusted her thick bifocals. "Well, I'm not sure. Just boxes and suitcases and whatnot."

"And the piano."

"Yes. He said it's been in his family for generations. His great-grandparents shipped it over from Europe." The older woman sighed. "What a shame. I do hate to see all these nice young couples splitting up. But that's life today; families just falling apart willy-nilly, and—"

Ellie clamped her hands over her ears.

Mara strong-armed Mrs. Hadwick out and turned the deadbolt. "Get a pen and paper and make a list," she directed. "We'll go take it room by room and write down everything that's missing."

Ellie collapsed on the upholstered bench next to the coat closet. "Honestly, who even cares at this point?"

"You do."

"No, I don't. I'm the woman who laid waste to the china cabinet, remember?"

Mara strode toward the kitchen. "I need a notepad, a list of all your credit cards, and a cordless phone, stat."

Ellie rolled her head back against the wall. "He's supposed to be in Dallas," she repeated. "I dropped him off at the airport."

"Well, evidently he missed his flight."

"But what about therapy? We were starting fresh. He…" She couldn't look away from the spot where the piano had been. "I will *kill* him, do you hear me? He's not going to live long enough to divorce me!"

Mara rolled up her sleeves. "I'm sorry to be so brusque here, but we're losing ground every second you sit there contemplating homicide."

"He can't do this."

"He already did."

"No, I mean, I have explicit legal rights to some of our stuff. We signed a pre-nup before we got married."

"You did?" This brought Mara up short. "Really? I would never have figured you for the pre-nup type."

"Oh, I'm not. But his family insisted."

"Yeah, well, rich people don't stay rich by blindly believing in happily ever after. Go get this pre-nup and let's see exactly what we're dealing with."

As Ellie led Mara back toward the safe in the master bedroom's walk-in closet, she realized that her friend was right to be cynical. Michael was nothing like the man she believed him to be, and maybe he never had been. There had been subtle signs along the way that she'd willfully ignored: the speeding tickets he'd "forgotten" to tell her about, his outspoken impatience with waiters and valets, his gloating when he got the upper hand in a business deal. She had managed to overlook all that because she desperately wanted her marriage to be as perfect on the inside as it appeared on the outside. So really, who was the bigger liar here: her husband or herself?

She discovered the answer when she opened the safe. Her copy of the pre-nup was gone, along with all the other legal documents and investment paperwork. The only things remaining were Hannah's birth certificate and Ellie's passport and social security card.

Ellie didn't have to say anything. Mara glanced from her face to the nearly empty safe and deduced what had happened.

"Son of a bitch! Well, we're not going to take this lying down. You're going to hire the best forensic accountant in the state and we are going to squeeze him for every dollar until he bleeds green!"

Ellie took a deep breath and began to list the things that Michael had taken from her. "My jewelry."

She grazed the cold metal walls of the safe with one finger and imagined the sparkly emeralds adorning the throat and earlobes of Dr. Victoria Locane. Then she pointed to the empty racks and rods on Michael's side of his closet. "All his clothes and his shoes. And his golf clubs."

"Good." Mara nodded. "Write all that down."

Ellie began cataloging material goods in her small, even handwriting. She worked calmly and methodically, and they were dismantling the drawers in Michael's study when she heard a key in the front door and Hannah's high, happy voice crying, "Mommy! What happened to the piano?"

Ellie turned to Mara. "Michael's mom is here. She was watching Hannah today."

"Is she aware that while she was baby-sitting, her son faked a business trip and ransacked your house?" Mara asked.

"No," Ellie said immediately. "Patrice would never condone that. She's like my second..." And then she had to remind herself how badly she'd misjudged Michael. "I don't *think* so."

"I'll take this as my cue to leave." Mara strode out into the hallway with a cheery "Hey, it's my little Miss Hannah Banana. Want to go get a Happy Meal? Your mom says it's okay."

"Yes! Yes!" Hannah adored Mara, who routinely let the little girl try on her high heels and jewelry.

Ellie waited until she heard the door close behind them, then emerged from the study to confront Patrice. As soon as she turned the corner and saw the older woman's expression, she knew Patrice hadn't been privy to Michael's duplicity.

"Oh Ellie." Patrice's hands hung limply at her sides and her face was ashen. "I'm so sorry. This is absolutely..." She closed her eyes and pressed her lips together.

Watching her mother-in-law's composure crumble set off fresh shockwaves of panic. "He took everything!" Ellie's voice was shrill with hysteria. "The piano, the paintings, all our valuables and financial records. What am I going to do?" She waited for Patrice to offer up advice, reassurance, or at the very least, a hug.

But Patrice didn't open her arms. She just kept repeating, "I'm sorry. I don't know what else to say."

"Will you talk to him?" Ellie begged. "He can't do this. It's wrong on every level. Someone has to make him see reason."

Patrice didn't reply. She backed away, still murmuring barely audible apologies, until she had retreated out the door. Seconds later, headlight beams bounced across the foyer as the Jaguar pulled away and Ellie was left alone to search for all the other things she never imagined she could lose.

Jen

Chapter 13

*T*hank God you're home." Jen ran out of her home office to greet Eric at the side door. "I was wondering when you'd get back. You didn't give me your flight information."

Her husband looked disheveled and in desperate need of a hot shower and a square meal. All the airport layovers and meetings in windowless conference rooms had taken their toll, and Jen couldn't suppress her impulse to nurture and revive him.

"You must be beat. Let me whip you up a smoothie. I just bought some fresh kiwi and mangoes and I'll—"

He sighed and rubbed the fine reddish stubble sprouting along his chin. "Don't make this harder than it has to be. I haven't changed my mind about what I said in New York."

That was when she noticed that he hadn't brought in his suitcase from the car.

"I'm just here to pick up some clothes. I'll stay at a hotel until we figure some things out."

Lotus strolled down the hall and rubbed against Jen's leg. She picked up the hefty black cat and cradled him against her chest. "Okay. I get it. You're still inexplicably upset about having hot, wild sex, but—"

"No, Jen, you *don't* get it. I'm not upset anymore. I'm not hurt or angry or crying on the inside, or whatever sensitive, New Age men are supposed to do. What I am is done."

"Done with me."

"You. Us. This farce of a marriage."

She sucked in her breath. "Why do you keep calling it that? I'm really trying here; I thought you were, too."

"And it's still not working." He looked her right in the eye.

She shrank away from the cold defiance in his gaze. "When did you stop loving me?" she asked softly.

"It doesn't matter if I love you, because you don't love me."

"Of course I do!"

"No, you don't. Not enough. And I know I said that wouldn't matter, but it turns out it does."

"This is crazy!" She exhaled sharply in frustration. "We are a team; we can't just quit when the going gets tough."

He took a step back toward the door. "You want to keep me around, but you don't care about keeping me happy."

Jen leaned against the wall, appalled by the image of her he portrayed. When they'd gotten engaged, he had described her as his ideal woman. Had she really changed that much, or had he?

"You gave me fair warning before we got married," he continued. "You love me, but you're not *in* love with me. And I can't stand it anymore. You checked out."

"Me? What about you?" Jen squeezed Lotus a bit too hard, and he wriggled free of her grasp and escaped down the hall. "You're always on the road, you never want to talk..."

He shrugged. "I guess we're both to blame."

"Ellie gave me the name of an excellent marriage counselor."

"No. I don't want to go to a shrink and sit around re-hashing all the reasons why we never should have gotten married in the first place. I'm finished."

"I don't even get a vote? It's my marriage, too."

He rolled his eyes. "Of course it is. It's *your* marriage, *your* company, *your* life. I'm just along for the ride."

She forced herself to ask the question she had been avoiding since he walked through the door. "Is this about what I said in the hotel room? About the company? Because I didn't mean that the way it sounded."

He hesitated a long time, then said, "Yeah, you did. You don't need me, or anyone else because you've got your work. And I respect that. I really do. But I can't live with it anymore."

Right on cue, the phone in her office started ringing. Eric smirked. "Duty calls."

"But I'm not answering!" she pointed out. "You have my full attention. See? You trump my company. Aren't you satisfied?"

"Nope. Neither are you. And since I got us into this

mess, I'll get us out." He jammed his hands into his pockets. "I'll be meeting with an attorney this week, and I'm going to file for legal separation." He held up one palm. "I don't want things to get nasty and ugly, but I have to move on with my life." He brushed past her and headed for the master bedroom. "And don't worry about what our pre-nup says; I have no interest in enforcing all the terms we agreed to."

She pushed off the wall and hurried after him.

"I know that I could take the company away from you," he threw over his shoulder, "but I won't. I don't want it. I just want out."

Jen tried to disguise her fear with outrage. "I cannot believe you'd bring up the pre-nup at a time like this."

"I'm packing up my clothes and meeting with lawyers. When else would I bring it up?"

The phone in her office started ringing again.

"Eight-thirty P.M. and your life is calling," Eric said. "Better answer."

"Jen! Thank God you picked up!" Deb the publicist sounded positively electrified. "I have big news. Huge. Sit down and brace yourself, 'cause your life is about to change forever."

Jen perched on the edge of her desk and cast a baleful look toward the vicinity of the bedroom, where Eric was busy packing his bags. "There seems to be a lot of that going around tonight."

"What?"

"Nothing." She sighed. "So what's up? You're certainly working late."

"I bust my butt for you twenty-four seven," the publicist said. "I told you when you signed on: I'm expensive but I'm worth it. Guess who I just got off the phone with?"

Jen took more than two nanoseconds to reply, which far exceeded Deb's patience.

"Rory Reid's booking agent!"

"Shut up!" Jen hopped off her desk. "*The* Rory Reid?"

"The one and only. I sent her people a big case of Noda and wouldn't let them eat, sleep, or pee in peace until they tried it. And they loved it! They want to feature it on the show. Rory might even interview you on-air."

Jen managed only a small squeak in response.

Deb crowed in triumph. "Who's working for you, babe?"

Another tiny squeak.

"Say something!" Deb commanded.

"I'm here," Jen breathed. "You wouldn't kid me about something like this?"

"I don't kid. Especially when it comes to national television. So what do you say? Are you ready for the big time?"

Jen waited for the thrill of victory. Deb was right; everything was about to change. She'd been fantasizing about this phone call since she sold the very first case of Noda to a tiny organic café near Sedona. She had always known that no matter how hard she worked, success was ultimately yoked to luck. Some random stranger in a random office had made a snap decision to give her everything she wanted. Just like that.

"Wow."

"That's the understatement of the millennium," Debra said. "Sometimes I'm so good I amaze myself."

Jen started laughing uncontrollably. "I think I might throw up."

"Go right ahead. And then uncork some champagne, because moments like this don't come along very often." Deb herself sounded ready to light up a postcoital cigarette. "Oh! My other line's ringing and I've got to take it, but I'll call you tomorrow. Congrats!"

Jen gently replaced the receiver and took a moment to let the news sink in. She heard a faint rustling behind her and turned around to find Eric standing by the door. Two overstuffed duffel bags rested on the rug behind him.

"Good news?" he asked.

"Great news." A dazed half-smile spread across her face. "That was the outrageously overpriced publicist I hired against my better judgment. Noda's going to be featured on the Rory Reid show."

Eric looked stunned. Even he, who couldn't pick Lindsay Lohan out of a lineup, had heard of Rory Reid. "She's that talk show host, right?"

"Mm-hmm." Jen wrapped her arms around herself and squeezed. "The 'Gen-X Oprah.' She's going to plug Noda on national TV. This is incredible."

Her husband placed his house key on the console

table under the hall mirror. "I'll call you when I need to come back to pick up more stuff. And congratulations. I mean it."

And with that, Eric exited her life as quietly and calmly as he'd first crept in.

Mara
Chapter
14

"Great news, Ellie, I've got a kick-ass lawyer for you." Mara waved her assistant away as the frosted glass door to her office started to open. At three-thirty on a Friday afternoon, she was juggling Ellie's phone call, four new urgent e-mails, and an oncoming tension headache. "Karen Hamilton. She's with Koeth and Godwin and she's supposed to be the best— What? Oh, don't worry about the retainer fee. I'll write you a check and— I won't take no for an answer, El. I've seen these things go bad too many times. You can't afford *not* to hire a shark. Trust me … Don't be ridiculous, no one thinks you're a charity case. If it'll make you feel better, you can pay me back after you settle and stick that jackass with your legal bills."

She sipped her coffee while Ellie spouted a litany of panicked protest and questions. "No, I can't represent you. Believe me, I wish I could, but I do trust and estate law and you need someone who specializes in family law.… Exactly; I can write a pre-nup, but I can't enforce it. Speaking of which, have you dug up a fresh copy of the one you and Michael signed? Uh-huh...Oh boy. Well, come over this weekend, and we'll go over the parts you don't understand. Listen, I have about fifteen phone calls to return before five o'clock, so I have to run. Call Karen Hamilton right now, okay? I just e-mailed you her work number....Right...Okay. And don't worry, El, everything's going to be fine. I promise."

She hung up and dug through her desk drawer for the bottle of ibuprofen she kept stashed for afternoons like this one. Everything was definitely *not* going to be fine for Ellie, but Mara knew that the only way to help her friend right now was to stay positive and try to find loopholes in a contract Ellie had signed when she'd trusted Michael to cherish and protect her for the rest of their lives.

Trust was a trap. Mara had seen that over and over again with her clients. They said they loved each other, but then they tried to conceal assets and impose all kinds of restrictions on one another. One groom had wanted a pre-nup clause stipulating that his bride-to-be would forfeit alimony if she gained more than fifteen pounds during the course of their marriage. Another requested that his fiancée agree to continue his family's tradition of naming the firstborn son after his great-great-grandfather— Hiram—despite the fact that she detested the name.

And now sweet, softhearted Ellie had to pay for placing her trust in the wrong man. It wasn't fair, but that was one of the first things you learned in law school: touchy-feely concepts like karma and fairness didn't count. The only thing that mattered was what was explicitly stated in the contract.

Mara typed up a terse response to an e-mail, then

poked her head out the door. "Sorry, Julie, I was on an important call. What's up?"

"The DeLorenzo documents just came in on the fax," her assistant reported. "And Josh is on line one. And your wedding planner is on line two. She wants to know if you've made a final decision about the chair covers."

Mara stopped skimming through her inbox. Josh hardly ever called her at work. "Josh is still holding?"

"I think so. The light's still blinking."

"Tell the wedding planner I'll call her back." Mara picked up the phone as if it were wired with unstable explosives. Then she jabbed the hold button and answered briskly, "Mara Stroebel."

"Hey." Josh sounded as hesitant as she felt. "Do you have dinner plans?"

"I do, as a matter of fact. Lukewarm Chinese takeout at my desk. Ever the slave to billable hours. Then, evidently, I may be forced to attend an emergency chair-cover summit with the wedding planner. Want to come?"

He paused. "So the wedding's still on?"

Mara tried to sound blithe and matter-of-fact. "I'm agreeing to a chair-cover summit, am I not?"

"Translation: You love me and you can't live without me?"

"Well. Yeah, basically." She tossed her hair to hide her discomfiture, even though there was no one to witness her. "Can we please just skip this part and get back to business as usual?"

He laughed. "Oh, you sentimental sap."

"If you want puffy hearts and frolicking kittens, you've got the wrong woman."

"Forget the kittens. How about a simple 'I love you'?"

"I do love you."

"Then I think we should try to reach a resolution on the pre-nup situation."

Mara counted to five, then exhaled. "I can't get into this right now."

"I know," he said patiently. "That's why we should get together tonight. How about dessert after you finish up at the office?"

"You think if you anesthetize me with enough chocolate, I'll agree to whatever you want," she accused.

"That strategy has proved successful in the past." She could hear the smile in his voice.

"I'm on to you." She glanced up as Julie came in with a fresh pile of paperwork. "Meet you at Sophie's at eight. I'll bring the chair-cover brochures, you bring the sparkling conversation. Let the good times roll."

Sophie's of Scottsdale was bursting with romantic ambience: harpists, flowers, and immaculately groomed couples making small talk through first dates. Mara knew she stuck out in her power suit and briefcase, but she didn't care. She and Josh were long past the point of trying to make a good first impression. By now, they both knew what they were getting into, for better or for worse. Which brought up a single, critical question:

"I have to ask you something," she announced as the maître d' pulled back a chair at a cozy corner table. "And I want you to be completely honest."

Josh, who was wearing the navy sweater she'd given

him last Christmas, grimaced. "Can't we at least order drinks before the interrogation begins?"

"No." She pushed aside her silverware and rested both hands on the table. "Okay, here goes: Why do you want to marry me?"

He returned her unflinching gaze. "Is this a trick question?"

"Everyone knows why I want to marry you; you're basically the nicest guy who ever walked the face of the earth."

"You forgot dead sexy," he pointed out.

"But why do you want to marry me? I'm snippy and high-maintenance and, let's be honest, kind of an emotional basket case."

"You forgot dead sexy," he repeated.

"I'm being serious." She rubbed her forehead and shrugged out of her suit jacket. "Face it: I'm terrible wife material. I don't clean, I don't cook, I'm a total control freak, and, as you're so fond of pointing out, I shun open displays of sentiment. Why would anyone want to sign on for a lifetime of all that?"

She stared at him. He stared back at her. "Are you finished?" he asked.

"I'm finished."

"Good. I want to marry you because I love you."

"But why?"

"Besides the fact that you're mind-blowing in bed?"

She sat back in her chair. "Josh . . ."

"What?" He grinned. "Don't think that's not a factor. But come on, you know why I love you. You're smart and fun and secretly do all kinds of nice, thoughtful things when you think no one's looking. Like all the charity stuff with Ellie and Jen."

"I only do that because they harass me until I'm teetering on the ragged edge of sanity."

"Trust me, you're very lovable."

"Well, frankly, I think you could do better."

"That's part of your problem," he said. "You're so hard on yourself. Whenever anything's less than perfect, you just want to write it off. Life doesn't work that way. You screw up, you move on."

"Well." Mara straightened up in her seat. "You say that, but sometimes it's not so easy to move on."

Neither of them explicitly mentioned the incident in San Diego, but they didn't have to.

"Oh no." He grabbed the cocktail menu. "Are we back on that again?"

"Of course. We're always going to go back to that, and it puts me at a permanent disadvantage."

"Where are you going with this?"

"The pre-nup," she said. "That's where I'm going. If you really forgave me, you'd—"

"Let you walk all over me and call all the shots?"

"No, but—"

"I'm not going to back down on this, Mara."

Googly-eyed couples at neighboring tables were starting to glance their way.

She forced herself to lower her voice. "I've been doing a lot of thinking since we had that argument last week. You think I don't listen, but I do."

He folded his arms and waited.

"Signing a pre-nup shouldn't really be about me

protecting myself or you protecting yourself. It should be about each of us protecting the other. We're a great team; we're going to be even more successful after we get married. A pre-nup ensures that we'll both have an equal stake in everything we acquire together."

"In the event of a divorce," Josh clarified.

"For the last time: we're not going to get divorced. But by including the cheating clause, you're negating the shared protection guaranteed by a pre-nup, which defeats the whole purpose. Plus, legally, Arizona is a no-fault state so your attorney is going to have a hell of a time enforcing that clause. *Plus,* as I believe I've mentioned previously, I'm not going to cheat."

"Then you have nothing to worry about," he retorted. "And don't get all lawyerly on me; you have your principles, and I have mine."

She slammed her palm down on the table, rattling the silverware. "You know what? I think I have the answer to all our problems. When's your bachelor party?"

"We fly to Vegas on Thursday night."

"All right, you go to Vegas with your buddies and while you're there, have a one-night stand."

He laughed. "Give me a break."

"I'm not kidding. I can't change the past, and obviously, you're never going to get over it. So go have sex with someone else and then we'll finally be even."

"Mara . . ."

"Find yourself a showgirl or a hot blackjack dealer or whatever. Hire a call girl if you want. Just get it over with already."

"You're insane. I'm not going to sleep with someone else."

"Why? Because then you won't have the moral high ground every time we fight? I want you to cheat on me, Josh. I'm begging you to!"

"Is this some sort of test?" He gave her a long, assessing stare. "Don't say it if you don't mean it."

"Oh, I mean it," she assured him.

"You're telling me to go to Vegas four weeks before our wedding and sleep with someone else?"

"Correct." She nodded crisply.

"Fine, then." He folded up his napkin. "I'll do it."

She blinked. "What?"

"If that's what you want, that's what you'll get. I'm taking you at your word." He got to his feet and tossed some cash on the table. "I'll talk to you when I get back from the bachelor party. When we're even."

Jen
Chapter 15

*J*en ran seven miles on Thursday afternoon, pounding across the sandy trail that bordered the desert preserve behind Mayfair Estates, trying to fatigue herself to the point where she could stop thinking about Eric.

Just pretend he's on another business trip, she told herself. *Just pretend his absence is temporary.*

But as she slowed from a sprint to a lope to a walk, she had to admit the truth: Eric had been absent for a long time now. Months, maybe even years. They both had. She had channeled all her passion into her work and he had... well, she wasn't exactly sure where he'd turned for fulfillment. Which just went to show how tuned out she'd been.

She mopped the sweat off her forehead with the sleeve of her baggy cotton T-shirt and squinted into the sunset. They hadn't even made it to their fifth anniversary. Before she got married, that had seemed like such an easy, unremarkable milestone. She'd had sports bras for longer than five years, for God's sake. Half a decade of marriage should be a foregone conclusion.

Everything had changed because of Patrick. He'd pushed Jen and Eric together when he left, and now that he'd returned, he was pulling them apart. And there didn't seem to be anything she could do about it. Patrick had sauntered in and usurped all the power. Again.

Power, when you got right down to it, was the real reason she'd held back a little part of herself from Eric. She'd always known he was more invested in their relationship than she was. She'd never abused that knowledge or given him any reason to waver in his commitment. But she also found solace in the disparity because it guaranteed that her husband could never hurt her the way Patrick had.

Until yesterday.

She trudged past the huge stucco mansions with shiny European cars parked in the driveways and wondered what had ever possessed her to move into this neighborhood. Ellie had been assimilated into the country club lifestyle of the Barton clan, and Mara viewed her golf course town house as a good investment with no landscaping maintenance, but Jen had never felt at home in Mayfair Estates. What exactly was she trying to prove with all that square footage?

Once upon a time, she and Eric had spent hours poring over maps and magazines ("travel porn," they'd called it), fantasizing about trips to Belize, Kenya, Malaysia. In between overseas excursions, they'd planned to hit all fifty states, starting with beach bungalows in Key West and progressing up to fishing lodges in Alaska. Of course, they had never put in the time or effort to do more than plan. Eric's travels had been limited to airports and interchangeable business hotels, and Jen hadn't left Arizona since the honeymoon. She'd barely left her home office.

Her post-workout endorphin buzz fizzled into a funk by the time she fished her house key out of the tiny pouch sewn into the waistband of her jogging shorts. Before she made it to the bathroom to rinse her face, the kitchen phone started ringing and she detoured down the hall to answer, hoping that it might be Eric.

"*Finally*," Deb barked on the other end of the line. "I've been calling your office, your cell—where on earth have you been?"

Jen grabbed a bottle of water out of the refrigerator and twisted off the cap. "Just out for a quick run. What's up?"

"What's up is that your run almost cost you your career. Rory Reid's people called. One of their scheduled guests canceled and they have an opening for tomorrow, but they need a definite answer from us in the next five minutes."

Jen choked on her water.

"You'll have to fly to L.A. tonight; the taping's at ten A.M. I told them you'd be there. Don't make a liar out of me."

Jen's endorphins kicked back in. "I'll be there. Absolutely. But what about my talking points? I mean, we haven't prepped for this kind of—"

"Don't worry about all that right now. Just get your ass to Los Angeles. Call me from the hotel tonight and we'll go over everything."

"But what should I wear?"

"Something stylish but athletic." Deb clicked her tongue. "Something that shows off your arms. You have biceps like freaking Madonna; might as well flaunt them."

Jen flipped through a mental inventory of her closet. "I have a short-sleeved brown shirtdress. It's not really season-appropriate, though."

"Who cares? You're selling an image. It's always summer in Noda land. They have a professional hair-and-makeup team on-set, so tell them to give you a sun-kissed glow. You want to look sporty. One of the Kennedy kids just back from Hyannisport."

"Got it," Jen said. "Call them back and confirm."

"Excellent. Now, go book your flight! Pack your bags! Move, move, move!"

Still lathered in sweat, Jen slammed down the phone and dialed the airlines. The doorbell rang in the middle of her negotiations to try to reserve a seat on a sold-out seven-thirty P.M. flight to LAX.

"I'll pay double," she offered the ticket agent. "Triple. Whatever it takes. I have to get to L.A. tonight."

"I'm sorry, ma'am, but that flight's overbooked."

"But I'm going to be a guest on the Rory Reid show!"

The ticket agent sniffed. "Is that so?"

"Yes! So you see—"

"And they're not even flying you out?"

"Well." Jen paused. "No."

"Then you should have booked this flight two weeks ago."

The doorbell chimed again. "Please. Isn't there anything you can do?"

"I can book you through to Orange County," the agent said. "You'd get in at midnight. That's the best I can do."

Jen dashed into the entry hall, phone in hand, and yanked open the front door.

Patrick Spillane was standing on her doorstep with a bottle of wine in one hand and a box of cigars in the other.

"Ma'am?" the airline rep prompted. "Do you want the flight to Orange County?"

"I'll call you right back." Jen hung up and regarded Patrick with suspicion. "What now?"

"I missed you, too." He laughed.

"This is my house." Jen blocked the doorway by raising one arm, which she immediately lowered when she realized that she might smell less than powder fresh after her run.

"I'm aware this is your house." Patrick's eyes gleamed with amusement. "Nice neighborhood. Although that gate is pretty useless; the security guard waved me right through. I could've been a serial killer for all he knew." He held up the wooden box of cigars. "Is Eric here?"

"Not at the moment." Jen was suddenly, acutely aware that her face was blotchy, her lips chapped, her hair windblown, and her baggy running clothes drenched in perspiration.

"Too bad. I brought these for him and this"—he hoisted up the bottle of wine—"for you. If memory serves, you're a sucker for a good cabernet."

"Don't," Jen said sharply. "Don't show up at my door

with your wine and your cigars and try to pretend like nothing ever happened between us."

"I'm not pretending anything."

"Well, good. Because things happened. Many things. Bad things."

"That's why I'm trying to start fresh. With you *and* Eric. The way we left—okay, the way *I* left—it wasn't right. And I apologize. You don't owe me anything."

"You got that straight."

"But I thought we should get reacquainted. As friends. You live in Scottsdale, I live in Scottsdale . . . it's a small city."

She thinned her lips. "Not that small."

He didn't seem at all offended by her hostility. In fact, he seemed to relish the challenge of winning her over. "I thought it would be better to face each other now, get everything out on the table so we can start over."

"I don't want to start over," Jen bristled. "And I don't have time to stand here and debate with you. I have to book a flight to L.A. tonight. So unless you happen to have a connection to a major airline, you can just—"

"I do, actually. My cousin's a pilot for Southwest. I can give him a call right now." He laughed at her expression. "Impressed?"

"No," she muttered.

He whipped out his cell phone. "What time do you need to leave?"

"Forget it." She shook her head. "You can't do this for me."

"It's not a problem." He punched a few buttons on his keypad. "Name your preferred time of departure."

"Patrick . . ." She ground her molars together, but ushered him inside.

"Yes?" He was the epitome of Mayfair Estates masculinity: confident, well-mannered, and socially bulletproof. No wonder the security guard had waved him through.

"We are never, ever going to be friends."

"Duly noted. Departure time?"

She hesitated a second longer before giving in. "Seven-thirty. But this doesn't change anything."

"Of course not." He turned away from her as he dialed the phone. "Hey, it's Patrick. . . . Right, just got back, so how are you? . . . Not much, but listen, I need a favor . . ."

Jen ducked into the guest bathroom and splashed cold water on her cheeks. She rinsed her hands under the faucet and combed her fingers through her short blond bob, trying to salvage some approximation of style.

There was a light knock on the door. "You just barely squeaked onto the passenger list for Southwest's seven-thirty flight to L.A. And I do mean barely; you may have to sit on a flight attendant's lap. But the good news is, no charge."

She knew a thank-you was in order, but all she could manage was, "How'd you finagle that?"

"Oh, you know me—ever the finagler. So. Am I allowed to ask why you have to fly to California on a moment's notice?"

Jen rummaged through the vanity drawer for lip balm. "No."

The phone in the kitchen started ringing again. "Want me to get that?" he asked.

She stepped back, assessed the results of her thirty-second makeover, and reached for the doorknob. "No, that's okay, I'll—"

Too late. By the time she reached the kitchen, Patrick had picked up the cordless extension. "Good afternoon, house of Jen."

And then he uttered the words that made Jen go from hot and sweaty to cold and clammy:

"Hey, Eric. Yeah, it's Patrick Spillane. From college. How are you these days?... Yeah, I was just in the neighborhood..."

Jen gasped, but Patrick continued smiling and joking, unaware that he had just detonated the marital equivalent of a hydrogen bomb in her kitchen. "Hey, I brought some cigars over for you. Cubans. I'll leave them with Jen.... Oh, we're just catching up on old times. You going to be back in town soon?" Then, suddenly, his face changed. "Oh. Okay. I'll tell her. Right. Hey, are you—" He jerked the receiver away from his ear and frowned. "Your husband just hung up on me."

Jen finally recovered her voice. "Oh. Shit."

"I don't remember him being so sarcastic," Patrick said. "What's his deal?"

"Get out. Get out, get out, get out." She marched back to the front door and held it open. "And take your contraband cigars with you."

"They're for Eric," he protested.

"They're illegal. You still think the rules don't apply to you. You still don't bother to think about how you're affecting other people."

"Why are you yelling? They're just cigars."

"This isn't about the cigars, Patrick! Just go." She shoved him out onto the stoop and slammed the front door so hard that the hall mirror fell and cracked against the floor. The she dashed back to the kitchen and tried to reach Eric, but he wasn't answering his phone.

According to the digital clock on the microwave, she had exactly twenty minutes to pack if she hoped to make it to the airport in time to catch her flight. She dragged her suitcase out of the closet and was in the process of cramming in a fifth pair of shoes (no way was she going to face Rory Reid without an arsenal of fabulous accessories) when Mara called.

"I don't have time to talk," Jen said.

"Make time," Mara replied. "This is an emergency."

"I have to get to the airport. I'm leaving right now."

Mara perked right up. "You're going to the airport? Perfect timing. Swing by and pick me up, will you? I have to get to Vegas before Josh sleeps with a showgirl."

As soon as she flipped on the garage lights, Jen started cursing. Her car sagged to one side with a flat tire, which, upon inspection, proved to be the result of a giant nail puncturing the rubber tread.

Eric had always predicted that sooner or later, all the debris from the custom home construction sites would wind up in their tires. But she hadn't spent a lot of time worrying about it; he coddled their cars and always stayed on top of the oil changes and tune-ups. Plus, he was an expert tire changer, so speedy and competent that she had never bothered to learn how to do it herself.

She hauled her suitcase out to the driveway and called the only person she knew she could count on for help.

"I wouldn't be asking you this if I weren't truly desperate," she wheedled. "We're talking the Rory Reid show here. My whole career is on the line and I don't have time to wait for a cab."

"I understand that," Ellie replied, "but Hannah finally went down for her nap and there'll be hell to pay if I wake her up."

"Why can't she just sleep in her car seat?" Jen asked.

"Spoken like a woman who has no children."

"I'll read her bedtime stories on the way!" Jen promised. "Sing with her, tell her stories, whatever you need."

"It's the middle of rush hour. The airport's forty minutes away with no traffic."

"Car pool lane," Jen said. "*Please!* If you do this for me, I will spend the rest of my life making it up to you. Money, slave labor, hit man duties, you name it."

"I might take you up on that last one. Guess what I got in the mail today? A certified letter from the brokerage firm that used to handle my retirement account."

" 'Used to'? That sounds ominous."

"Yeah, they were forwarding a notice from the IRS demanding a bunch of penalty taxes for liquidating my account before reaching retirement age."

Jen sucked in her breath. "He *didn't*."

"Of course he did. So now, on top of all the legal fees I can't pay, I have a bunch of tax bills I can't pay, and no IRA."

"We'll plot revenge on the road."

Ellie sighed. "Oh, all right. But you better offer me early buy-in when the Noda corporation goes public. I'm gonna need some lucrative investments to support me in my old age."

"I love you," Jen gushed. "Oh, and uh, one more thing: We have to make a quick stop on the way."

"Why does it smell like rancid chocolate in here?" Mara wrinkled her nose as she climbed into the backseat of Ellie's BMW.

"I threw up," Hannah announced proudly. The little girl was strapped into her car seat wearing a pink princess nightgown and clutching a battered stuffed fox. "Mommy's mad."

"Hey, cute outfit." Mara blew her a kiss. "What's new, kangaroo?"

"Daddy doesn't live at our house anymore," Hannah said. "Do you have gum?"

"Go to sleep, honey," Ellie urged. "It's naptime, remember?"

"I'm not sleepy."

"I have some Xanax in my bag," Mara offered.

"I'll take some," Jen said.

"What's Xanax?" Hannah asked.

"Go to sleep!" all three women chorused.

And finally, after ten minutes of inching along the

freeway and several rounds of "The Itsy Bitsy Spider" in three-part harmony, Hannah's eyes fluttered closed.

Ellie glanced at her napping daughter in the rearview mirror and announced, "You wake her up, you walk the rest of the way to the airport."

Jen turned to Mara and whispered, "Okay, so what's the deal with telling Josh to——"

"Shhh!" Ellie hissed.

"She's sleeping," Jen pointed out.

"She's *drowsing*. Big difference."

"I'll try to keep it down, but aren't you dying to know why Mara told Josh to go have a torrid affair?"

Ellie gasped. "You what?"

"A one-night stand," Mara corrected. "Not an affair. Don't exaggerate."

"Spill your guts," Ellie commanded.

Mara glanced pointedly at Hannah. "Can't, sorry. I don't want to walk the rest of the way to the airport."

"You'll walk the rest of the way if you don't start talking right now."

"There's a word for this, you know: extortion."

"Good to know, counselor." Ellie winked at Jen. "Now out with it."

Mara cleared her throat. "Well, Josh and I may or may not have had a fight about the pre-nup."

"Again?"

"And I may or may not have told him to go, uh…" Mara glanced sideways at Hannah "…engage in carnal relations with someone else in Vegas."

"Why on earth would you do that?" Ellie asked.

"Because I was piss—pardon me, highly vexed. I told

him he should do to me what I did to him and then we'd be even."

"And he *agreed*?"

"Well, not at first. He kept saying I didn't mean that, so I said oh yes I did."

"But you didn't mean it!" Jen said.

"Well, no, not really, but once I'd said it, I couldn't back down."

"Why not?"

Mara coughed. "That would be because of my foolish pride."

"Aren't you the one who always says to keep a level head in a romantic crisis?" Ellie said.

"Turns out it's a lot easier to do that when it's somebody else's romantic crisis. Anyway, the point is, now Josh isn't answering my calls so I need you to give me Eric's cell number."

Jen frowned. "You want to call Eric? *My* Eric?"

"Well, yeah. He's at the bachelor party, isn't he?"

"I have no idea."

"You have no idea where your husband is?" Ellie asked.

Jen didn't reply.

"Jennifer?" Mara said. "Anything you'd care to share with the rest of the group? Before Ellie starts with the extortion threats again?"

"I can't talk about this right now," Jen murmured.

Ellie reached over and gave Jen a maternal pat on the head. "You might feel better if you talk about it. Or, you know, smash a stack of plates."

"No, I have to stay focused. Tomorrow is Noda's national TV debut."

"Forget Noda," Mara said. "Does Noda keep you warm at night? Does Noda promise to love and cherish you for as long as you both shall live?"

"No. But neither does Eric." Jen covered her face with her hands as the SUV came to a stop in a snarl of gridlock. "He moved out on Monday. And as for Noda... Mara, I have a pre-nup question for you. A big one."

Jen

I didn't know you and Eric signed a pre-nup," Mara marveled. "All these years and you never said a word? I'm your best friend!"

"*We're* your best friends," Ellie chimed in.

"True, but you both kept your little secrets. And my pre-nup was nobody's business." Jen scrunched up into a semifetal position in the front seat.

"Then why are you telling us now?" Mara asked, obviously offended. "Seeing as you're such the paragon of privacy and all?"

"Because Eric said he's filing for separation, and our fifth anniversary is next week, and..." Jen screwed her eyes shut and clutched the door handle with both hands. "If we don't make it to the five-year mark, it's possible that I could lose the company."

"That's stipulated in your pre-nup?"

Jen nodded.

Mara whistled through her teeth. "Why on earth would you ever agree to that?"

"It was my idea," Jen wailed.

"I'm so confused," Ellie said.

"Me, too," Mara said. "The whole point of a pre-nup is to protect you when the shit comes down. So why would you deliberately screw yourself over..." She trailed off as realization dawned. "Oh boy. Please tell me this isn't going where I think it's going?"

"Why does it have to go anywhere?" Ellie said. "I understand completely, Jen. You got married when you were young and madly in love, and you never even considered the possibility of—"

"I wasn't in love," Jen whispered.

Ellie tapped the brakes hard, and they all pitched forward. "Come again?"

"I wasn't in love with Eric." Jen swallowed. "When we got married. I did love him, but it wasn't...we weren't *in* love."

"Well, he was definitely in love with you," Mara said. "His face at your wedding...If I could have bottled the bliss and sold it on the street, I'd be set for life."

Jen curled herself up even tighter. "I never should have said yes when he proposed. It wasn't right. I tried to talk him out of it, a month before the wedding. But he got so upset. He insisted that my feelings would grow over time, and he was so emphatic, I started to believe it, too. Plus, by then he'd given me all this money to start Noda, and I felt so guilty. Hence, the pre-nup. I got married on the rebound."

Ellie nosed the SUV into the right-hand lane. "It all comes back to Patrick? But you and Eric were so happy. Even when you were just friends."

"That's the problem; I think we're better at being friends than at being spouses. And it's my fault," Jen concluded gloomily. "I never should have let him talk me into taking it to the next level."

"It's no one's fault," Ellie said. "You can't help who you fall in love with."

"Yeah, but you can help who you marry," Jen said.

"True. But there were mitigating circumstances," Mara said. "And you didn't do anything to lead him on. He took one look at you at freshman orientation, and bam! Poor bastard never had a chance."

"Yeah, he knew what he was getting into," Ellie agreed. "You told him that there was no chemistry."

"Well…" Jen hedged. "I wouldn't say we have *no* chemistry."

"I would," Mara said. "Considering it took him six years and practically an entire bottle of Absolut to wear you down."

"No! Wrong, wrong, wrong," Jen protested. "That's not what happened."

"That's what you told me," Mara said. "You said you two went to a bar, you went a little crazy with the vodka tonics, and then you finally took pity on the guy and put out."

Ellie frowned. "Why have I not heard this story?"

"You were probably too busy with your secret law school applications," Mara said.

"Maybe," Ellie mused.

"Listen." Jen was practically frothing at the mouth. "Not that it's any of your business, but I will have you know that Eric happens to be excellent in bed. Excellent."

"Were you still in love with Patrick when you married Eric?" Ellie wanted to know. "Truth."

"No!" Jen exclaimed.

"It's okay," Mara said. "You can tell us. We won't judge."

"No. When I say I got married on the rebound, I don't mean I was still in love with Patrick. I wasn't in love with anyone."

"So why couldn't you love Eric?" Ellie asked softly. "Considering how great he is, not to mention excellent in bed?"

"I could have," Jen said. "Lots of times. But I *wouldn't*. Do you remember how awful that breakup was?"

"I remember," Ellie and Mara said in unison.

"Stupid Patrick Spillane with his stupid perfect body and his stupid medical degree and his stupid humanitarian crap." Jen paused. "I would have waited for him, you know. If he had just asked, I would have done the long-distance thing for years. I would have put everything on hold. But he never asked me to wait."

Ellie cleared her throat. "So you're making Eric wait instead. For you."

Jen lapsed into a long, moody silence. Finally, when it became apparent she wasn't going to offer any more details, Mara said, "Okay, then. So the pre-nup?"

Jen sighed. "Right before we got engaged, Eric invested almost every penny he had in Noda. I was trying to get the company off the ground, and I really needed the capital, but my bank was not too enthused about the market prospects for an 'antisoda.'" She finally cracked a smile. "I was way ahead of my time."

"How much money are we talking here?" Ellie asked.

"Enough," Jen said. "Enough that I didn't feel right about taking it with no strings attached, which is what he wanted. He kept saying I should consider it a wedding gift or an investment in our joint future, but I said that if something, you know, unfortunate happened in our joint future—"

"Something like what's happening right now," Mara clarified.

"—that he deserved to be protected. I mean, he was ready to just hand over his life savings and the inheritance he got from his grandparents, but I couldn't let him do that. So we drew up some papers."

"And you didn't even consult me?" Mara sniffed.

"My engagement wasn't exactly the high point of my life," Jen said. "I didn't want to admit to myself or anyone else what a huge mistake I was making."

"So to make up for not loving him enough, you gave him a majority stake in your company," Mara translated.

"Only in the event of divorce. The deal was, if we made it to our fifth anniversary, the money he staked me would be considered a gift."

"But since you're just shy of five years . . ."

"It's still technically a loan. I'll have to pay it all back. Plus interest. Plus half the current value of the company, since Arizona is a community property state. And I can't afford to cash out his initial investment right now, never mind the company's value, because I have to pay the bottlers, the drivers, the warehouse, the publicist . . . the list just goes on and on. I'd need to get a loan to repay him, but no one wants to back a business whose co-owners are about to split up. I've already put out feelers. Too many 'unforeseen risks' is the party line. 'Come back after the divorce.' By which time it'll be too late. I'll have lost my husband *and* my career." Jen rubbed the back of her neck. "But Eric says he doesn't care about enforcing the pre-nup. He says he wants a clean, civil separation."

"Yeah, right." Mara snorted. "That's what they all say in the beginning. When's the last time you met anyone who had a clean, civil divorce?"

They both looked away from Ellie, who said, "I'm sure things will be different for you, Jen."

"I don't want a divorce, civil or not." Jen felt the unexpected sting of tears in her eyes. "I want to stay married."

"Did you tell him that?" Ellie asked.

"Of course!"

"Then why did he leave?"

Jen gazed out the window. "Take a wild guess."

"Patrick *again*?" Ellie shook her head.

"I know that face," Mara said. "You saw him, didn't you?"

"Against my will," Jen said. "But yes. He tracked me down. Last week outside the bakery and today in my own house. He answered the phone when Eric called."

Ellie and Mara gasped. "No!"

"Yes. He says he wants to start fresh and be friends."

"Could you pull over?" Mara asked Ellie. "I have to vomit."

The traffic ahead came to a complete standstill.

"Argh!" Jen launched into a meltdown in the front seat. "Move, damnit, everyone *go*!"

"Well, look on the bright side," Mara said. "At least

your fiancé's not about to sleep with some random hoochie because you dared him to. The glass is half full."

"Of Noda." Jen scowled. "And now Noda is all I have left. I have to make this flight."

"You'll make it." Ellie jerked the car onto the shoulder of the road and gunned it for the nearest exit.

Mara yelped and made the sign of the cross. Hannah stirred in her car seat. Jen burst into tears.

"Why are you crying?" Ellie asked, alarmed. "You said you need to go; we're going."

"Okay, but if it's not too much trouble, do you think we could get there alive?" Mara cringed as they rumbled over a discarded piece of plywood.

Ellie didn't answer, just floored the accelerator and switched on her turn signal as they neared the airport turnoff. They were only a few yards away from the exit when they heard the police siren wailing behind them. "Uh-oh."

"What's happening, Mommy?" a fully awake Hannah demanded.

"Mommy's gone rogue," Mara replied.

"Don't worry, sweetie." Ellie sounded calmer and more confident than Jen had ever heard her. "Everything's going to be fine."

"Stop the car," Mara urged. "Before they shoot out our tires and I get disbarred for aiding and abetting a fugitive."

"And you say *we* exaggerate," Ellie said, but did as Mara asked. When a tall, burly policeman walked up to the SUV, she rolled down the window and greeted him with a cheery "Evening, Officer."

The cop peered in at the BMW's occupants with evident dismay. While Jen wept silently into her shirtsleeve, Hannah started flailing against the straps of her car seat, and Mara yelled, "I told her not to do it, sir!"

The officer rested one hand on his gun holster. "What seems to be the trouble here?"

Ellie smoothed back her long dark hair. "In a word? Pre-nups."

"Pre-nups," Mara seconded darkly.

"Pre-nups." Jen sniffled.

Hannah leaned forward as far as she could and yelled, "I threw up!"

The policeman stared at them for a moment, then straightened up and took a step back. "I'm going to let you ladies off with a warning. But, ma'am, be advised that this lane is reserved for breakdowns and emergencies only."

Ellie nodded and flipped on her hazard lights. "Trust me, Officer, we qualify on both counts."

Mara *Chapter* 17

Mara spent the majority of the sixty-five-minute flight from Phoenix to Las Vegas peering out the window at the dark expanse of desert and torturing herself with mental images of Josh entangled in Kama Sutra poses with various femmes fatales, each more wanton and limber than the last. She didn't even realize she was tapping her fingernails against the metal plate on the seat divider until the passenger next to her finally spoke up.

"Excuse me." The scrawny teenage girl in tight jeans and a vintage Ramones T-shirt fixed Mara with an exasperated stare. "Are you planning on doing that the entire trip?"

Mara blinked, dissipating a vision of a lingerie model unfastening her flimsy bra and using the straps to bind Josh's wrists to wrought-iron bedposts. "Doing what?"

"That." The girl pointed out Mara's twitchy fingers.

"Oh. Sorry. Didn't even realize." Mara turned back to the window.

Two minutes later, she felt a tap on her shoulder. "Ahem. You're still doing it."

"Well, a thousand apologies, but I've got a lot on my mind," Mara snapped. She recommenced tapping, and threw in a little ankle-jiggling for good measure.

The teenager heaved a mighty sigh, then dug out her mp3 player and headphones and cranked up the volume. For the remainder of the flight, Mara's sexed-up scenarios were set to a musical score of frenetic drumbeats and soaring guitar solos.

She dialed Josh's cell phone the minute the plane touched down, but he still wasn't answering. Fine. If he wanted to play hardball, she'd play hardball. She freaking *invented* hardball.

She reached into her bag and retrieved the contact information Jen had given her back at the airport.

"Hello?" Eric picked up on the third ring.

"Hi, it's Mara Stroebel," she said breezily. "I got your number from Jen—"

"What's going on?" he demanded. "Is she okay?"

"Yeah, Jen's fine, but . . ." Mara trailed off as she heard the rhythmic thump of pounding bass on the other end of the connection. "Where are you guys?"

He didn't answer.

"Hello?" She frowned into her headset. "Eric?"

"Uh . . ." There was a lot of muffled rustling as he stalled for time. "What?"

"I asked where you were." She grabbed her hastily packed valise and charged through the terminal.

"We're, um, out," Eric hedged. "Just having a few drinks."

"Where, specifically?"

"Oh, you know, here and there. Garden-variety bachelor party stuff. Playing cards, smoking cigars..."

Mara sighed. "Which strip club?"

"Whoa, hey, no one said anything about strip clubs."

"Look, I'm at the airport and I need to talk to Josh. Right now."

"The Vegas airport?" He sounded appalled, and more than a little panicked. "You're *here*?"

"Where is he?"

"Why are you in Vegas?"

"Stop stalling and put Josh on the phone."

"I can't do that right now."

Her impatience snowballed into desperation. "Why not?"

"Hey, is it true you told him to hook up with someone else this weekend? Because I gotta tell you, that's pretty—"

"Eric, as God is my witness..." She forced herself to stop and take a deep breath. "Okay. All right. I'm a reasonable woman. What do you say to a little information exchange? You help me, I help you."

"What do you mean?" He sounded suspicious.

"I've got the latest dirt on Patrick Spillane. Interested?"

"No," he said in a laughably unsuccessful imitation of disinterest.

"Fine. Then I guess you don't want to hear about what happened between him and Jen this afternoon."

"That's right."

"Yeah, I probably wouldn't want to know either. You're very wise to spare yourself the drama. Especially since I know every last detail, and I'm not known for pulling my punches. Anyway, nice talking to you."

Eric caved. "All right, all right. We're at the Black Diamond. It's right around the corner from the Luxor."

"Thank you," Mara said sweetly. "And Josh is with you?"

"He just went back into the VIP area with the stripper who was talking to him all night."

She forced a laugh. "But nothing happens in the VIP area, right?"

"Uh…"

"I mean, no one actually has *sex* in the VIP rooms, right? That's only in the movies?"

"Well…"

"Listen to me, Eric. You put your drink down right now and go get him."

"I don't think I can do that," Eric said. "The bouncer back there looks pretty tough."

"Damn it." Mara balled up her fists and quickened her pace, darting through throngs of luggage-laden tourists. "I have to do everything myself."

"So what happened this afternoon?" Eric prompted. "With Jen and Patrick?"

Mara made a guttural noise in the back of her throat. "Oops, I'm losing the connection."

"Hey!"

She let her voice drop. "Can't…hear…bad…bye!" She snapped her phone closed, dashed out the doors to the curb, and flagged down the first cab she saw. "I need to get to the Black Diamond," she told the driver. "And step on it."

The exterior of the Black Diamond didn't look like the den of iniquity Mara had envisioned—no garish neon, no tattered posters advertising cut-rate peep shows, no frat boys urinating in the gutter. The club looked like any other upscale bar. There was even a valet stand staffed with uniformed attendants and a red velvet rope cordoning off the entrance from the sidewalk.

The interior was another story. Mara begrudgingly forked over the twenty-dollar cover charge the doorman demanded, then stepped into a dizzying display of strobe lights, mirrors, and sequins.

Breasts and blond hair. For a moment, that was all she could process. Tanned, toned women, most of them clad in G-strings that amounted to little more than two Post-its fastened together with rubber bands, writhed around a veritable forest of stripper poles. After her eyes adjusted to the dim house lights, Mara surveyed the groups of men gazing glassy-eyed up at the floor shows. Most of these guys wore suits or collared shirts and had plenty of crisp dollar bills to dole out. One or two glanced her way when she walked in unattended, but they quickly lost interest when it became apparent she wasn't going to be gyrating out of her jeans anytime soon.

She spotted Eric at the bar, brooding over a beer, so she made her way over to him and yelled over the pounding rock ballad blaring through the speakers. "Hey!"

He whipped around, his expression startled and guilty.

"Where's Josh?" she hollered directly into his ear.

He hollered back something that sounded like "This is the suckiest bachelor party ever."

"Where's Josh?" she repeated.

He scowled and launched into a rant, the only words of which she could make out were "Patrick Spillane."

"Oh my God, I don't have time for this. Where's Josh?"

Eric didn't answer, but he didn't have to. Mara watched a tall, leggy stripper entice a customer up from a lap dance and lead him back to a black velvet curtain in the corner.

She charged after them, threw back the curtain—and found herself up against a stony-faced Goliath in a tight black T-shirt.

He crossed his arms and blocked her path. "This area is restricted."

She tried to hold her ground as his massive head loomed over hers. "VIP rooms, right?"

"That's right. I'm going to have to ask you to step back."

"But my fiancé is back there!"

"Then I'm definitely going to have to ask you to step back."

"But I need to see him!" Mara pleaded. "Right now! He...I...Before he does something we'll both regret!"

"Only paying customers are allowed past this point." Goliath shuffled forward, forcing her back into the main room.

"I understand, but—"

"House rules, no exceptions." He wedged one bulging biceps against the door frame. "Paying customers only."

"Fine. Be that way." Mara turned and raced over to the nearest mini-stage, where a petite brunette was finishing up her set.

Mara cleared her throat. "Um, miss? How much for you to go back to a VIP room?"

The dancer adjusted the strap of her bejeweled red thong and tilted her head. "With you?"

All the men within earshot were suddenly paying rapt attention. Mara lifted her chin and tried to look nonchalant.

The dancer pursed her glossy lips. "Two hundred."

"*Dollars?* Why don't you just rob me at gunpoint?"

"That's the going rate." The woman rolled her shoulders and jiggled her ample breasts. "Don't worry; I'm worth it."

Mara glanced away from the frontal nudity toward the black velvet curtains separating her from Josh. "Is there any way I can get a discount if I don't want you to dance?"

"You don't want a dance?" The stripper narrowed her eyes. "Then what exactly do you expect me to do back there?"

"Oh, forget it. Here." Mara opened her wallet and counted out a stack of twenties. The testosterone-charged crowd grunted their approval as the brunette took Mara by the hand and sashayed back toward the curtains.

When they passed through, the dancer nodded to the bouncer, who melted away into the shadows.

"Here we are." The dancer led the way down a narrow, mirrored hallway, then drew back another set of curtains. She smiled and winked. "Ladies first."

Mara stepped through the doorway into a sumptuous, gold-trimmed Vegas version of a Moroccan oasis. A bar lined one wall, and the rest of the room was comprised of private, fabric-draped cabanas that could be closed off for privacy. The atmosphere in here was much more intimate than the aggressive exhibitionism out on the main floor. The music was softer, the air warmer, the lights dimmer.

The dancer nodded toward the bar. "Care for a drink?"

"No, I'm good." Mara edged closer to the nearest cabana and tried to catch a glimpse of what was happening inside. She could hear female giggling and what sounded like male moaning. But not Josh. She knew Josh's sex noises.

"Naughty, naughty," the dancer trilled, steering her toward an open cabana on the far wall. "No peeking."

Mara dug in her heels and fumbled for an excuse. "I, uh, have to use the ladies' room."

The dancer tapped one five-inch Lucite platform stiletto and gave her a shrewd once-over. "What's going on?"

"Nothing. I just really have to——"

"Listen, honey, I don't know what you've heard, but Black Diamond girls are class acts. If you try anything kinky, I'll get you tossed out of here so fast. I don't care how much money you throw at me."

"I'm relieved to hear that." Mara's ears pricked up as the sound system paused between songs. Amid all the clinking glass and rustling fabric and creaking leather, she thought she heard the low undertones of Josh's voice.

She dashed over to the corner cabana and, before her diminutive escort could intervene, ripped aside the gauzy gold veils. "Aha!"

Josh was cozied up on an overstuffed velvet banquette with a bottle of champagne, a silver platter of strawberries, and the most beautiful woman Mara had ever seen in real life.

Not to mention the most buxom.

Not to mention completely nude except for a handful of silver sequins strategically scattered across her pubic bone.

Now Mara knew how Ellie had felt while comparing herself to the infamous Vixen_MD. The woman currently hanging off her fiancé was the flesh-and-blood nightmare of every bride-to-be who sent her fiancé off to Vegas for one last hurrah: flowing hair the color of freshly burnished copper, huge doe eyes, and abs so toned they almost looked airbrushed. Her skin was flawless and deeply tanned, save a tiny patch of white in the shape of a flower near her hip, where she had obviously placed a decorative decal while tanning.

Mara had braced herself for any number of sordid scenarios. Bumping, grinding, possibly even a blow job; she had, after all, basically dared Josh to do it. What she was not prepared for was the sight of this flame-haired hussy gazing soulfully into her man's eyes . . . and her man gazing soulfully right back.

"*I knew it!*" Mara rolled up her sleeves and prepared to release her surging adrenaline via senseless violence. "I caught you! You're caught!"

Josh and the sequined seductress stopped cooing at each other and blinked up at her.

Josh was the first to recover his composure. "What the hell are you doing here?"

"I might ask you the same question," Mara said. "How could you?"

"Hey!" The dark-haired dancer caught up with Mara and sank her manicured talons into Mara's forearm. "You can't do this! I'm calling security!"

"No, no, it's okay." Josh turned to his companion. "This is her."

The stripper sized up Mara through heavily mascaraed eyelashes. "You don't say."

"Yeah." Josh reached into his pants pockets, produced his wallet, and took out a few bills, which he handed to Mara's escort. "She can stay here with us. It's fine."

The brunette consulted the redhead. "You okay with this?"

The world's most gorgeous female nodded. "If he says it's okay, it's okay. Don't worry."

The brunette made a face but retreated, leaving the other three to face off over berries and bubbly.

Mara opened her mouth to rip into Josh, but the stripper beat her to the punch. "So you're Mara. You have some nerve, showing up like this. Ever heard of boundaries?"

Mara leaned across the tiny round table and got right up in the other woman's face. "First of all, I don't need boundary talk from someone who bares her booty for tips. Second of all, I don't think we've been properly introduced, you little—"

"This is Bentlie," Josh said quickly, before Mara could finish her sentence. "She's—"

"Oh, I know what she is." Mara glared at the dancer, who glared right back. "Now back off; this guy's engaged."

"So what?" The stripper lounged back against the banquette and took a slow, leisurely sip of champagne.

"So obviously you don't care about oh, you know, *morality*, but I do."

The stripper stopped smiling. Her hazel eyes glittered coldly. "From what I hear, you've got no room to talk about morality. In fact, from what I hear, this guy's not engaged anymore. You know, I meet a lot of men in my line of work. A lot of low-down, no-good, lying, sexist, bottom-feeding assholes. But not this one." She trailed her fingers from Josh's wrist up to his shoulder. "He's a nice guy."

Mara's blood pressure skyrocketed. "Hands off."

"Why do you care?" the redhead challenged. "Didn't you tell him to go sleep with another woman?"

"What exactly have you two been doing back here?" Mara demanded.

Josh straightened up in his seat and tried to avert the head-on collision. "We should go."

"Not so fast." Bentlie nibbled on a strawberry. "Josh and I have been talking. He has lots to say, and obviously, you don't listen."

"Oh, now you're a therapist in a thong?"

"I get paid a lot more than a therapist," Bentlie said loftily. "And I don't need a psych degree to see that you treat him like dirt and he'd be better off without you."

"You can't talk to me like that!"

"I'll talk to you any way I want." Bentlie raised her eyebrows to Josh. "Why do you put up with this?" She turned her attention back to Mara. "Do you have any idea how hard it is to find a guy who actually respects women? I don't think so. Sounds to me like you're spoiled and selfish. You don't deserve him."

"That is not—"

"Still talking." Bentlie smirked. "I can't believe you threw away a catch like this."

"I didn't throw him away."

"Hello? You sent him off to Vegas and told him to have sex with someone else. Face it, babycakes, the engagement is over." She smiled at Josh. "You're lucky you escaped before it was too late." The two of them exchanged a meaningful look.

"All I asked for was a pre-nup," Mara said faintly. "All I wanted was—"

"Blah, blah, blah, you, you, you." Bentlie examined her lacquered red fingernails. "*You* want, *you* need. You're an idiot."

"I see where this is going. You think you should have him instead?"

"Hell, no." Bentlie helped herself to another strawberry. "I've had enough of marriage to last me a lifetime."

"Her ex-husband was terrible to her," Josh informed

Mara. "Verbally abusive, compulsive liar, gambling problems."

"I can't believe this." Mara snatched up Josh's champagne flute and drained the contents. "I am not going to sit here trying to justify myself to some random stranger—"

"I have a name," Bentlie said.

"Give me a break. Bentlie's not your real name and we all know it."

Josh looked disappointed. "It's not?"

"Of course not!" Mara couldn't wait to deflate the dancer's mystique. "Her real name's probably something like Sarah or Kristen or—"

"Alex," Bentlie admitted, twirling a lock of red hair around one finger and amping up her expression of wistful vulnerability. "But I don't tell customers that. Only real friends."

"I understand." Josh's eyes shone with gallantry. "You have to keep some things private."

"Enough." Mara circled the table, grabbed Josh's elbow, and hauled him to his feet. "Tonight's therapy session is officially over."

Josh waited for the next break between songs before telling Alex, "You have my card. Give me a call and we'll figure something out."

Mara stopped yanking at his sleeve and punched him in the shoulder. "*Figure something out?* What is that supposed to mean?"

He started toward the exit. "Let's go."

"Oh no. I'm not going anywhere with you until you tell me—"

Josh lowered his voice and regarded her with flinty detachment. "Let's. Go."

Her protests died halfway to her lips and she found herself trailing along behind him.

"Bye!" Alex called after them. "It was great to meet you, Josh. Stay strong! I'll talk to you soon."

"I don't even know where to begin," Mara said to Josh's back as they made their way into the smoke and mirrors of the club's main floor.

"Then don't."

"Well . . ." She tried to figure out exactly when she had lost the upper hand. "Aren't you going to explain yourself?"

"Nope." Josh waved to Eric and started across the room toward the bar. "I'd say the situation's pretty self-explanatory."

"Hey!" She stumbled after him. "Don't just walk away from me!"

"Hurts, doesn't it?" He kept going.

"Wait! Let's just talk this through for a second."

"Mara." He stopped long enough for her to catch up. "Why are you here?"

She lowered her eyes and forced out the words. "I came to apologize."

He ignored all the tits and ass and mirrored disco balls surrounding them on all sides and watched her closely. "Really?"

She studied the worn maroon carpet. "Yes."

"Well, go ahead then."

Her head snapped back up. "What's that?"

"Apologize."

"I just did."

"No, you didn't. You said you were *going* to apologize."

Her cheeks burned. "I was. Until I saw you with the minx with no tan lines."

"Don't talk about her that way. She's a very nice girl. In fact, I was hoping you could talk to her. She's having some legal issues with her divorce——"

"Did you have sex with her?" Mara blurted out.

His brows snapped together. "Of course not."

"Did you kiss her?"

He rocked back on his heels and stared at her.

"Well? I'm waiting."

"Do you not remember what you instructed me to do before I left Phoenix?"

The rivulets of cold sweat started up again on her neck. "So you did kiss her."

"I'm not going to answer that." Josh resumed walking toward Eric and signaled the bartender for a beer. "But I'll tell you one thing: I'm finished with this push-me-pull-you bullshit. Bentlie was right——"

"Alex," Mara corrected.

"Whatever you want to call her, she was right. You're punishing me for something *you* did, and I've had it." He dusted off his hands. "You're scared to make a commitment? You refuse to get married without a bunch of legal loopholes? Fine. We won't get married." He opened his mouth to continue, but she was so terrified to hear his next pronouncement that she cut him off with "Let's do it. Right now."

"Do what?"

"Get married."

"Can we please be serious here?"

"I am serious. Let's do it! Come on!" She was starting to hyperventilate a bit, but tried to parlay this into giddy enthusiasm. "We can be at a drive-through chapel in less than ten minutes. No muss, no fuss, no pre-nup. You win."

"Get real." He let out a harsh bark of laughter. "You're not ready to get married tonight. Neither am I. I don't think we'll ever be ready."

"What are you saying?" She reached out to touch his face, but he flinched away.

"I'm saying good-bye, Mara." He changed direction and headed for the exit. The dancer's words echoed through her mind: *You're spoiled and selfish. You don't deserve him.*

So Mara let him leave and realized too late that a woman with a fake name, fake breasts, and a fake hair color knew her better than she knew herself.

Ten minutes and several sodden tissues later, Mara emerged from the restroom and scanned the bar area for Eric. But he had abandoned his earlier post, and she finally located him by a small round table in the middle of the room, slouched deep into a black leather chair and surrounded by a bevy of undulating blondes.

She sat down next to him. "I'd offer to buy you a lap dance, but I'd say you've already got an embarrassment of riches here."

"Yeah. So?" Eric threw some cash down on the tablecloth without even looking up from his Scotch and soda. "At least they're not pretending to care about me because they feel sorry for me."

"Oh boy." Mara settled in and made herself comfortable. "You know, for a guy surrounded by hot, naked chicks, you seem pretty depressed."

"No offense, but I'm trying to have a little guy time here."

She nodded toward the stack of money. "Well then, I should probably tell you that you're supposed to put those in their G-strings."

He glanced up at her long enough to notice her red-rimmed eyes. "What happened to you?"

"That is a long and ultimately pointless tale. Let's focus on someone who actually has a shot in hell of saving their relationship: you."

"Where's Josh?" He finally gave her his full attention, and the dancers, sensing that the cash flow was drying up, drifted off toward more promising prospects at neighboring tables.

"He left," she said flatly.

"Where'd he go?"

"He didn't say."

He indicated his Scotch. "Want the rest of that?"

"Nah, I think it's best for everyone involved that I self-medicate with carbs instead of alcohol tonight. Where's the rest of the bachelor party?"

Eric shrugged. "They're around here somewhere. Or not. Maybe they went back to the casino. It was every man for himself after Josh went in to the VIP room."

"Clearly, men do not share the strict no-desertion

code of honor that girlfriends do." She shook her head. "Jeez. Who leaves a guy in your condition alone with a bottle and a bunch of strippers?"

"I *want* to be alone. If you wouldn't mind..."

"Sorry. I can't just abandon you to the vagaries of the Black Diamond."

"Sure you can. It's easy."

"Nope. Jen would never forgive me."

Eric's expression darkened. "Say her name again and I'm outta here."

"Look. I know you're not in the mood for this, but the thing you have to realize about Jen is—"

"Isn't there a no-harassment code of honor? You don't hear me yapping about Josh."

"That's because there's nothing left to yap about. He's done. I made it impossible for him to love me."

"Lucky bastard."

"Oh, that's nice."

"No, I mean, I wish I could just turn it off like that." He snapped his fingers. "Being in love sucks. It's like a drug. It's like...diet soda."

"Well, you know, there's a cure for that now."

Eric set his jaw. "So tell me about Patrick. Just get it over with. Is she seeing him again?"

"No," she said emphatically. "Forget Patrick. Let me tell you about Jen instead."

He paused for a moment. The strobe lights onstage threw glints of gold across his face. "I could take her company away from her. In the divorce. Part of me really wants to do it. Just so she'll know what it's like to put in all that time and effort and get nothing back."

Mara nodded and waited.

"I won't actually do it." He prodded the ice cubes in his glass. "Probably."

She sighed and waved away an approaching dancer. "Jen and I go back a long way. Almost as far as you and Jen go back."

"Yeah," he said. "I was her BFF before you and Ellie were her BFFs."

"You're not her BFF; you're her husband."

"Soon to be ex-husband."

"Hear me out, Eric. It's not that she doesn't love you."

"Actually, that's exactly what it is."

"She's afraid. But she's trying. Aren't you going to give her a chance?"

"I gave her five years' worth of chances. If Patrick wants her so bad, he can have her."

"But she doesn't want him, she wants you."

"Then how come she's off in L.A. promoting Noda instead of trying to win me back?"

"That's not fair," Mara objected. "The Rory Reid gig is a once-in-a-lifetime—"

"*You're* here, aren't you?" He challenged, his eyes flashing with anger. "You had problems with Josh and you took action. You didn't sit around waiting for him to come to you."

"I wouldn't use Josh and me as the benchmark for a healthy relationship."

"Still, you're trying."

"And you're not."

"Not anymore," he agreed.

"But you love her."

He shrugged. "Irrelevant. You've got the right idea. You have to protect yourself."

She leaned forward and put on the game face she used when preparing to negotiate with a fellow attorney. "What would it take? What would Jen have to do to show you that she really wants to be with you 'til death do you part?"

He drained the last of his drink and put the glass down with a thump. "Nothing."

"Don't be difficult."

"I'm not. I'm being literal. She'd have to do nothing. Stop letting Noda and Patrick and everything else consume her whole life."

She sat back. "You want Jen Finnerty to do nothing?"

"Yep. Talk about a long shot, huh?"

"Well, sometimes long shots pay off. And when they do, you win big."

"But most of the time, you lose."

"Take a look around, my friend." She opened her arms to encompass all the drinks and debauchery. "We're sitting smack dab in the middle of the world capital of long shots. Are you feeling lucky?"

He half smiled. "Is that an invitation to the poker table?"

"Hey, as long as you're throwing money away, I'd be happy to let you stake me."

"You're on."

Jen

Chapter
18

*Y*ou have bone structure to die for," raved the makeup artist as she daubed rosy cream blush onto Jen's cheeks. "And your complexion! Flawless! What's your secret?"

Jen gazed glumly into the brightly lit mirror set up in Rory Reid's backstage greenroom. "Oh, you know. Water. Vegetables. Clean living."

"Well, you must save a fortune on facials." The stylist finished up with the blush and moved on to mascara. "The smog out here absolutely chokes my pores. And it doesn't help that I practically live on take-out and diet soda."

A few days ago, Jen would have seized this opportunity to spread the gospel of Noda, but this morning, she couldn't muster the enthusiasm.

Apathy and pessimism had definitely set in. She knew that she was poised at the top of what would probably be a long, slippery descent into depression. She would have to take preventative measures. Soon. Maybe tomorrow. But today . . . eh, who really cared?

"Hi there! What're you in for?" A taut-faced brunette in a spangly red sweater and white jeans slid into the revolving chair next to Jen.

Jen's confusion must have shown on her face, because the woman laughed and offered up a dainty hand dripping in diamonds. "I'm Whitley Westphal, here to worship at the altar of Rory and shill my new jewelry line."

Jen nibbled her lip and tried to place the name. "Whitley Westphal? Aren't you the—"

"Divinely talented diva who sang the one-hit wonder 'Something in the Water' back in 1997?" the woman rattled off. "Why, yes I am. You probably recognize me from the bargain bin at Best Buy or on VH1's *Where Are They Now?*"

"No, no." Jen furrowed her brow. "You married a baseball player, right?"

Whitley shrieked with delight. "Oh, sugar, you've just made his day! Brick! Brick, get over here! This woman knows who you are. I *told* you you still had groupies!"

A gangly, elderly man shambled over from the corner. He clutched a white Chanel handbag in one hand and a steaming cup of coffee in the other. "Brick Milton. Pleased to make your acquaintance. You must be a true-blue Dodger fan, young lady."

Brick Milton. *That* name clicked right away. "You're a pitching legend," Jen gushed, breaking every self-imposed rule she had about fawning over celebrities. "Number seventy-eight, right?"

"That's him!" Whitley sat back in her chair and

patted her husband's forearm as if he were a particularly clever poodle performing a trick.

Brick smiled shyly. "You really know your stuff. That was decades ago."

"My husband worships you." Jen reached down, grabbed her handbag, and searched for something to write on. "I hate to be a nuisance, but would you mind signing an autograph for him? He'll be devastated that he missed meeting you. He's going to die!"

Her smile wavered as she remembered that Eric wouldn't be there when she got home to hear tales of her brushes with the rich and famous. She didn't even know where he was staying.

But it was too late to call off Brick. He accepted the airline ticket jacket she'd handed over and paused, his pen at the ready. "What's your husband's name? Anything special you'd like me to write?"

"Um..." She fumbled for words. "His name's Eric. And you can just write...um..."

Whitley regarded her with creaseless, Botoxed concern. "Are you all right, sugar? You look a bit peaked."

Jen shrugged one shoulder. "Just stage fright, I guess. I've never done a live national TV show."

"You'll do fine," Whitley assured her. "Why, I remember when I sang the national anthem at the World Series. I was a nervous wreck."

"Is there a Jennifer Finnerty in here?" An intern holding a huge vase of red and pink flowers bustled through the door.

Jen raised one hand. "Right here."

"These are for you." The intern plopped the vase down without ceremony, tossed a tiny white envelope at Jen, and hightailed it back out to the hallway.

While Whitley and the makeup artist oohed and aahed over the bouquet, Jen opened the card with shaking hands and read a single, simple sentence:

Knock 'em dead

"Are they from your hubby?" Whitley asked. "That is too precious for words." She turned to Brick. "Why don't you ever do anything romantic like that for me?"

"I just bought you a house in Santa Ynez," Brick protested.

"Yeah, but that's a good investment." Whitley pouted. "I'm talking about gentlemanly tokens of love and affection."

"I'm holding your purse, aren't I?"

Jen blocked out their bickering and focused on the three little words typed on the white card. Maybe Eric had decided to give her one last chance. Maybe he'd started to miss her the way she missed him.

She excused herself from the makeup chair and hurried into the ladies' room. She dialed Eric's cell number, crossed her fingers, and sighed with relief when he picked up.

"'Lo?" he slurred after a few seconds of static.

"What's wrong with you?" Jen demanded. "You sound—"

"Hungover." Eric groaned. "In Vegas."

"Ah, yes. The bachelor party." She knew she should leave well enough alone, but she had to ask. "And how was the strip club?"

"Naked. Depressing. Expensive. The usual." He didn't seem surprised to hear from her, which she took as an auspicious sign. He *had* sent the flowers. Love! Hope! Second chances!

"So, listen." She lowered her voice. "You'll never guess who's in the greenroom with me."

"Greenroom?" He paused. "Oh, right. You're doing that show today."

And the Lord taketh away.

"You forgot." She crumpled up the card in her hand and pitched it into the wastebasket next to the sink.

"I've been busy," he said, a tad defensively. "Doing crazy things. Things that would shock you."

Jen smiled in spite of herself. "Really? Like what?"

"Losing money, mostly," he admitted. "Mara kicked my ass at the poker table."

"Wait, why were you playing poker with Mara? I thought she was going out there to talk to Josh."

"Josh wasn't available, so she had to talk to me. We stayed up all night gambling and eating. Well, she ate. I drank. Which didn't help my poker game."

"May I ask what you two discussed?"

"It'd be better if you didn't." He coughed. "Is Patrick with you?"

"No! Why would you even think that?"

"Gee, I don't know. Maybe because he answers the phone when I call my own house?"

Jen took a deep breath. "I didn't invite him yesterday, he just showed up on my doorstep. *Our* doorstep. I didn't do anything wrong."

There was a soft knock on the door. "Ms. Finnerty? Is everything all right?"

Jen covered the phone mouthpiece and called back, "Everything's great, thanks!"

"Okay, well, you're on in a few minutes, so..."

"I'll be there!" Jen double-checked the lock on the door and waded back into the argument at hand. "You have every right to be upset, but I love you, honey. Come home. Please. At least let me explain what happened."

Another knock at the door. "Ms. Finnerty? We really need you on-set right now."

"Go ahead," Eric said. "Take Noda national. You deserve this."

"But it's half yours," Jen choked out. "*More* than half yours."

"All I really did was write a check. You did the work. You made the sacrifices."

"But—"

"Bye, Jen."

She emerged in a daze from the restroom and allowed the production assistant to usher her down the hall.

"We're set for your segment as soon as we come back from break," the P.A. informed her. "Rory will introduce the product; we've put a few bottles of it out on the coffee table for close-ups. And please remember we're live, so watch your language."

Jen nodded numbly and tried to recapture the frisson

of excitement she'd felt when Deb had first called her about appearing on the show.

"All right, you're on." The production assistant shoved Jen out of the shadows, and a smattering of applause broke out in the audience. "Good luck."

Knock 'em dead.

She threw back her shoulders and strode into the spotlight with a bright smile on her face and a twist of despair in her heart.

Ellie

Chapter 19

Stay calm and let me do the talking." Karen Hamilton, Ellie's divorce attorney, adjusted the tasteful pearl and platinum brooch affixed to the lapel of her gray suit jacket. "These are just initial negotiations. We've got a long way to go before we hammer out a final settlement."

"I'll stay calm," Ellie promised, though her heart rate accelerated at the prospect of facing Michael for the first time since he'd kissed her good-bye at the airport. "But I just got the water bill in the mail. And the mortgage statement and the car lease note. So do we just pass those along to him, or...?"

"Don't worry. We'll get to all that in good time."

Mara hadn't been kidding when she praised Karen Hamilton as unflinching and unflappable. Ellie had met with her lawyer several times now and had yet to see her express any hint of emotion.

"I won't panic," Ellie chanted softly. "I won't panic."

"Good." Karen led the way into the hushed,

sumptuously appointed conference room of her down-town legal firm.

Ellie glanced at the heavy blue drapes and gleaming dark wood bookshelves until her gaze locked on to Michael. He was seated across the wide mahogany table with Terry Dawes, a ruddy-faced, squinty-eyed lawyer whom Mara had described as "the unholy love child of a pit bull and Giorgio Armani."

While their attorneys exchanged cordial hellos, Ellie and Michael sized each other up like prizefighters circling in the ring.

Stay strong, Ellie admonished herself. *Stay focused on the long-term goal: security for Hannah. Don't get distracted by love or anxiety or grief.*

Emotion was a waste of energy. The only thing that mattered, according to Karen, was money. Ellie had forced herself to stop thinking about her impending divorce in terms of bitter betrayal and start framing it in terms of billable hours. Of which Karen had already amassed a heart-stopping number.

We are gathered here today to put an exact dollar amount on your value as a wife, mother, and human being.

After an office assistant ferried in a tray heaped with pastries, a crystal carafe of water, and a silver pot of coffee, Michael's attorney helped himself to a scone and whipped out a sheaf of papers. "Shall we get started?"

"Absolutely." Karen took a seat next to Ellie. "I'd like to begin with a few questions about the financial documentation your office provided me with."

"Of course." Mr. Dawes looked directly at Ellie, who flushed and started to fidget.

"According to the terms of the pre-nuptial agreement, my client is entitled to half of all assets acquired during the course of the marriage, in addition to the cash value of three percent of the Bartons' family business." Karen glanced down at the documents in front of her. "But per this accounting report, your client..."

"Actually lost money during the course of the marriage. Correct." Mr. Dawes nodded. "He supported his wife and daughter primarily with the interest from his trust fund, the principal of which, as you know, is exempt from the terms of the pre-nup."

Karen scribbled down a few notes. "So your contention is that Mr. Barton's salary did not contribute to the family finances in any substantial way?"

"Correct. Most of the couple's assets, including the down payments for the house and vehicles, were attained via cash gifts from Mr. Barton's parents."

Ellie's head snapped back up. "What? That's not true!"

Karen silenced her with a light touch on the wrist. "And what about Ms. Barton's share of the real estate development company?"

Terry Dawes initiated a brief, whispered consulation with Michael. Then he nodded and turned back to Karen and Ellie. "Ms. Barton signed a buy-sell agreement, stipulating that in the case of divorce, she must sell back her share of the company at current market value."

"I'm well aware. And your contention is that Ms. Barton's share is worth...?" Karen raised one eyebrow, inviting the opposing counsel to finish the sentence.

Michael's lawyer named a dollar amount so low that

Ellie couldn't stifle her gasp. The attorney shrugged in a theatrical display of helplessness. "As you know, the real estate market is severely depressed right now. And, even assuming the market was booming, three percent doesn't amount to much, especially when we have to account for reserves for depreciation, rising taxes and insurance costs, and falling rents. The fact is, my client's family business is in the red and has been for some time."

Michael murmured in agreement while tugging down his shirt cuff to conceal the Cartier watch on his left wrist.

Ellie snorted. "Give me a break. His country club membership alone costs like ten thousand dollars a year. He spends money like it's water!"

Karen hastened to rephrase this: "I must agree that the Bartons did seem to enjoy an extremely comfortable lifestyle. Luxury furnishings, vacations, new automobiles every two years. If the records that have been supplied are complete, then clearly my client and her husband were living far beyond their means."

Terry Dawes chuckled. "They certainly wouldn't be the first couple to do so. Their cars were leased, the house was purchased with a negatively amortized mortgage, and Mr. Barton took out several sizable lines of credit to finance various remodels and furniture purchases. In fact, my client is now living in one of his parents' investment properties for economy's sake."

Ellie mirrored her lawyer's stony-faced demeanor and said, "He's lying."

Michael's jaw dropped. Terry Dawes's eyes bugged

out. "Ms. Barton, that is a very serious accusation! For you to imply—"

Karen cut him off. "Frankly, I have to agree that this summary of Mr. Barton's accounts seems incomplete. Your client has an obligation to produce all financial records: pay stubs, bonuses, preexisting bank accounts, investments, tax returns. *All* the money for the course of the marriage."

"I understand my client's obligation, counselor. If you'd like to take this before a judge, we're happy to go to court."

Karen didn't miss a beat. "You do realize that if the court finds that you've been less than forthcoming about the true state of your client's finances, you'll be held in contempt?"

"My client has fully divulged all financial records in good faith. I assure you, he's practically bankrupt."

Ellie covered her mouth and pretended to cough. "Bullshit." Michael reddened.

With a flourish, Terry Dawes produced a stack of documents and slid them across the table. "Ms. Barton, isn't this your signature on the tax returns filed jointly by you and your husband during the course of your marriage?"

Ellie glanced through the tax forms. "Yes, but—"

He jabbed his index finger toward the ceiling. "Are you asserting that these tax returns do not fairly and accurately reflect the financial situation of Mr. Barton and yourself?"

Ellie realized too late that Michael had trapped her. Again. "Well, I—"

"Surely you're aware that it would constitute perjury to file a falsified or incomplete tax return with the IRS?"

Ellie looked to Karen for direction while Terry settled back and poured himself a cup of coffee.

"The profit and loss statements included in these tax returns corroborate my client's account of monetary distress. So the question before us, Ms. Barton, is: Were you lying to the IRS for the past seven years about the state of your finances? Or are you lying to counsel about the state of your finances now?"

Karen held up her hand. "You're way out of line. This is a gross mischaracterization of what's going on here!"

"Then let's get down to brass tacks," Terry said to Karen. "We're willing to cede any remaining equity in the house to your client; in exchange, my client would retain ownership of the house's contents. Furniture, exercise equipment, appliances, et cetera. It's more than fair."

Ellie swept aside the tax returns. "He's already looted all the expensive stuff! The grand piano, the paintings, my jewelry."

Michael brushed off his lawyer and addressed her directly. "Those are family heirlooms."

"Your mother gave me those emeralds!" Ellie insisted. "They were a gift."

"They were a gift predicated on your union with my client," Terry Dawes said. "Those emeralds have been in the Barton family for several generations. And speaking of family heirlooms…" He did his best to feign reluctance. "We'd like to request the return of Ms. Barton's engagement ring. Immediately."

"Not going to happen," Karen said. "An engagement ring's a gift, free and clear."

"Not in this case," Terry said. "If the marriage dissolves, ownership reverts to the Bartons."

"According to whom?" Karen demanded. "There's nothing in the pre-nup about the engagement ring."

Terry dug out another stapled stack of papers. "I happen to have with me a copy of the current insurance policy on the diamond ring and the emerald pieces. Notice the name of the policy holder." He pointed out the text for them: *Heath Barton.* "While it was indeed generous of your father-in-law to let you wear the jewels, the duration and amount of this policy clearly establishes ownership."

Ellie looked Michael right in the eye and asked, "Who *are* you? When did you turn into such a—a—"

"Stay calm," Karen said under her breath.

"Have a shred of decency!" Ellie said. "Even if you don't care about me anymore, think about Hannah."

The opposing attorney nodded. "On the subject of your daughter."

"Stay calm," Karen repeated.

"Ms. Barton will be entitled to court-mandated spousal support only for the length of time that it would take her to complete career training and reenter the workforce. She's young, she has a college degree, she's certainly capable of supporting herself. Clearly, my client is in no position to provide a lump-sum settlement to Ms. Barton at this time, but he is prepared to do whatever it takes to support his daughter."

"Well, I should hope so!" Ellie exclaimed.

Michael and his lawyer both ignored her. "We do understand that as a working mother, Ms. Barton will necessarily undergo a drastic change in lifestyle. My client is more than willing to assume full physical custody of his daughter."

Ellie, who had never so much as swatted Hannah's behind, had to fight the sudden and overwhelming urge to lunge across the table and physically rip out Michael's jugular. She gripped the tabletop with both hands and said, "Never. Over my cold, dead body. I mean it, Michael. If you try to take Hannah, I will—"

"My client has proven himself to be a devoted father. Furthermore, he can show that he'll have the monetary and practical means; his family will guarantee educational and financial assistance, provided Hannah lives with their son."

"They should be willing to do that, anyway!" Ellie said. "She's still their grandchild, no matter who she lives with."

"Oh, we agree," Terry Dawes oozed. "Sadly, Mr. Barton's parents do not."

"Patrice would never . . ." Ellie's hands started to ache. At this rate, her fingertips were going to leave permanent indentations in the wood. "Does your mother know about this?"

"You're never going to get full custody." Karen sounded bored. "My client is an excellent mother, and you know as well as I do that any court-appointed intermediary is going to side with her."

"Ms. Barton might want to consider the needs of her daughter above her own. Were her daughter to live primarily with my clients and his parents, her standard of living would be significantly—"

"This line of negotiation isn't worth pursuing." Ellie's lawyer tapped her pen against the tabletop. "My client will never agree to that. Let's move on."

Ellie's entire body was trembling with fury. Michael avoided her searing glare and pretended to study the yellow legal pad next to his attorney.

"Fine. We'll table the custody issue until our next meeting," Terry Dawes said. "As to the matter of the house contents and the vehicles—"

"Before we continue," Karen interjected, "I do realize that my client is bound by the terms of the pre-nuptial agreement, but I'd like to point out that if both parties didn't fully disclose all assets at the time the pre-nup was signed, the agreement is not binding."

Mr. Dawes frowned. "Where exactly are you going with this? I already told you that my client is in dire financial straits. We've accounted for all of his income and holdings. Ms. Barton signed tax returns that corroborate his accounts. You have absolutely no grounds to suggest that my client has ever hidden any assets, before or after the marriage."

"I have the firsthand account of my client."

He rolled his eyes. "Well, no offense, but I'd venture that Ms. Barton's current perspective is somewhat colored by emotion."

"I'll go to court for an injunction if I have to," Karen warned.

"Go right ahead. You have no evidence, and we have nothing to hide."

"You're sure?" Karen said. "No offshore accounts, no assets recently transferred to family members?"

"Absolutely not."

"Not even Ms. Barton's recently liquidated retirement accounts?"

Terry Dawes didn't even blink. "My client used those funds to pay off jointly held debts before they separated. It inured to the benefit of both of them."

"Check his computer files," Ellie said to Karen. "His laptop. That's where the real dirt is going to be."

For the first time since he'd sent her off for the spa day from hell, Michael's face registered the tiniest flicker of guilt. He immediately reached down and clamped a proprietary hand on his briefcase, which never left his side and which always contained the laptop in question.

Karen tapped her pen against the table. "If you have nothing to hide, certainly you wouldn't object to a forensic accountant reviewing your client's computer files?"

"Out of the question," Michael's lawyer blustered. "First of all, my client has no undisclosed accounts and any suggestion to the contrary is malicious slander. Secondly, before we would even consider granting access to his personal files, my client would need ample opportunity to go through and redact all private and unrelated material."

Michael tightened his grip on his briefcase.

"My client has sensitive information on his computers," Terry said. "Correspondence that is protected by attorney/client privilege, medical records, contact information for his new girlfriend. Plenty of fodder for harassment. No judge is going to grant that injunction, and you know it."

Ellie tuned out the attorneys' sniping and stared down the tall, dark and handsome conniver she had mistaken for Prince Charming. She knew he was lying about the money. A few hours alone with that laptop would blow their pre-nup to hell. But how would she ever persuade him to turn it over to her?

Her husband had always underestimated her. She'd been too sweet and soft to ever pose a threat. But that had been before he'd uttered the words that were going to seal his doom: *full custody.*

Prince Charming was about to find out that, when pushed far enough, even Snow White had a dark side.

Mara
Chapter 20

Hey, Julie, have you seen the DeLorenzo documents?" Mara gave her overloaded assistant a hopeful look. Monday mornings were always hectic at the firm, but today was especially crazy with deadlines and demands.

Julie didn't look away from her computer screen. "Sorry, but no."

"Are you sure? I thought I gave them to you to proof-read."

"You did, but then you asked for them back, remember?"

"Vaguely." Mara conducted a mental inventory of her town house and office, trying to puzzle out where she might have left the contract drafts.

Julie squinched up her face before sneezing into a crumpled tissue.

"Bless you," Mara said.

"Thanks. I think I'm coming down with something. My throat tickles and my nose has been running—"

"Well, take it easy," Mara said. "Lots of fluids. Cough syrup. Zinc. You name it, I'll have it messengered over ASAP."

Julie grinned and blew her nose again. "You just don't want me to take a sick day."

"You wound me." Mara glanced at the pile of Kleenex heaped in the wastebasket under Julie's desk. "Take a nap at lunch. You can use the couch in my office."

Her assistant looked shocked. "Aren't you working through lunch?"

"Not today." Mara drummed the fingers of her now ringless left hand on the door frame. "I think I just remembered where I put the DeLorenzo files."

Good thing she had hung on to her key to Josh's apartment. She'd tried to return her engagement ring via messenger, but Josh had refused delivery, and so now it was moldering in her safety deposit box at the bank.

She hadn't spoken to him since he'd dumped her at the Black Diamond. She had, however, spoken to the wedding planner. And the caterer. And the florist. And her mother, who had said, "You couldn't have decided this *before* invitations went out?" and then hung up in a huff.

Mara knew that she should try to glean a bit of wisdom from the smoldering wreck that had once been her love life. She should track down Josh and tell him everything she knew to be true: that she wished him well, that she accepted full responsibility for sabotaging the only semihealthy relationship she'd ever had, that she would never entirely get over him. She should finally say what she meant and mean what she said.

And she would.

Someday very soon.

But on this chilly, overcast Monday afternoon, it was all she could do to force herself to drive over to his apartment building and cruise the parking lot to ensure that his car wasn't in its customary spot. Then, just to be sure the coast was clear, she dialed his home number and held her breath while the phone rang four times before his answering machine clicked on.

She climbed the carpeted stairs to the third-floor apartment and tried to remember precisely where she'd left the drafts she needed. Probably in the huge chrome bread box on the kitchen counter. Josh had picked up the hulking relic from the 1950's at a garage sale, and had offered it to Mara as a makeshift filing system since "you get mad when I use your work papers as coasters, and now, when you're at the firm and your paperwork smells like doughnuts, you'll think of me."

The mere thought of doughnuts made her stomach lurch. She hurried down the hallway, slipped her key into the deadbolt on Josh's door, and told herself that she must be coming down with Julie's bug. Queasiness and headaches were classic flu symptoms. Same with soul-crushing remorse and the urge to weep openly.

"Josh?" A female voice called out when the lock clicked open.

Mara froze.

"Josh?" The voice sounded closer this time, and Mara

heard rustling on the other side of the door. The key started to swivel as someone turned the deadbolt from the inside, and then, before she could flee or even attempt to disguise her expression of horror, the door swung inward and Mara found herself face-to-face with the perfect, petite, auburn-haired stripper from the Black Diamond.

Bentlie/Alex's eyes widened when she recognized Mara, but she quickly recovered her composure. "Well, well, well. Fancy meeting you here."

Mara didn't bother trying to dredge up a witty rejoinder. She was too busy hyperventilating. "What are you wearing?"

The dancer had traded in her sequins and platform heels for a comfy ensemble of gray sweatpants, a navy sweater rolled up at the sleeves, and an Arizona Diamondbacks cap pulled low over her tousled red hair.

"What?" Alex glanced down at the outfit with evident amusement. "I'm still not covered up enough for you? Wow, you *are* the jealous type. What do you want, a burka?"

"That's Josh's hat," Mara said. "And his sweater. I gave him that sweater."

"Yeah, and?" Alex shrugged. "I don't go prancing around in Day-Glo spandex on my days off, you know."

"What exactly are you doing here?"

Alex volleyed back with "What are *you* doing here?"

"I asked you first."

"Didn't twist the knife enough in Vegas?" Alex shook her head in disgust. "Had to come back to make sure he's miserable without you?"

Mara tried to barge into the apartment, but the tiny

dancer wouldn't back down. "There'd better be a good explanation for this."

"Oh, there is." Alex's face was solemn, but her hazel eyes sparkled. "A very simple one. Come on, use your brilliant lawyer brain to connect the dots."

"No. Uh-uh. There is no way," Mara said with more conviction than she felt. "Josh would never take up with—"

All humor vanished from the other woman's expression. "With a skank like me? Is that what you're trying to say?"

"No." Mara shook her head and backpedaled furiously. How had she been relegated from offense to defense in the space of two minutes? "But, I mean, we just broke up."

"Trust me, babycakes, I'm the perfect rebound girl." Alex pursed her plump, pink lips into a sexy pout. "Fun, frisky, and no mind games. Now, if you'll excuse me, I'm right in the middle of *Law and Order*, so . . ." She started to close the door.

"I do mind, actually." Mara shoved the door back open and darted into the apartment, which smelled of freshly microwaved popcorn. The kitchen and living room were tidier than she'd ever seen them. Either Josh had finally hired a cleaning service or his houseguest had marked her territory with a Swiffer and a bottle of Windex.

The DeLorenzo documents were still safely nestled inside the bread box. Mara retrieved them without comment, then marched back toward the door. "This is not over," she informed Alex icily.

"What's that?" Alex eyed the file folder.

"None of your business."

"Actually, it is my business if you rob the place while I'm standing right here." Alex made a surprise grab for the file folder and a brief, high-pitched scuffle ensued on the threshold.

Mara gasped and flailed wildly as Alex caught a fistful of her hair. "You—ouch! Let go!" She dug her nails into the sleeve of Josh's sweater.

Alex yelped. "I'll let go when you do!"

"Ow!"

"Ow!"

"Shuddup or I'm calling the cops!" a deep voice boomed from down the hall.

"Good! Tell them I'm being robbed." Alex wrestled Mara out into the hall, then snatched the file folder, pivoted, and triple-locked the apartment door before Mara could regain her balance.

Mara leaned against the wall for a moment, panting and swearing under her breath. Then she pounded on the door until the ornery neighbor down the hall started yelling again.

"Open up," she demanded, pressing her cheek up against the cold metal door panel.

No response from Alex.

"Just give me that file folder and I'll leave you alone," she tried.

Nothing.

"Please?"

All she could hear from inside the apartment was the upbeat music from a television commercial.

"Fine. *Fine!* I didn't want to drag Josh into this, but you leave me no choice. Pack up your pasties, woman, 'cause you're going to be on the first flight back to Vegas."

Mara charged into the Second Dawn Center and headed straight for Josh's makeshift office next to the break room. Cosmetically, the nonprofit center was the polar opposite of her posh law firm: industrial green paint on the walls, haphazard stacks of papers atop battered filing cabinets, the scent of coffee and chemical cleansers ground into the carpets. The staff here didn't get bloated expense accounts or private bathrooms. Instead, Mara imagined, they got a sense of fulfillment and good karma, though Josh had often remarked that the day-to-day reality of his job—writing grant proposals, monitoring investments, navigating political bureaucracies, and hitting up corporate donors for money—was more tedious than transcendent.

His office door was ajar; he sat inside with his back to her. She could see the very beginnings of a bald spot peeking through his brown hair. The small, pale patch of skin stopped her in her tracks for a moment as she realized how vulnerable he was underneath his outward demeanor of affable capability.

She shook off her apprehension and announced herself with crisp efficiency. "Question: What is that stripper from Vegas doing in your apartment?"

Josh jumped about a foot and banged his knees on the underside of his metal desk. "Mara! God! What are you doing here?"

"Considering filing assault charges," she answered.

"Your busty little friend practically bludgeoned me to death this afternoon. She's a lunatic and probably a felon. I hope the sex is worth it."

He grimaced and rubbed his knee. "You went to my apartment?"

"I needed some work documents I'd left in the kitchen. I still need them, actually, because when I tried to recover what was rightfully mine, she attacked me. She's violent, I tell you, and I...I will *sue!*"

Josh looked like he was trying to suppress a smile. "You're going to sue?"

"That's right! Do you have any idea how much I spend every month on my hair? Cut, color, conditioning? And she ripped out half of it, at least."

Josh's chair squeaked as he leaned back to assess the damage. "You look fine to me."

"Well, you can't see the emotional pain and suffering I've endured," Mara blustered. "She's devious and unstable and *what the hell is she doing in your apartment wearing the sweater I gave you for Christmas?*"

"Ah." Josh nodded. "So that's what this is about." He templed his fingers under his chin and gave her a long, appraising look.

"You said nothing happened between you two! Liar!"

"Don't jump to conclusions. She asked for help; I'm helping."

"Helping her. I see. Is that what they're calling it these days?"

"You should try to have a little compassion. Not everyone has had the advantages you have."

"That doesn't mean you have to move them into your

apartment and dress them up in the double-ply cashmere sweaters that your 'compassionless' ex-fiancée gave you! And stop laughing, it's not funny."

"I can't tell which you're more upset about," Josh said. "Me or the sweater."

"She's a menace to society."

"She's probably going to be my new volunteer coordinator."

Mara's dismay intensified. "You're hiring her?"

"I might. She wanted a career change, and she's having trouble getting back on her feet after—"

"I don't believe this. Why can't you just come home from Vegas with an STD or a tattoo like everyone else?"

"She deserves a chance to start over."

"You know what your problem is?" Mara fumed. "You're too good for your own good. She's taking advantage of you!"

"Hey." For the first time, his tone was tinged with anger. "Back off. I'm allowed to have a houseguest, and you... Well, you don't get a say anymore."

She gazed up at the water-stained ceiling tiles. "I know. And I'm sorry, Josh. I really am. I hate myself, if that makes you feel any better."

"It doesn't."

"See? Too good for your own good." Charged, heavy silence fell over them for a moment, then Josh started rearranging the contents of his desktop.

"Anyway, Alex's got nowhere else to stay. She can't afford a hotel and she doesn't have enough saved for a deposit on her own place."

"How can that be? She got two hundred dollars for

every sucker she could lure back to the VIP room. Plus pole dances, lap dances.... She probably makes more money than I do."

"I get the feeling prudent financial stewardship isn't her strong suit. So unless you're offering a spare bedroom..."

Mara's eyes lit up. "I'm offering four, as a matter of fact. Your sweater will be back in your closet by nightfall."

"Look who's a humanitarian all of a sudden."

"I'm Mother Teresa in a miniskirt. Leave everything to me."

Ellie

Chapter
21

*H*i, is Patrice there?" After sitting in the lobby of her lawyer's office building for an hour, reeling in disbelief and zoning out to the steady splash from the indoor waterfall, Ellie finally shook off her stupor and took action. "It's Ellie."

Tina, Patrice and Heath's housekeeper, paused on the other end of the phone line. "Mrs. Barton's not at home right now. But I'll be sure to let her know you called." Her voice sounded formal and distant, as if she had never met Ellie. As if the last seven years of chatting and snacking together after Patrice's lavish dinner parties had never happened.

Ellie pretended not to pick up on the cold undertone. "Well, it's kind of urgent. Do you know where she is? Because she's not answering her cell phone, and I need to speak with her right away."

"I'm not sure," Tina hedged.

Ellie sighed. "Look. I get that this is awkward, but

you know I wouldn't press you on this if it weren't an emergency."

Tina finally cracked a little. "Is Hannah all right?"

"Don't worry, Hannah's fine." Ellie racked her brain, trying to remember what she would have been doing today if her marriage hadn't suddenly jumped the track. "Patrice is at a committee meeting, isn't she? For the cancer benefit?"

A looong pause. "It's possible."

"I'll take that as a yes. Did she mention who's hosting today?"

"I can't tell you that," Tina said.

"Please?" As the word left her lips, Ellie realized that she had found herself in a position of supplication with alarming frequency since Michael left. This would have to stop. Soon.

"I don't want to get involved in all this," Tina said.

"Well, neither did I, but here I am. Come on, just give me a name."

"Oh, all right. For you." The housekeeper lowered her voice to a whisper. "Caroline Surbaugh."

"Oh crap, not Caroline." Ellie cringed. "Thanks, Tina. And don't worry; if anyone asks, I'll say you hung up on me before I could even finish saying hello."

"I'd appreciate that." And then Tina did hang up on her. Ellie listened to the dial tone, stunned at the speed with which she'd been demoted from the level of chummy confidante to telemarketer. Then she put on her coat and prepared to face the clique of elder stateswomen that she, Jen, and Mara privately referred to as "the gold-plated Gestapo."

———

Caroline Surbaugh epitomized the expression "A woman can never be too rich or too thin" and was both reviled and revered throughout Mayfair Estates as the sun around which the social solar system revolved. She had a tendency to overindulge at cocktail parties (not difficult, considering she probably tipped the scales at less than a hundred pounds) and expound on topics of questionable taste. Mara hated her because she had once opined that "anyone worth less than five million dollars is only 'beer and pretzels' rich," and Jen hated her because she had once offered to send Jen some special herbal tea that would help Jen (who had just finished training for a triathlon) "lose those last five stubborn pounds." Ellie had no reason to hate her, as she had Patrice as a buffer. Until now.

Ellie arrived at the front door of the Surbaughs' sprawling Spanish-style hacienda and tried to comfort herself with the thought that her life could not possibly suck any more than it already did. Let the ladies who lunch do their worst.

She rang the bell and began the countdown to her official excommunication from polite society. In five... four... three...

"Ellie Barton!" Caroline exclaimed, louder than was strictly necessary. "What a surprise!"

All conversation in the living room immediately ceased. Ellie could hear the clink of a demitasse spoon against a china cup, and then total silence.

"We're so glad you could join us," Caroline gushed, motioning Ellie in for an air kiss. "But I have to say, I didn't think you'd make it, considering..."

Sharp staccato footfalls echoed off the coffered wood ceiling as Patrice rushed to join Caroline in the foyer. "Ellie, darling." Her voice was also loud and cordial, presumably to convey to all assembled that she and her daughter-in-law were still on good terms.

The sight of her mother-in-law broke Ellie's heart all over again. Losing Michael had been bad enough, but in some ways, losing Patrice would be worse.

Ellie kept her posture rigid when Patrice attempted to hug her. "We need to talk."

Patrice dropped her arms and nodded. She appeared perfectly put together, as usual, in a crisp white blouse and brown herringbone trousers, but her face bore evidence of strain. Her gray eyes had lost their customary snap and the fine lines around her mouth had deepened. "Of course. I have an appointment this afternoon I simply can't cancel, but let's try to find time this weekend."

"Now." Ellie tried to ignore the crescendo of scandalized whispers building in the next room. "This can't wait."

"Very well." Patrice's smile remained firmly in place under Caroline's watchful gaze. "Let's step out to the patio. Caroline, may we?"

"Of course." Caroline led them back through the dining room and opened the French door leading out to the gardens.

Ellie waited until the glass doors closed completely before she opened her mouth again, but Patrice surprised her by initiating the conversation. "I know you met with our lawyers, and I'm sorry. From the bottom of my heart."

Ellie let her shoulders slump as her spirit wilted. "So you knew? You knew what he was going to say about wanting full custody of Hannah?"

"Well, no, not precisely."

"Then why don't you seem surprised?"

"I don't know all the details, darling." *And I don't want to*, was the unspoken implication. "Please believe me when I say I would never participate in the legal machinations. I'm trying very hard not to get involved."

"Great. One more person who doesn't want to get involved. Meanwhile, Michael is screwing me over and no one is stopping him."

Patrice touched her lightly on the shoulder. "I am so, so sorry, Ellie."

"Don't be sorry!" Ellie pulled away. "Be on my side!"

Her mother-in-law didn't reply.

"I'm still the same person, you know. I haven't done anything wrong."

"I know."

"You're the one who told me to give him another chance."

"I know."

"And now he's trying to weasel out of paying alimony and threatening to take my baby away and he's saying you and Heath are in full agreement! How could you?"

Patrice sidestepped this with "Surely you know how highly Heath and I both think of you."

"Then how can you sit by and let him do this to me?"

"I really . . ." She waved her hands helplessly. "I'm not privy to the details. The lawyers . . ."

"Don't give me that, Patrice! You're the linchpin of this family. If you say stop, he'll stop." She would not beg. She would not beg. Okay, maybe just a teeny bit. "*Please* help me out here."

Patrice raised one hand to touch the strand of pearls around her neck. "It's not that simple."

"Think about how you would feel, Patrice, if Heath had left you and tried to take your sons away."

"Michael's not going to take Hannah away from you. And he's not going to let her go without. He wouldn't do that, and even if he wanted to, Heath and I would never allow it."

"Then what the hell?"

"It's just legal negotiations. That's how the game is played."

"Oh. I see. To you guys, this is a game. But to me, this is my *life*."

"Try to understand. This isn't personal. It's not under my control and it has nothing to do with how I feel about you."

"That's even more disturbing."

"I adore you, Ellie, and I never imagined it would come to this." Patrice lowered her eyes. "But, in the end, Michael is my child. We're family."

"And I'm not. Got it. But let me remind you that I gave up my chance to attend law school for the sake of your family. I could have been one of those attorneys you're so happy to let do your dirty work. Instead, I did what was best for Michael and helped him build his career, and now, I'm supposed to start all over with nothing because he kicked me out of the family? I don't think so."

Patrice dabbed at her eyes with the cuff of her pristine white sleeve. "Oh, Ellie, I understand how difficult—"

"Trust me, you have no idea."

"—but I hope that someday, in the future—"

"No wonder you guys insisted on that pre-nup." Ellie crossed her arms tightly. "It makes it so easy to take everything back: vows, jewelry, obligations. If you can find the right attorney to negotiate, it's like my marriage never existed. Who cares about feelings as long as you get your precious piano back." She turned and yanked open the French doors, surprising a trio of eavesdroppers, who scurried back to the living room. This time, the ladies didn't bother whispering. They murmured and gasped and snickered, and Ellie had to go right through the gauntlet of gossip on her way out the door.

"Leaving so soon?" Caroline called after her.

Ellie didn't bother with any more phony social niceties. She slammed into her car and peeled out, leaving tire tracks across the queen bee's front lawn and plenty for everyone to buzz about.

When Ellie pulled up to her house, she was shocked to see Mara standing on the front step, repeatedly jabbing at the doorbell.

She rolled down the window and yelled, "Perfect timing. I could use a drinking buddy right about now. Hop in and we'll go for margaritas."

"No can do." Mara didn't move from the doorstep, so Ellie turned off the car with an exasperated sigh.

"Since when do you turn down margaritas?"

Mara waited until Ellie joined her under the portico, then muttered, "I tried to call, but you weren't picking up."

"What's up with the monotone and shifty eyes?" Ellie asked.

Mara jerked her head toward her car, which was parked at the curb by the mailbox. Ellie followed her gaze and noticed the woman in the passenger seat: a tiny slip of a female with the face of an angel, the cagey eyes of a fox, and the bustline of Pamela Anderson. When the stranger saw them both staring at her, she got out of the car and started toward them. Her small stature was only emphasized by her outfit of baggy sweatpants and an enormous blue sweater.

"Pleased to meet you." Ellie extended her right hand and slapped on the sweet, superficial smile that had gotten her through countless benefit luncheons. "I'm Ellie Barton."

The other woman regarded her with obvious suspicion and made no move to reciprocate the greeting. Ellie withdrew her hand and threw Mara a questioning glance.

"This is Alex," Mara announced. "She's a friend of Josh's from out of town and she needs a place to stay for a few days."

Ellie immediately saw where Mara was going with this and did her best to head her off at the pass. "I see. Well, there's a lovely bed-and-breakfast that just opened by the Frank Lloyd Wright estate, and of course, the Fairmont is divine this time of year."

"Yeah, that's not gonna work." Mara turned to Alex. "Could you excuse us for one moment? Thanks." She waited for Ellie to unlock the door and followed her into the house, where she delivered a quick rundown on Josh, the stripper, and the navy sweater. "And she refuses to let me pay for a hotel, and Jen's still in L.A., so if you could—"

"Oh, no." Ellie shook her head so fast, the room spun. "No, no, no, no, no. I have more stress than I can handle already. I do not need sweater subterfuge and strippers added to the mix. I have a child, for heaven's sake."

"'Stripper' is such a pejorative label," Mara said. "Think of her as Josh's potential trainee. Come on, don't you want to do your bit to better the community?"

"I'm no longer part of this community. Caroline Surbaugh and the gold-plated Gestapo are crucifying me over canapés as we speak. I need a few minutes alone to have a nervous breakdown before I pick up Hannah at preschool, and then I need to hire a forensic accountant."

"Want me to get you some names?" Mara offered. "I'll help any way I can. Money, baby-sitting, you name it."

"Thanks. And under normal circumstances, I'd do the same for you. But I don't know the first thing about this woman. What if she's a drug addict? What if she steals? What if she murders me in my bed and then kidnaps Hannah?"

"Now you're just being ridiculous. Who in their right mind would want a three-year-old?"

"It's okay." Alex's voice was directly behind them, and Ellie and Mara both were startled. "I wouldn't want me for a houseguest, either, if I lived in a neighborhood like this."

Ellie whirled around, clutching her coat lapels. "No, no. It's not you; it's me. I'm dealing with a few personal issues right now. My husband just left me."

Alex nodded. "I've been there."

"And my daughter's having trouble adjusting and—"

"No explanation necessary." Those big hazel eyes glittered. "I get it. People like you don't associate with people like me."

Ellie flushed.

"But just for the record." Alex unwrapped a piece of gum and popped it into her mouth. "I don't do drugs and I don't steal. And I definitely don't kidnap."

Mara blanched. "No, of course not."

"I'm not just some waste of space." Her posture took on a defensive swagger. "And I can take care of myself, so if you're waiting for me to beg..."

Something inside Ellie snapped at the word "beg." "You can stay."

Mara blinked. "But you just said—"

"I know what I said. And now I'm saying I'd love to play hostess for a few days. It'll keep me from sitting around feeling sorry for myself. I'll put fresh towels in the guest room and whip up some muffins." This time her smile was genuine. "I just hope you don't mind the *Dora the Explorer* theme song blasting at six-thirty A.M."

"I probably won't even hear it." Alex assured her. "I trained myself to go deaf at will after I heard 'Girls, Girls, Girls' one too many times backstage. If I can block out Mötley Crüe, I can block out anything." She scuffed the toe of her sneaker against the marble floor. "But you don't have to do this. I'll figure something out. If all else fails, I can always go back to Josh's couch."

Mara kept her mouth shut, but her forehead veins bulged.

"Please stay," Ellie said firmly. "You'd be doing me a favor. Honestly."

"I love you, El," Mara said. "Save me a muffin?"

"Greedy, greedy." Alex rolled her eyes. "Don't touch my fiancé, don't wear that sweater, save me a muffin—"

"I have to get back to the office," Mara snapped. "And he's not my fiancé anymore, as you know." She was out the door before Alex could offer a rebuttal.

"She's really very sweet," Ellie told Alex. "Underneath all the bluster."

"I'll have to take your word for it." Alex pointed to the conspicuously vacant patch of living room carpeting and asked Ellie, "So what happened in here?"

"Oh, that's where the grand piano used to be. Before my husband absconded with it while I was at the spa he sent me to." She ticked off Michael's offenses on her finger. "This was after he cheated on me, while he canceled my charge cards, and before he served the divorce papers."

"Ouch." Alex nodded in sympathy. "My husband took the pool table and the plasma TV. He was a cheater, too. And the worst part was, the chick I finally caught him with wasn't even pretty. I mean, what's worse than being left for some stumpy, stringy-haired lounge singer?"

"Being left for a physician who looks like Angelina Jolie."

"Yeah, okay, that might be worse."

They paused for a moment of quiet introspection.

"God, I miss that plasma TV," Alex finally said. "Hey, were you serious with that muffin offer?"

"Absolutely." Ellie led the way into the kitchen. "Although I must say I'm jealous that you can eat muffins and keep that figure."

"Oh, I can't. That's the good thing about giving up dancing; I'm going to stop tanning and starving myself and totally let myself go. I can't wait."

Ellie grinned. "So you're not one of those women who worries about how many calories are in a grape?"

Alex laughed wickedly. "Who has time to worry about calories when there are ratbag ex-husbands to be dealt with?"

The phone rang while Ellie was toweling Hannah off after bathtime. Hannah had taken an immediate liking to their new houseguest when Alex suggested an "all orange dinner" consisting of mac and cheese, baby carrots, and milk tinted with red and yellow food coloring, and she was all wriggles and giggles despite the late hour.

"Can you get that?" Ellie called to Alex. "I'm knee-deep in shampoo and toothpaste over here."

"Sure." Alex, who had insisted on washing the dishes and then disappeared into the den to watch a rerun of *CSI* (apparently, she, too, had considered a career in law enforcement once upon a time), picked up the phone.

Ten seconds later, Alex appeared in the bathroom doorway. "It's someone named Patrice."

"Gramma!" Hannah squealed. "Mommy, Mommy, let me talk!"

Ellie and Alex locked eyes in the mirror over the sink.

"You can talk to Gramma after you've brushed your teeth," Ellie said. "Alex, would you mind taking over in here for a few minutes?"

"No problem."

Ellie grabbed the phone and hurried out of her daughter's earshot. "Hello?"

"Hello." Patrice's tone was frosty. "Thank you for taking my call."

"Well, of course." Ellie matched her mother-in-law's brisk formality. "I know I was upset this afternoon, but it's only fair to give you a chance to explain."

"I'm not calling to explain anything, just to let you know that although we all appreciate the hard work you've done for the cancer benefit, it might be best if you declined your invitation."

"Best for whom, exactly?"

Patrice sighed. "The entire committee agrees. We'd prefer that the focus of the event remain on raising awareness for a good cause and not on unsavory rumors."

"I haven't done anything to spark unsavory rumors," Ellie pointed out. "So if anyone's bowing out, it should be Michael."

"Michael and Heath have already bought a table for their clients."

"Oh my God." Ellie sat down on the edge of the bed. "He's bringing his new girlfriend, isn't he? That's what this is about."

"There's no reason we can't be civilized about this. I'm merely pointing out—"

"Don't worry. I wouldn't be caught dead at your precious benefit ball. Thanks to your son, I won't be able to afford a new gown anyway, and heaven forbid I be seen in the same dress twice. What would the *committee* say?" She hung up the phone and started pounding the receiver against the mattress.

"Everything okay?" Alex cracked open the door.

"*No.*" Ellie sent Hannah off to choose a bedtime book, then continued seething about the blacklist. "It's not enough to leave me humiliated and penniless. They have to take away my social life, too?"

"Hold up," Alex said. "He can't leave you penniless if you can prove he's hiding lots of money, right?"

"Yeah, but like I said before, how am I ever going to prove that if he won't give up access to his computer?"

"I think I just figured out what to give you for a hostess gift," Alex rubbed her palms together. "All you have to do is get my name on the guest list for that benefit ball."

Ellie frowned. "But why?"

"Manipulating men is my business. Your fairy godmother has arrived."

"And you have a plan already? It's only been thirty seconds."

"The less you know, the better off you'll be. Just score me an invite and prepare to be amazed."

Jen *Chapter* 22

Ellie, you know I'm happy to make a donation to the cancer society, but there's no way I'm going to that ball," Jen said as she, Mara, and Ellie began their walk around the golf course. "For one thing, I don't want to deal with all the questions about why Eric isn't with me, and for another, I have nothing to wear."

"You have nothing to wear?" Mara asked. "Come on. We've all seen the inside of your closet. You've got enough evening gowns to outfit the entire Miss America pageant."

"I know." Jen quickened her pace. "But I've been very upset since Eric moved out, and..."

"You lost weight, didn't you?" Mara stayed right on her tail. "I knew it! Woman, you are wasting away. How many times must I tell you: Sometimes you need to take a break from all that macrobiotic, organic crapola and eat a damn cheeseburger."

"You do look thinner," Ellie agreed. "Kind of gaunt, actually. Your cheeks are hollowing out."

"I already have a mother, ladies. When I want a lecture

on my nutrition, I'll call her. Besides, I don't have time for society soirees right now. I'm busy with work."

"You're always busy with work," Ellie said.

"Even busier than usual."

"Well, that's great!" Mara said. "So that means your whirlwind publicity tour worked?"

"Yeah, apparently." A huge understatement, but Jen wasn't in the mood to divulge details right now. Since her appearance on the Rory Reid show, orders had started pouring in from all over the country, along with interview requests from magazines and newspapers. Her publicist was euphoric. Her accountant was salivating. And every time Jen looked at the skyrocketing sales projections for next quarter, she felt totally apathetic.

"Then what's with all the doom and gloom?" Mara demanded as they veered off the asphalt path to avoid the sprinklers. "You look like you just spent a month in solitary confinement. Have you been talking to Patrick again?"

Once Mara mentioned his name, Jen realized she hadn't even thought about her ex-boyfriend since leaving Los Angeles. "No. Although he did send me flowers backstage at the Rory Reid show."

Ellie threw out her arms, bringing all three of them to a halt. "Why didn't you tell us?"

"Because I threw them in a Dumpster and I never want to think about them again. Like I said, Patrick's not the problem. The problem is Eric."

Mara buried her hands in her hair. "You still haven't called him? What are you waiting for? You must call. Right now. Here, want to borrow my phone?"

"Don't push her; she'll call him when she's ready." Ellie waved away Mara's cell phone, then muttered to Jen, "Why haven't you called him?"

Jen shrugged. "What am I going to say to him? Sorry our marriage is DOA, but the good news is, I'm about to make a ton of money and you're entitled to at least half of it? He'll just shut me down again."

Ellie furrowed her brow. "I thought he said he wasn't going to go after Noda."

"Maybe he will, maybe he won't." Jen squinted into the morning sun. "I could care less at this point."

"Don't let his attorney hear you say that," Mara warned.

"Yeah, she's right," Ellie agreed. "*All you need is love* only applies if you've got a hefty trust fund to fall back on. I'm learning that one the hard way."

"Duly noted." Jen seized on the chance to change the subject. "So is Michael still crying poor?"

"Totally. According to him, we've been living on credit cards and a prayer for the last seven years. He's planning to stick me with half the debt and go riding off into the sunset with his mommy and daddy's money." Ellie beseeched Jen with her big brown eyes. "That's why I need you to go to the benefit ball, so I can prove that he's lying."

"I don't get it," Jen said. "Am I supposed to pick-pocket his bank card out of his tux?"

"Nah, he already cleaned out all the bank accounts," Ellie said. "I need you to take Alex as your plus one."

"Who's Alex?" Jen asked.

"That would be the stripper who came home from Vegas with Josh," Mara said.

"*What?*"

"She's not a stripper anymore!" Ellie cried. "She's starting a new phase of her life, and we should all be supportive!"

Jen called a time-out. "Enlighten me. Why exactly am I taking a stripper—pardon me, *former* stripper—to a black-tie charity event?"

"So she can bust Michael and make him pay!"

"But how is she going to do that?" Mara asked. "Especially if he's bringing the new girlfriend?"

Ellie nibbled her lower lip. "Well, she kind of glossed over the details. But she assured me that she's very good at this kind of thing. And you know the gold-plated Gestapo would never add her name to the invitation list. She's new in town, she's not old money, she's not even quote-unquote 'beer and pretzels rich.' "

"She's a *stripper*," Mara added.

"This is not gonna end well," Jen predicted.

"Don't worry about what to wear," Ellie said. "Just get Alex in the door, then turn around and go straight home. She can take care of herself."

Jen put one hand on her hip. "But I still don't understand how—"

"Fore!" a golfer bellowed across the green.

"Mara!" Jen tried to shove her friend out of the little white ball's trajectory, but it was too late.

Thwack!

"I'm *fine*," Mara repeated for the hundredth time while she, Ellie, and Jen waited for the emergency room staff to call them in. "I didn't even pass out. I have an incredibly thick skull. Just ask Josh."

"You're not fine," Jen said. "You dropped like a rock. We thought you were dead!"

"I was momentarily surprised, that's all." Mara rubbed her temple.

"Don't touch it!" Ellie cautioned. "You might have internal injuries."

"Give me a break. I'm *fine.* Can we please go now? I have a hair appointment at two."

Jen rolled her eyes. "Oh yeah, chemicals and blow-drying. That'll heal you up in a jiff."

"Mara Stroebel!" yelled a nurse in pink scrubs.

"That's us!" Jen grabbed Mara's elbow. "Right over here!"

"Wait, wait!" Mara's unwitting assailant, a tall, lanky man in a cabled white sweater and atrocious plaid pants, rushed in through the front entrance. "I just wanted to make sure you got here okay and, well, I got you these." He handed Mara a cellophane-wrapped bunch of wilting carnations. "Best I could do at the gas station. Again, I am so sorry. My grip was off and I sliced left and ... well, I'm a terrible golfer. The scary part is, this was actually an improvement over my last game. Might be time to take up fishing instead."

Once you got past the garish ensemble, the guy was actually very attractive, Jen decided. And she wasn't the only one who noticed; Ellie was eyeing the golfer with evident interest.

"How are you feeling?" he asked Mara. "Still dizzy? Are you bleeding at all?"

Jen smiled. "Don't worry, she's spent the last fifteen minutes explaining how utterly and completely fine she is."

"I am," Mara insisted. "Give me a couple ibuprofen and I'll be good as new."

The nurse in pink scrubs started tapping her foot. "Mara Stroebel?"

"We're coming," Ellie said.

The golfer shifted his weight from one cleat-clad foot to the other. "I feel awful. Here's my contact information; I insist on reimbursing you for the medical bill, insurance co-pay, all that."

Mara glanced down at his business card, then handed him one of hers.

His expression went from anxious to appalled. "You're an attorney?"

"Yes, but a very nice one," Ellie assured him. "Who doesn't believe in frivolous personal-injury lawsuits. Right, Mara?"

Mara raised one eyebrow. "Define 'frivolous.'"

"She's joking," Jen said. "Let's go." She steered Mara toward the nurse, who led them back to a small curtained partition and took Mara's blood pressure. "A doctor will be with you shortly."

Two minutes later, Ellie joined them. "His name is Ben," she announced. "He's new to Arizona and he seems very nice." She rounded on Mara with an accusatory glare. "And you better not sue him."

"Ooh." Jen winked at Mara. "Sounds like someone has a thing for plaid pants."

"What? Don't be ridiculous!" Ellie's entire face flushed. "First of all, I didn't even notice his pants—"

"How could you *not*?" Mara snorted. "I'm blinded for life."

"—and second, I'm never going to have a 'thing' for anyone ever again. I'm done with men."

"Famous last words," Jen said.

"No, I mean it. After everything with Michael..." Ellie trailed off as footsteps approached the other side of the thin white curtain.

A tall female doctor stepped into the little partition. Her baggy blue scrubs and starched white coat couldn't disguise her willowy figure. "How are we doing today?" She consulted the patient chart. "Head injury?"

"Golf ball to the forehead," Mara confirmed.

Jen heard a tiny squeak, and turned to see Ellie's face freeze in a silent rictus of horror.

"Okay, well, let's take a look." The doctor leaned forward and extended her right hand. "I'm Dr. Locane, by the way."

"Why does that name sound so familiar?" Mara asked, oblivious to Ellie's distress.

"Mara." Jen made frantic throat-slashing gestures with her fingers. "Drop it."

"No, hang on." Mara tilted her head and regarded the doctor with great interest. "I know I know you."

Jen stepped in between Mara and Dr. Locane. "No, you don't."

"Yes, I do," Mara insisted. "What's your first name? Veronica? Something with a *V*."

Dr. Locane looked surprised. "Victoria."

"See?" Mara shot Jen a look of triumph. "I told you I know her. How else would I know her name starts with a *V*?"

"We have to leave," Jen hissed. "Now."

Mara peered over Jen's shoulder at the doctor. "What are you talking about? We just got here."

Jen jerked her head toward Ellie and willed Mara to understand. "Because—"

"My husband said you were looking for commercial office space." Ellie snapped out of her state of shock and was edging around Jen toward Victoria. "But you don't work in an office."

Victoria tucked one hand in the pocket of her white labcoat. "Why on earth would I be looking for commercial office space?"

Ellie stared at her for a long moment. "I guess you don't remember me. I'm Ellie Barton."

Victoria's right eyelid twitched ever so slightly, but otherwise she maintained a perfect poker face.

"Michael's wife," Ellie said, loudly enough to be heard beyond the curtains separating the exam area from the rest of the ER. "You've been having an affair with my husband."

Mara's mouth formed a perfect O. "I tried to tell you," Jen said.

Victoria took a moment, then cleared her throat. "Ah yes, the lunatic who keyed my car. I'll send over the repair bill."

Ellie choked. Jen cringed. Mara absolutely lost her mind. She leapt off the exam table and tackled the other woman. "You bitch!"

Victoria staggered backward, caught her shoe on a monitor cord, and fell to the ground. Her stethoscope and medical chart clattered against the scuffed floor tiles. "Security!" she screamed.

"Time to go," Jen announced.

But Mara wasn't finished with Vixen_MD. She lunged down after the doctor and shoved her index finger up under Victoria's chin. "Marriage vows mean something, you know. Marriage is *sacred!*"

Victoria recommenced yelling for security. Mara was unimpressed. "I have a head injury, remember? I can kick your ass right now and claim temporary insanity."

A nurse yanked back one of the curtain panels.

"She started it!" Mara cried. "She's a husband-stealing harpy!"

Jen grabbed the back of Mara's blouse and hauled her upright. "We were just leaving."

"Anytime, anywhere!" Mara waved her fist as Jen dragged her back into the waiting room. "Don't worry, Ellie, I'll avenge you!"

"Ladies, I'm going to have to ask you to calm down." The nurse ushered them out through the huge double doors.

Mara was shaking with outrage. "But she—"

"I heard," the nurse assured her, then turned to wave off the uniformed security guard who had approached with a walkie-talkie in his hand. "It's okay. They're on their way out. Just another wife looking for Dr. Locane."

Ellie's eyebrows snapped together. "*Another* one?"

"Oh yeah." The nurse lowered her voice. "She's got

a thing for collecting married men." She regarded Ellie with great sympathy. "It was your husband?"

Ellie nodded. "You say she does this a lot?"

The nurse exchanged a pointed look with the receptionist behind the admittance desk. "Honey, half the staff stopped bringing their husbands to the holiday parties because of her. Do you have kids?"

"A daughter. Three years old."

"What a shame. But Locane'll get bored and move on to her next victim. Don't worry; he'll come crawling back."

"I don't want him back," Ellie said. "I'm done with him."

But that was the problem with misbehaving men, Jen mused as she drove home from the hospital—they kept showing up, no matter how much you wanted to deny their existence. When she pulled up to her house, there was an unfamiliar sedan parked at the curb and an all too familiar figure waiting on her front step. She hesitated for several minutes before getting out of her car, then decided that there was no point in delaying the inevitable.

She strode toward her front door with her hands in her coat pockets and her head held high. "Why won't you leave me alone?"

"We need to talk," Patrick said.

"No, we don't." She turned her face into the cold wind sweeping down from the mountains. "I'm through with you. I thought I made that clear."

She should walk into the house she'd shared with Eric and lock the door behind her and never again wonder about what might be waiting for her outside the big, empty fortress of her marriage. She should accept that if she couldn't make it work with Eric, she couldn't make it work with anyone, because her husband had loved her so much more than Patrick ever could.

But she just couldn't bear to barricade herself anymore. So she looked into Patrick's eyes and drank in the desire and approval she'd been craving.

"Meet me for dinner," he urged. "Hear me out. That's all I ask."

"Okay. Fine. I give up." Jen's keys slipped out of her fingers and fell onto the thick woven welcome mat. "I'm listening."

Mara
Chapter 23

Marriage is sacred.

The words she'd screamed at Dr. Victoria Locane reverberated through Mara's mind as she drove home from the emergency room. She'd been out of control, spitting mad, but her anger wasn't all on Ellie's behalf.

A lot of it was directed at herself.

When she lashed out at the notorious Vixen_MD, she'd been striking a blow against women who didn't take commitment seriously. Women who couldn't be trusted. Women, in other words, like herself.

Marriage is sacred. She truly believed that. And that's why, even though she was devastated that Josh had given up on her, she was also secretly relieved. Because now she didn't have to be afraid she would let him down again.

The gorgeous vista outside her windshield was in complete contrast to her mood: The sun was shining, the palm trees were swaying in the breeze, and not a single cloud appeared on the open blue horizon. Her cell phone rang and she snatched it up, grateful for any distraction. "Hello?"

"Hi! This is Pam from the Happily Ever After bridal salon. I'm just calling to let you know that we've finished all the alterations on your gown and it looks fantastic!"

Mara paused. "Didn't my wedding planner call you guys a few weeks ago?"

"Not that I know of. Anyway, it's all steamed and ready to go. When would you like to come pick it up?"

"Well. About that…"

"We're open this afternoon 'til five."

Mara's temples started to throb as if she'd just taken another golf ball to the head. "It's already hemmed?"

"Let's see…" Mara could hear papers shuffling on Pam's end of the line. "The seamstress took in the waist, moved the back buttons, and shortened the hem."

"So there's no way I could, you know, *return* the dress?"

"Pardon?" Pam's chirpy tone suddenly dropped about an octave. "I'm afraid not. This gown was custom sewn in London especially for you. Final sale. We'll need the rest of your deposit as soon as possible."

"I know, but…" Mara sighed. "The wedding's off."

"Oh, I am so sorry to hear that." Pam allowed two seconds of respectful silence, then continued, "We accept Visa, MasterCard, and American Express."

"Can't you just hang on to it and see if anyone else might be interested? I'd like to recoup some of my costs if at all possible."

"We'll see you before five," Pam said firmly. "Thank you for allowing us to help create the wedding of your dreams!"

"I'm here to see Pam, please." Mara slunk into the bridal salon with the penitent posture of a bride gone bad. Swaths of white tulle and clusters of silk roses festooned every available surface, and sweeping violins played softly over the sound system.

"Pam's with a client." A short, eager-looking young woman stepped out from behind the decorative table that served as a counter for the cash register. "I'm Suki. Is there something I might be able to help you with?"

"I hope so. I ordered a wedding gown six months ago and Pam just called to tell me it was in, but——"

"Ooh! How exciting!" Suki squealed and clapped her hands. "What's your name?"

"Mara Stroebel. But I don't——"

"One second!" The clerk's ponytail swished as she hurried into a back room. She emerged minutes later with a long, baby blue garment bag. "Let's try it on and make sure it fits."

Mara crossed her arms. "No need."

"But you have to!" Suki insisted. "We should make sure it fits perfectly; it better, considering what it cost!"

"Here." Mara shoved her credit card across the counter. "Would you just ring it up, please?"

Too late. Sukie unzipped the garment bag, revealing the elegant ivory silk georgette sheath that Mara had selected after trying on and rejecting countless other options. The fabric was unadorned but artfully draped to create a graceful silhouette.

"So chic," Suki said, watching Mara's expression change. "Let me open up a dressing room for you. Aren't you dying to know how you'll look on your wedding day?"

As soon as the saleswoman said this, Mara realized that she did indeed want to know. Trying on this gown would give her a tiny glimpse at what her future might have been like if she hadn't forced Josh to give up on her. Trying on this gown would also tear the scab off wounds that were still raw and fresh. The smart thing to do would be to turn around and leave this shop posthaste.

Five minutes later, Suki was doing up the delicate row of buttons on the back of the gown and Mara was gazing at herself in the mirror. She had chosen this gown because, when she walked down the aisle toward Josh, she hadn't wanted to look like an uptight lawyer, or a sweet little princess, or anything less than a—

"Grecian goddess," Suki confirmed, kneeling down to smooth out the fabric at the bottom. "Wow. Your fiancé is a lucky guy."

Mara stepped away from Suki's ministering hands and gathered up her bag and change of clothes. "Can I please just pay now? I have to go."

"Right now? But you'll ruin the gown!"

"Oh, it's already ruined." Mara powered toward the cash register, credit card in hand. "And there's not a seamstress alive that can fix it."

It took her a five full minutes to summon the courage to knock at Josh's apartment. She loitered in the hallway, plucking at the soft silk of the gown, until a pizza delivery boy appeared in the stairwell and gaped at her.

"What are you looking at?" Mara flushed and rapped her knuckles against the metal door.

Ten seconds later, she was staring at her former fiancé.

"Don't worry, you don't have to get a restraining order," Mara announced by way of greeting. She reached into her handbag and produced a small white box. "I just wanted to give you this, and then I'll be on my way."

Josh accepted the box but didn't open it. "What are you wearing? And what happened to your face?"

"What do you mean?"

He pointed to her cheek. "You're got a huge cut right there."

"I do?" She raised her hand to her cheek and felt a long, thin ribbon of raised skin. She hadn't even noticed the wound in the mirror at the bridal salon; she had only looked at the dress. "Vixen_MD must've gotten in one good scratch before I pinned her. She's a feisty one."

"You got in *another* catfight? Didn't you learn anything from that brawl with Alex?"

"I'd hardly call that little dustup with Alex a brawl. Anyway, that wasn't my fault; she forced my hand," Mara said. "And the one this morning was for Ellie."

"I'm not asking any more questions." Josh shook his head and leaned against the door frame. "I don't think I can handle the answers."

"Probably wise." Mara straightened her shoulders. "Anyway, I know we didn't leave things on a very good note, so I wanted to apologize again for, um, slightly over-reacting in Vegas. That wasn't my finest hour. Oh, and when I showed up at your office ranting and raving about how dare you let Alex crash on your couch? That wasn't my finest hour, either. But you'll be happy to hear that she's found excellent living accommodations. And…"

"And?" he prompted.

"And I'm sure she's a lovely person," she muttered through clenched teeth.

His whole body relaxed when he smiled. "That's quite a turnaround."

"Yeah, well, I'm starting fresh." She glanced down at her gown. "I'll be incinerating this on my patio later, along with the veil and all the drafts of the pre-nup. A ceremonial bridal bonfire. I might even make s'mores."

"Sounds fun."

"You know it. So if you have any wedding parapher-nalia you'd like to unload, you can pass it along now. Think of it as cleansing."

"Cleansing," he repeated.

"Closure. Whatever. I'm not a psychologist. All I know is, I don't want to think about this wedding any-more. Ever. So here we go." She threw out her arms and offered up her ensemble for inspection. "I'm in my dress, you got your watch, *voilà*. Closure."

"This is a watch?" He opened the lid of the box to re-veal the antique Swiss timepiece she'd bought from an es-tate jeweler. At the time, she'd imagined him passing it down to their future child.

"I was going to give it to you after we got married, but that's never going to happen and you deserve to have it. Consider it a war medal." She closed her eyes and took a slow, measured breath. "Closure."

He waited for her to open her eyes, then asked, "Feel better?"

"A little bit." She picked up her purse. "Anyway, I should be on my way. You know, places to go, lighter fluid to buy . . ."

"I'm surprised the home-owners' association allows bonfires."

"Oh, they don't. But I'll be putting the town house on the market next month, so let them cite me to their hearts' content."

"You're moving?"

"That's phase two of the cleansing process. Plus, I'm not impressed with the way the neighbors have been treating Ellie."

"You're serious about starting over."

"Absolutely. It's way past time."

He stared at her in silence for a long moment, but all he said was, "Have a s'more for me."

"I'll do that." Her whole body felt lighter as she started to walk away, as if the silk gown had evaporated into thin air.

Ellie

*H*ow do I look?" Alex twirled out of Ellie's master bath-room wearing a slinky, low-cut gold evening gown.

Ellie rocked back on her heels and whistled. "Very fashion-forward."

"Are you sure?" Alex frowned down at the décolletage swelling over the gown's neckline. "I don't look like a . . . I mean, it's not over the top?"

"I don't *do* over the top." Jen, clad in a brilliantly cut black ball gown, followed Alex out of the bathroom. "And neither does Zac Posen."

Alex looked horrified. "This is Zac Posen? *Real* Zac Posen? On my body? Right now?"

Jen nodded.

"You can't lend me this! What if I accidentally rip it? I gotta tell you, I'm not sure the bodice is going to hold."

Jen shrugged. "I'll take it to a tailor."

"Well, what if I accidentally spill wine on it?"

Jen peered into the mirror above Ellie's dresser and touched up her mascara. "I'll take it to the dry cleaner."

"But what if... what if something happens? Things happen, you know."

"If something happens, something happens," Jen said. "I've worn that dress a grand total of twice. If you don't wear it, it'll just hang in my closet, collecting dust. Oh, and I almost forgot." She reached into the cosmetics case she'd toted over from her house and extracted out a gray leather jewelry box. "I brought you these to wear with it."

Alex opened the box with trepidation and pulled out a string of large, lustrous chocolate-colored pearls. "They're gorgeous. And they probably cost even more than this dress. No way am I wearing this."

"Oh, wear it," Ellie urged. "And look, I have shoes that go perfectly." She produced a pair of dainty sandals from her closet. "Can you fit into a seven and a half?"

Alex stopped protesting and just looked at Jen and Ellie for a moment. "God, it must be nice to be rich."

"I'm not rich," Ellie reminded her.

"You will be after tonight." Alex grinned, and a glimmer of her usual moxie resurfaced. "You're just a few hours away from those computer files you need."

Ellie wasn't so sure, and her doubt must have shown on her face, because Alex tossed her head and said, "All Jen has to do is get me into the cocktail reception and point out that cheating dog and I'll work my magic. Yes, girls, I really am *that* good."

"But he's not going to bring his laptop to a black-tie event," Ellie pointed out.

"No kidding." Alex joined Jen at the mirror and fastened the pearls around her throat. "That's why I'll be going home with him at the end of the night."

Jen's eyebrows shot up.

"You're going to sleep with him to get the files?" Ellie couldn't hide her horror. "Alex, I can't let you—"

"No! Ew!" Alex sounded even more horrified than Ellie. "I'm a stripper, not a hooker!"

"Well, then, how—"

"Who needs sex when you've got booze?" Alex said. "I make a mean gin and tonic, and I do mean *mean*. I add a few secret ingredients to give it a little extra oomph."

"Don't add too many," Jen said. "The last thing we need is a body to hide."

"Relax, I know exactly what I'm doing." Alex pouted into the mirror. "His liver will bounce back. Eventually. But don't be surprised if he looks a little jaundiced at your next arbitration meeting."

"Well, you can flirt with him at the ball and you can ply him with drink 'til the sun comes up, but you'll never pry him out of the clutches of Vixen_MD," Ellie said gloomily.

"Have you met me? That Ivory Tower tramp doesn't have a chance. See you in the morning, babycakes. Don't wait up." She waggled her fingers in Ellie's direction and swept out of the bedroom like a postmodern Scarlett O'Hara.

Ellie looked at Jen. "This may have been a mistake."

Jen laughed. "I guess we'll find out tomorrow. Aren't you excited? Revenge will be sweet."

"I don't want revenge, I just want my life to go back to the way it was two months ago." Ellie started collecting the perfume bottles and bobby pins scattered across the countertop. "And if I can't have my old life back, I just want to make sure my future is secure enough to support Hannah through adulthood. Jeez, listen to me, talking about security. You'd think I would have figured out by now that there's no such thing."

"Hey, you do what you have to do to protect yourself. And if that means sending an exotic dancer out on the battlefield, then so be it."

"You know, if he would just play fair and honor the terms of the pre-nup ..." Ellie scowled. "It's *his* fault that I have to resort to strippers and skullduggery."

"Absolutely," Jen agreed. "He drove you to this, and now he and his liver must pay the price."

"Hey!" Alex called from the foyer. "Tick tock. Are we going or what?"

"Coming," Jen called back and started for the door.

"I want a full report," Ellie told her.

"But of course. I'll call you tomorrow morning and dish."

"Tomorrow? Can't you just come back over here after you drop her off?"

Jen coughed. "I have a meeting."

"Tonight?" Ellie frowned. "Who schedules a business meeting for eight P.M. on a Saturday?"

"Well." Jen lowered her eyes. "It's not exactly a business meeting."

"A *date?*"

Jen didn't confirm or deny this.

"You and Eric are trying to work things out? That's so great! See, I told you ..." Ellie trailed off when she realized that her optimism was entirely one-sided. "You're not meeting Eric tonight?"

"I would, if he'd return any of my phone calls!"

"But then, who——?" Ellie sucked in her breath as the obvious answer clicked into place. "Oh."

"Don't say 'oh' like that! It's a perfectly innocent dinner between old friends. Nothing's going on." Jen fiddled with her bracelet. "Not yet, anyway."

"I thought you said you were over Patrick," Ellie said gently.

"I did. I am! Do I look like I'm happy about all this?" Jen flung out her arms. "But he keeps showing up, insisting he has to see me. He sends me flowers, he calls me, he won't take no for an answer."

"I've dated a few like that." Alex didn't even bother to pretend she hadn't been eavesdropping. "The question you have to ask yourself is, when you finally say yes, will he still be interested or will he get bored?"

"At least he's interested now." Jen's full, layered skirt rustled as she paced the foyer. "My husband . . ." Her face crumpled. "I just can't take any more rejection."

Alex considered this for a moment. "Well, how many times did you make *him* take no for an answer?"

Ellie half expected Jen to pull a Mara and devolve into fisticuffs, but Jen just sighed and shrugged. "Once too many times, I guess. Now come on, let's go. Even if it's too late to salvage my marriage, we still have a chance to salvage Ellie's divorce."

Jen | *Chapter* 25

"There he is." Jen nudged Alex and pointed across the bar toward Michael, who was knocking back a whiskey on the rocks and ignoring a jovial older man's attempts to strike up a conversation.

"Cute." Alex gave him a brisk once-over and nodded. "Very cute. I can see why a girl like Ellie would fall for him. Look at that jawline."

"A girl like Ellie?" Jen repeated.

"They must have been like Ken and Barbie in their dream house. Let me guess: They hosted a lot of barbecues?"

"Well, yeah, actually. How'd you guess?"

"I told you: I'm just that good." Alex was still sizing up her mark. "Is it me, or is Ken looking a little rough around the edges? I mean, I know you people do these swanky shindigs all the time, but he didn't even bother to shave?"

Jen took another look and realized that Alex was right. Michael's classic chiseled jaw was dotted with dark patches of stubble, and his eyes were bloodshot and watery.

"Does he have a drinking problem?" Alex asked.

"No," Jen said. "At least, he didn't when he was with Ellie."

"Or maybe she just never told you about it."

Jen shook her head. "Trust me, those two had the perfect marriage. Well, you know, except for all the cheating and the lying."

Alex gave her a crooked little half-smile. "You wouldn't believe how many perfect husbands I've had proposition me during lap dances."

The old man gave up trying to talk to Michael and walked away from the bar. Jen now had a better view of the crowd across the ballroom, and what she saw nearly made her drop her evening bag. "Oh my God."

Alex crunched an ice cube from her glass of club soda. "What?"

"I know why Michael looks like death warmed over. Look." Jen jerked her chin in the direction of a statuesque brunette laughing up at a bronzed, dimpled hottie who looked about twenty-five.

"Now *that* guy looks like Ken," Alex decreed. "For real. Same hair, same face, same everything. I hope for her sake he's anatomically correct."

"That's her!" Jen whispered. "Vixen_MD!"

Alex stared blankly back at her.

"The woman Michael left Ellie for!"

"Well then, why is she draped all over Monsieur Beefcake over there?"

"I have no clue." Jen glanced back at Michael. "She

must have broken up with him. The nurse at the E.R. said she had a habit of seducing married men and then dropping them flat."

"The nurse at the...?" Alex held up her palm. "Forget it, I don't want to know."

"I have to tell Ellie." Jen yanked open her sequined evening bag and rummaged for her phone.

"You do that." Alex flexed her hands and rolled her head like an athlete warming up. "I'm going in. He's down, he's vulnerable...I almost feel sorry for him. Almost."

"Does this bring back memories or what?"

Jen slid into the narrow, beer-sticky booth across from Patrick. The wooden benches and tabletops at Jasper J's Bar and Grill in Tempe were scarred with carved initials, fraternity letters, and cryptic messages. The crowd tonight was loud and boisterous, and the music pounding out of the speakers over the bar was almost drowned out by raucous laughter and conversation.

Jen tried to ignore all the emotions that came flooding back as she glanced around the college watering hole where she and Patrick had spent countless evenings playing pool, dancing to the jukebox, and making out. Even the smell of this place—that classic college-bar combo of cheap booze, sweat, and liberally applied drugstore cologne—seemed instantly friendly and familiar.

She took a tiny sip from the frothy mug of beer Patrick had waiting for her and sighed. "Wow. I feel so... old. And so overdressed." After leaving Alex at the charity ball, she'd run home to change out of her ball gown and into a casual denim skirt, but her makeup and hair were still styled to perfection.

"You look great," Patrick assured her.

"Yeah, but I feel like I should be back in my old ripped jeans and a Gin Blossoms T-shirt." She laughed. "Now I *really* feel old. Do you think any of these whippersnappers have even heard of the Gin Blossoms?"

"Probably not." He grinned. "Gin Blossoms, De La Soul, Soul Coughing... we're dinosaurs."

"With excellent taste in music."

He watched her face carefully. "What are you thinking about?"

"Oh, nothing. Remember when my biggest tragedy in life was getting a C on my philosophy midterm?"

"How could I forget? Mara and Ellie had to put you on round-the-clock suicide watch."

"Philosophy was never my strong suit." She smiled wryly. "Give me facts and numbers in black and white and I can work miracles, but when it comes to the big questions in life..."

They lapsed into silence until the server came to check if they needed another round. "We're fine," Patrick told him.

"Fine," Jen echoed.

Patrick looked across the table and regarded her with an expression she'd never seen on his face before. He seemed guarded, almost shy.

She swilled the rest of her beer with exaggerated gusto and set down the mug. "What's going on? You look so... I don't know, intense."

He caught and held her gaze. "It's great to be here with you again."

Jen didn't reply, but she didn't look away, either.

"I picked this place for a reason," he continued. "I wanted you to remember how it used to be with us."

Like I could ever forget. But all she said was, "Patrick, that was years ago. I'm married now. Well, I *was* married. Well, I still am until——"

"About that." He reached across the table. "Whatever you have going on—or not going on—with Eric, I have to tell you——"

She shifted in her seat and snatched her hands away. "Don't say it."

"You don't know what I'm going to say."

She was terrified to tip the balance in this precarious state of limbo they'd created. "We don't need to have this conversation right now."

"Yes, we do." He looked even more determined. "I don't have many regrets in life, but letting you get away was one of them." He paused. "I hope that doesn't ruin dinner."

She opened her mouth, but before she could put together a coherent response, he charged ahead with, "I know it's too early, you're not ready, you're still wondering what happened with you and Eric."

"Yes," she said. "Yes to all of the above."

"But we were great together and we still could be."

There it was, out in the open, right next to the beer mugs and water-spotted silverware. A straightforward statement in black and white. No philosophical nuancing necessary.

She let the pulsing beat of the background music fill the silence for a minute, then asked, "Why couldn't you have had this revelation before you left me and went trekking off to a whole other continent?"

He rubbed his forehead. "I was an idiot. I admit it. But out of everyone I've ever met, everywhere I've traveled...you're it, Jen. You're the perfect woman."

"I'm not perfect," she said. "Not by a long shot."

"You're perfect for me," he insisted. "You know what you want. You know who you are. That's why we fit; you don't need anyone."

"Knowing who I am and what I want doesn't mean I don't need anyone."

"You know what I mean."

"I do." She rolled her empty glass between her palms. "And I used to think that I could love you enough for both of us."

"You did. I'm finally figuring that out."

"No. You're wrong. Love doesn't work that way. It has to be equal. I'm finally figuring *that* out."

His confidence had returned; he looked expectant. "So...?"

"So I have to go." This time she was the one who reached out. She gave his hand a quick, tight squeeze, than let go. "But thanks for the memories."

Ellie

Chapter 26

"Mommy. Mommy! I *said*, do you want some more tea?" Hannah's exasperated voice pierced through the fog of worry and wild speculation that had engulfed Ellie all morning.

"Hmm?" Ellie forced her attention back to the impromptu tea party Hannah was hosting on the living room floor with assorted dolls and stuffed animals. "Why, yes, I'd love another cup."

"You're not paying attention," Hannah accused. For a tiny blond pixie in lavender pajamas and a tinfoil tiara, she looked quite formidable. "Stop looking out the window."

"I'm sorry, honey, I thought I heard a car in the driveway."

Hannah dropped her blue flowered teapot onto the carpet and peered out the window. "Is Daddy coming over?"

"No, not today."

"Is Gramma?"

"No. But Alex is coming back, and—"

Hannah's lower lip jutted out. "Don't like Alex."

"Yes, you do! She made orange milk for you, re-member?"

"I don't want anyone else to live here but you and me and Daddy." Hannah sucked on the tip of her index fin-ger, a habit from infancy that Ellie thought she had given up months ago. "I want Daddy."

"I know you do, sweetie." Ellie gave up on trying to hug her daughter and let Hannah scowl and stomp her feet. "But he doesn't live here with us anymore, remem-ber? We talked about this. You're still going to see him lots and lots, and you're still going to see Gramma and Grandpa, and all of us love you so much."

"I hate you!" Hannah punted her teapot into the head of a bedraggled stuffed panda. "And I hate Alex, too."

Eight-thirty A.M., and Ellie was ready to trade in her cup of imaginary chamomile for a tall, icy Long Island Iced Tea. She did her best to calm Hannah down and was reading *A Bargain for Frances* aloud for the fifth time in a row when finally, *finally*, she heard a car engine outside.

Hannah raced back to the window. "Why's Alex in a taxi? I hate her."

"I heard you the first time." Ellie opened the door. Alex sashayed in with her gown wrinkled, her eyeliner smeared, and her hands clutching a black laptop com-puter and a large paper bag.

Ellie gasped. "Is that . . . ?"

"It is."

"Oh my God. Oh my God." Ellie wiped her suddenly damp palms on her jeans. "So what should we do now?"

"Now?" Alex placed the computer on the coffee table

in the sitting room and cracked her knuckles in gleeful anticipation. "Now we copy the hard drive and nail this S.O.B. to the wall."

Ellie glanced sidelong at Hannah. "Little pitchers have big ears."

Alex rolled her eyes. "Give me a break. Do you really think little pitchers know what S.O.B. stands for?"

Hannah sidled up to Ellie and tugged at her jeans. "Mommy, what does S.O.B. mean?"

Ellie patted her daughter on the back. "Go to your room and start getting dressed, sweetie. I'll come help you in a few minutes."

Hannah dawdled for a moment, until Ellie followed up with a stern "Right now, please."

When she heard the door to Hannah's room close, Ellie turned to Alex, who shrugged and said, "Listen, I can either set a good example or I can get stuff done. Take your pick."

Ellie ran her hand along the top of the laptop. "So I guess I should call my attorney now."

Alex snatched the computer away and hugged it to her chest, crinkling the bodice of the gold gown. "Are you crazy or just stupid?"

"Well, she needs the information on there, and—"

"And what are you going to say when she asks how you convinced him to hand it over?"

Ellie frowned. "Oh."

"Keep the lawyers out of this. Words to live by."

"But how are we supposed to find all the information by ourselves? We don't even know what we're looking for."

"Luckily, that's not our problem." Alex's crafty grin reappeared. "I just happen to have a . . . *connection* that can take care of all that."

Ellie raised one eyebrow. "What kind of connection?"

"One of my regulars from the Black Diamond. Nice guy, hopelessly nerdy. But smart. Very smart. He does a lot of high-tech work."

"Why is this sounding shadier by the second?"

"Trust me, all we need to do is turn on this computer, copy the hard drive, and give this guy a call. He'll take it from there."

"Are you sure? Mara says we'll need a forensic accountant to find all the files. Michael's very sneaky."

Alex smirked. "My guy hacked half a dozen casinos. I think he can handle a few personal firewalls."

"But if we're not going to hire a forensic accountant, and we're not going to tell the lawyers, how exactly are we going to convince Michael to break the terms of the pre-nup?"

"It's called blackmail, and it's next on my list of things to do after we finish up here."

Ellie covered both ears. "I'm not hearing this."

"Fine by me. Now start 'er up and let's see what we got." Alex flipped open the laptop and pressed the power key. The screen lit up and a long, thin box materialized in the center of the screen with a blinking cursor and a prompt that read: *Please enter password.*

"Okay." Alex positioned her fingers over the keyboard. "Hit me."

Ellie "Uh . . ."

Alex clicked her tongue. "I'm waiting."

Ellie fiddled with the cuff of her sweater. "Can't your hacker in Vegas figure out the password?"

"He doesn't have ESP!" Alex sat back in disgust. "I can't believe you don't know your own husband's password."

"I didn't know lots of things about him! Computer passwords don't even crack the top ten."

"Well, you lived with the man for like ten years. Take a guess!"

"Try his birthday." She recited the numerals corresponding to the day, month, and year.

Alex typed this in. "Nope."

"How about 'Hannah'?"

"No dice."

"Um..." Ellie racked her brain. "'Rufus'? That was his childhood dog."

"Uh-uh."

Ellie concentrated on the blinking cursor. "Let me think..." She was startled when she heard Hannah's voice behind her.

"What are you doing, Mommy?"

"I thought I asked you to go get dressed," Ellie said.

"I did." Hannah rounded the corner wearing ballet slippers, a pink tutu, a green bathing suit, and a threadbare white T-shirt covered with cartoon cats that Michael's parents had brought back from a trip to Greece. "Whatcha doing? Is that Daddy's computer?"

"Well." Ellie looked to Alex for assistance. "Yes."

Hannah clapped her chubby little hands. "I wanna play the ABC game."

Ellie struggled to put all her panic and guilt on hold. "What ABC game?"

"The one where you find the ABCs in the jungle. Daddy put it on there for me. Can I play?"

"Maybe a little later. Right now, Mommy and Alex are—"

"But *whyyy*?" Hannah whined. "I wanna play *now!*"

"That's enough," Ellie said. "Unless you'd like a time-out."

"Sorry, kiddo," Alex told Hannah. "Anyway, we can't even get into the main menu, so unless you happen to have Daddy's password..."

"Moodle." Hannah looked expectantly up at Ellie. "Now can I play?"

"What's Moodle?" Alex asked.

"The puppy that lives in my closet."

"Imaginary," Ellie explained. "Because her cruel, highly allergic mother won't let her get a real dog."

"Moodle starts with *M.*" Hannah helpfully pointed out the letter on the keyboard.

"Try Moodle," Ellie said, and Alex typed it in.

"Bingo." Alex nodded. "We're in. Good work, Hannah."

Adrenaline surged through Ellie's veins. She was going to *win*.

"Can I play now?" Hannah asked hopefully. "Find the ABC's?"

"In a little while." Ellie shepherded Hannah back toward the bedrooms. "First Alex and Mommy are going to find numbers."

Forty minutes later, Alex finished copying Michael's hard drive and was preparing to send off the information to her contact in Las Vegas. "All right. Phase one of Operation: Pre-Nup Payback is now complete. Now I'll get this computer back and have a little chat with him before he wakes up and calls the cops."

"Please hurry." Ellie blotted a thin sheen of sweat off her face. "We could be arrested for this."

"But we're not gonna be." Alex twisted her arms back and reached for the zipper on her gown. "I better change." The dress slithered off her lean, tanned body and pooled on the floor in a shiny gold heap.

"What are you doing?" Ellie shrieked. "My daughter is in the next room!"

"Little pitchers have big eyes, too?" Alex sauntered toward the guest room in high heels and minuscule ivory underpants. "Relax, I'll be out of your hair soon. I'll find my own place and walk around naked all day. Ah, sweet freedom!"

"No, it's okay." Ellie was instantly contrite. "You're more than welcome to stay. As long as you want. Well, until we have to move to a house with a much smaller mortgage."

Alex stopped halfway down the hall, turned, and faced Ellie. "Do you really mean that? I can stay?"

"Of course."

"That's darn decent of you."

Ellie knew they should bask in this moment of sisterly strength, but she couldn't tear her gaze away from

Alex's huge, pert, perfect breasts. They were a marvel of medical engineering. "It's the least I can do. And if there's anything else I can ever do to repay you, please let me know."

"I'm so glad you said that, because actually, I need to borrow an outfit. Something classy. Like a twinset-and-pearls-type deal. I have a lunch date after I finish putting the fear of God, your lawyer, and the IRS into Michael."

Ellie rummaged through the contents of her closet and handed Alex a conservative petal pink cardigan and knee-length gray skirt. "Will this work? It's from my pre-baby days. I keep hoping I'll fit into it again someday."

"Perfect." Alex wriggled into the sweater sans bra, which somewhat detracted from the ladies-who-lunch effect.

"Who are you meeting?" Ellie asked. "Anyone I know?"

"Yeah, as a matter of fact." Alex had one foot on the front step and the door halfway closed behind her before she finished answering Ellie's question. "Josh."

Jen   *Chapter* 27

"Holy charred rubble, Batman." Jen surveyed the black-ened debris strewn across Mara's flagstone patio. "You weren't kidding around with that bridal bonfire."

"I may have gone a little overboard with the lighter fluid." Mara approached from the kitchen with two cups of coffee and a foil-wrapped packet of toaster pastries. Since Ellie had her hands full with houseguests and legal strategy sessions, Jen and Mara had decided to forgo their usual Monday morning walk in favor of a quick breakfast powwow before work. "Barbecueing's not really my forte. I'm more of a peruse-the-steakhouse-menu-and-point kind of girl."

"You scorched the stonework." Jen indicated the dark streaks marring the paving slabs that bordered the edge of the golf course. "Is that going to hurt your resale value?"

"Probably. But it was worth it. Pop-Tart?"

Jen made a face at the very thought of all that white flour and refined sugar. "I haven't seen you so Zen since you first got engaged. Did you finally start taking that yoga class we talked about?"

"No, I just incinerated everything that reminds me of the ex." Mara handed Jen one of the coffee mugs. "Dramatic results in a tenth of the time. And no sweating. Speaking of exes, how was your dream date with Patrick?"

"It wasn't dreamy at all. More like a wake-up call," Jen said. "He took me to Jasper J's."

Mara brightened at the mention of their old college hangout. "Jasper J's is still there? Hey, are our names still carved in that ceiling beam over the jukebox? Is that crazy bartender with the Fu Manchu and the grizzly bear tattoo still working there?"

Jen sipped her coffee and watched as the golf course sprinklers came on, creating hundreds of tiny glittering prisms in the rising sun. "Yeah, it was just like old times. But I don't fit in there anymore. And I definitely don't fit with Patrick."

"You're not attracted to him at all? Drool-inducing man beauty leaves you cold?"

Jen lifted one shoulder and tried to explain. "I'm still attracted to him, but more on an abstract level. Like, I *should* be turned on, but I'm not."

Mara bit into her Pop-Tart. "Has anyone ever told you that you're impossible to please?"

"I believe the man I married might have mentioned something along those lines."

"Eric is one tough customer," Mara agreed. "Asking you to do nothing——"

"Nothing." Jen tightened both hands around the warm mug. "That doesn't even make sense! How am I supposed to do nothing? He wants me to sit motionless in a dark room?"

"I know what will make you feel better." Mara nodded out at the ashes. "May I recommend a white gown and a Zippo?"

"I'll stick to yoga, thanks." Jen pushed up the sleeves of her black jersey shirtdress. "All right, it's been lovely, but I better get back home. Duty calls."

"You're so disciplined," Mara marveled. "If I worked from home, I'd never change out of my pajamas."

"Yes, you would. How else would you manage to justify buying all those handbags and shoes?"

"I'd just buy swankier pj's. Which I'm going to have to do anyway, now that I can't swipe Josh's T-shirts to sleep in. What *do* they put in men's T-shirts to make them so comfortable?" Mara started packing files, notepads, and a few extra Pop-Tarts into her briefcase. "You know, you have the right idea. If I'd spent my free time working this year instead of planning a wedding, do you have any idea how many billable hours I'd have accrued by now? I'd probably be up for partner! Why should I be miserable and heartbroken when I could be rich and successful?"

"Why can't you be rich, successful, and still have a happy relationship?" Jen said.

"Life doesn't work that way. Exhibits A, B, and C: you, me, and Ellie. At least when you put time and effort into your job, you're guaranteed to get something back.

Look at everything you've done with Noda this year. You were on the Rory Reid show, for God's sake. You've arrived!"

Jen drained the remainder of her coffee. "Yes, I suppose I have. And now that I've arrived, where else am I supposed to go?"

"What are you talking about?"

"I'm talking about the future. I think I'm burned out."

Mara shook her head. "You can't be burned out. You're my new role model."

"Oh, well, in that case…" Jen clasped the empty coffee cup to her heart and gushed, "I love my life. I love having no free time and hardly any friends. I love the fact that I haven't had a vacation in over five years."

"That's more like it."

Outside, they heard the squealing of tires, then a series of loud, staccato horn honks.

"Doesn't the HOA have rules against noise pollution before breakfast?" Mara groused. "I can't believe that I get harassed for having a tiny little bonfire on my own property but the overprivileged teenage hooligans are allowed to roam the neighborhood, wreaking havoc in their Escalades."

Jen started to laugh. "You do realize that you're dangerously close to adopting a dozen cats and standing on the front porch with a broom, screeching, 'Get off my lawn!'"

"I look forward to it."

Then a voice started shouting. A loud, insistent, male voice.

"That's it." Mara picked up the phone. "I'm calling the gate guard."

"Hang on," Jen said. They both lapsed into silence. "I think he's saying your name."

"Yeah, that's real likely."

"No, really! Listen." And sure enough, the voice started up again.

"Mara!" This time, it was unmistakable.

Jen and Mara raced through the town house and threw open the front door to see Josh's Toyota idling in the driveway.

He greeted Jen with a friendly wave and Mara with a curt "Get in."

Before either woman could recover their composure enough to ask questions, Jen's cell phone started ringing.

"Go." Mara shooed Jen back down the hall. "Answer it."

"But—"

"*Go.* I need a moment."

Jen didn't recognize the area code blinking on her caller ID, but picked up anyway. "Jen Finnerty."

"Hello." The woman on the other end of the line sounded supremely smooth and self-assured. "This is Sheila Geiger. I'm a senior VP of business development with—" And then Sheila Geiger named a soft drink corporation so massive, so global and ubiquitous, that Jen sucked in her breath. She had always known she would face them sooner or later: the dark forces that had gotten her hooked on diet soda in the first place. *The evil empire.*

"We saw your segment on the Rory Reid show and

all of us here want to congratulate you on your product. Very original."

"Thank you," Jen croaked.

"Your innovation—Noda, is it?—creates a brand-new niche in the soft drink market. As you know, that's no easy feat."

"Well." Jen hesitated. "I try."

"We're interested in discussing what kind of synergy can be forged between your brand and ours," Sheila said. "We'd like to set up some meetings, maybe as early as next week."

"Synergy," Jen repeated. "But Noda is the antisoda. That's the whole point. That's the official slogan, in fact."

"And we love that! Healthy soda. It's genius."

"But, actually, it's not soda. At all. So I'm not sure how merging with a soda company could—"

"Listen, Ms. Finnerty, I'll get right to the point." The executive started to sound a tiny bit testy. "We'd like to buy Noda from you. The name, the recipe, everything."

"Oh, it's not for sale," Jen said instantly.

"We're prepared to offer a very generous buyout package. Plus stock options, consultant salary, you name it. We'd like to talk to your business partner, as well."

"My, uh . . ." Jen's throat went dry. "How did you—?"

"We did a quick check with the corporations division of Arizona's secretary of state. An Eric Kessler is listed as cofounder. Do you have his contact information?"

"I have to go." Jen hung up and glanced out the

window to see Josh's Toyota pulling away with Mara in the passenger seat. But she didn't have time to speculate about where they were going or why. She had to get to Eric before the evil empire did.

She dialed his number with shaking hands. He didn't pick up (no surprise there), so she left a voice mail: "I know you're screening but this is important. Call me back right now. Strictly business, I promise."

Thirty seconds later, her phone rang.

"Oh, thank you, thank you, thank you." She closed her eyes in a rush of relief. "Listen, Eric, I understand you're less than thrilled with me right now, but I really need to talk to you."

"I need to talk to you, too." He sounded wary and tired. "I have separation papers for you to sign."

She forgot about the evil empire for a moment. "Oh."

"So?" he prompted. "What can I do for you?"

She tried to match his clipped, businesslike tone. "Well, it's about the company."

"I don't want to talk about your company, Jen."

"It's ours, actually, not just mine. That's what we need to discuss."

"Noda is *yours*," he said emphatically. "I don't want anything to do with it. Not now, not ever."

"But because of the pre-nup—" she started.

He cut her off as soon as she said the *P* word. "Screw the pre-nup. Tell you what: I'll sell you my share of the company for a dollar."

She blinked. "You're willing to relinquish all claims?"

"Yep. Have your accountant draw up a bill of sale.

Consider it your divorce gift. Anything that happens to Noda from now on is your deal only."

She put down the phone for a moment, stung by his indifference.

"Hello?" he prompted.

She put the receiver back to her ear. "Are you sure this is what you want?"

"I'm sure." He sounded even more burned out than she was.

"Well, I'll pay back the personal loan," she promised. "Plus interest."

"I don't care about that, either."

"I insist."

"Take your time. I know you don't have that kind of capital on hand right now. Next year, ten years from now ... don't sweat it."

"Actually." She cleared her throat. "It might be a lot sooner than you think."

"Whenever. Can I come over with the papers tonight, or should I have my lawyer send them to you?"

Before she could reply, her call waiting beeped. The evil empire was nothing if not persistent. She ignored the call and kept talking to Eric. "Listen, before you make any final decisions, you should know that I just got a call about Noda from—"

"I'm hanging up now," he warned. "Can I come over tonight or not?"

"Fine." Anger at his total dismissal swept away any twinge of remorse. "You're going to get exactly what you wanted: nothing."

"What?" He seemed genuinely confused.

She didn't bother explaining. Eric was right. Noda was all hers: her time, her passion, her life. She was entitled to reap all the rewards. But not legally. Not yet.

"Come on over," she told him. "As soon as possible. I'll have some papers for you to sign, too."

Mara *Chapter* 28

*W*here are we going?" Mara asked as Josh drove out through the automated gateway of Mayfair Estates. Pale morning sunlight streamed through the windshield, which was still streaky from the weekend rainstorm.

He stopped for a red light, but kept his eyes on the road. "You'll see."

Mara studied his face, but couldn't decipher his expression. He looked...resolute. Well, that made one of them. "This doesn't involve a shredded pre-nup and a shallow grave in the desert, does it?"

He laughed. "It involves breakfast, and don't worry, I'll get you to work before your first meeting starts. I already called Julie to check your schedule."

"I'm impressed. And intrigued." She settled back against the nubby gray upholstery and tried to be patient, but patience had never been her strong suit. "So what are we having for breakfast? Are we going to that place on Seventh Street with the killer beignets?"

"Nope." He maintained his cyborg face. "We're going

someplace new. Consider it a first date. Pretend we've just met and we still need to get to know each other."

She stared at him, trying to decide if he was being sincere, then extended her right hand. "Hi, I'm Mara Stroebel. Pleased to meet you. I should warn you, you're in for some unpleasant surprises."

"Should I drop you off now, or are you going to take this seriously?"

"I'm taking it very seriously," she said. "But what happened to 'We'll never be ready?' I thought we were done."

Now he gave her his full attention. "Are you done?"

"I didn't have a choice! You were pretty clear in Vegas that you wanted out."

"I thought I did." He seemed lost in thought for a moment. "But then I had lunch with Alex. She had a lot to say about the importance of second chances."

"Since when does Alex like me?"

"She doesn't." One corner of his mouth tugged up. "I do, though."

This sudden, earnest declaration demolished what was left of her equanimity. "Well, I like you, too."

"This whole marriage thing…" Josh continued, and her heart constricted. "…is a bad idea. We're not ready. Not even close. I never should have proposed."

Instead of being offended, Mara nodded and said, "I never should have said yes."

"And the pre-nup definitely didn't help."

"Be honest, though. Our problems started way before the pre-nup."

"Hang on a sec." He slowed the car, pulled onto the

shoulder of the residential road, and gave her his full attention.

"The real problem was the night in San Diego," Mara said, watching the traffic pass. The outside world was business as usual, hectic and harried, but they were standing still. Getting ready to go into reverse, even. "San Diego ruined everything after."

"If we hadn't had problems to begin with, San Diego wouldn't have happened."

"But it did happen. And we can't change that. So now we have no trust and no future."

He reached across the console and took her hand. "Hence, the first date."

They sat in silence, holding on to each other, letting go of their old defenses and expectations.

Finally, Mara ventured, "Well, then, since we just met and all, I should tell you that I don't usually hop into cars with men I don't know and let them spirit me away to undisclosed destinations."

He put the car back in gear. "I predict that this time around, you're going to be doing a lot of things you don't usually do."

"Ooh. Sounds kinky."

Five minutes later, he parked in front of a residential building in Old Town Scottsdale. "Okay. We're here."

She looked around at the art galleries, jewelry boutiques, and salons flocking the building. "I thought you said we were having breakfast?"

"We are. Follow me."

He led her through the building's front doors, into the elevator, and up to the top floor.

Mara followed him, with growing trepidation. "Please tell me this isn't Alex's new apartment and she's going to be serving us omelets and giving us relationship counseling."

Josh ushered her down a corridor and opened a locked door to reveal a spacious, empty apartment with high ceilings, a wall of windows, and a view of the mountain range in the distance. Mara could smell the fresh paint still drying on the walls.

"After you." He stepped back to let her inside.

She took a quick inventory of the vacant bedrooms, bathrooms, and airy living area. The modern, streamlined kitchen looked sterile and bare, except for a dewy silver bucket filled with ice, a carton of orange juice, and a bottle of champagne.

"What's all this?" She crossed the living room to find a stack of flimsy paper cups and a box of Pop-Tarts tucked behind the champagne bucket.

"The question isn't 'What is this?'" Josh corrected. "The question is: 'What could this potentially be?'"

She traced a bead of moisture as it trickled down the surface of the ice bucket. "Okay, then, what could it potentially be?"

"This could be our new apartment."

She snapped to attention.

He nodded. "I put down a deposit to hold it until the end of the week. If you want to sign the lease, it's ours."

"How long is the lease?"

"Twelve months."

Her brain buzzed with *if*s and *but*s and *why*s and *wherefore*s. "But what about my town house?"

"You'd have to sell it."

"What about your apartment?"

"My lease is up at the end of the month."

"You know, the last time we talked about moving in together, the end result was less than desirable."

"That's true. But we're starting over, remember? Good thing we got all that closure."

"Good thing." And then she looked him in the eye and asked the scariest question of all. "What if things don't work out between us?"

"It's a possibility. No guarantees."

She ripped open a packet of strawberry Pop-Tarts and nibbled off a corner. "I don't make the same mistake twice."

"I'm counting on it."

He watched her and waited. She pondered and ate pastry.

Finally, she said, "I'm not exactly easy to live with."

"No kidding."

"I have some very annoying habits."

He grinned. "Me, too."

"You really want to give this another shot?"

"I do."

"I do, too." She grinned back. "Although, isn't shacking up together moving a little fast for a first date?"

"That's why we have to establish some ground rules." Josh reached into his jacket pocket and produced a pen and notepad.

"Oh yeah?" She kissed him and prepared to negotiate. "What kind of ground rules are we talking about here?"

PRE-*Pre-Nuptial Agreement*
Agreement between Mara ("Party 1") and Josh ("Party 2") as they enter into the state of blissful cohabitation. In consideration of the mutual promises in this Agreement, the parties agree to the following terms and conditions:

1. Party 2 shall not leave his beard shavings clinging to the bathroom sink every morning.
2. Party 1 shall not appropriate more than two (2) of Party 2's T-shirts—without the express and uncoerced permission of Party 2—citing grounds that "they're so much more comfortable than my pajamas."
3. Party 1 shall not leave loads of clean clothes in the dryer after such time as the dry cycle has completed, thereby impeding Party 2's laundry progress.
4. Party 2 shall not leave the tiny stickers peeled from fresh fruits on the kitchen counter, but shall instead place them directly in the trash receptacle.
5. Party 2 shall not interrogate Party 1 as to the extent and necessity of her clothes shopping excursions, and shall specifically avoid the phrase: "Do you really need *another* pair of black boots?"

6. In the event that either Party shall become ill, that Party shall wield full albeit temporary power over both the TiVo and remote control. (N.B.: Claims of illness shall not be exaggerated and/or wholly fabricated in an attempt to abuse this Agreement.)

7. Party 1 shall not subject Party 2 to the "ice cream bait-and-switch," i.e., when Party 2 asks Party 1 if she would like him to pick up ice cream at the grocery store, Party 1 shall not respond "no" but then dig through the grocery bags as soon as Party 2 returns and demand ice cream. Similarly, Party 2 shall not formulate any "psychic grocery list" and expect Party 1 to divine that Party 2 used the last coffee filter but neglected to notify her.

8. All terms and conditions of this Agreement are subject to change at any time, for any reason, except for the following Paragraph, which must be upheld regardless of any other circumstance:

9. Both parties shall kiss the other good night, good morning, and good-bye. In good faith and in perpetuity.

Jen

Chapter 29

*L*et's keep this short and sweet." Eric strode through the front door with the expression of a soldier about to go over the wall. He handed a stack of papers to Jen. "My attorney stuck Post-its everywhere you need to sign and initial. This is all just to get the ball rolling. He's going to file a petition for the dissolution of marriage next week. There's plenty more where this came from. We have to divvy up retirement accounts, health benefits, equity in the house, all that stuff."

"Oh."

"Yeah. Apparently, there's a mandatory sixty-day waiting period before anything's finalized, but the sooner we start, the sooner we'll finish, right?" Eric rubbed the bridge of his nose with his thumb and index finger. "Should be pretty cut-and-dried. I think we should just stick to the standard, no-fault party line."

Jen's head snapped up. "Well, of course. What other grounds would we have?"

Eric glanced away. "Oh, my lawyer kept yapping about 'abandonment.'"

"Excuse me?" She slapped the documents down against her leg. "I'm not the one who's out of town forty weeks a year on business. If anyone's an abandoner here, it's you!"

"*Emotional* abandonment," he clarified, looking pained. "Forget I said anything."

"For someone who wants to keep this short and sweet, you're doing a horrible job," Jen fumed. "And your lawyer sounds like a total—"

"That reminds me," Eric interrupted. "Did you hire an attorney yet?"

She balled up her fist, crinkling the papers in her hand. "No. I haven't even started looking."

"Well. Could you please get on that?"

She forced herself to take the count of five to re-group, then said, "Would you like to know why I haven't started looking yet?"

Panic flickered across his face. "Is this a trick question?"

"There's something I need to tell you. About the company."

Eric's panic was instantly replaced by irritation. "Oh, right, the bill of sale. I'll sign right now. Do you have a dollar?"

"The last time I saw you I was getting ready to go on the Rory Reid show, remember?"

"Yeah," he muttered. "You did a great job."

She paused. "You saw the interview?"

"I . . . Yeah." His shoulders hunched down even far-ther. "So what?"

"I had no idea you were watching."

"I TiVoed. Now you know." He regained his air of impatience. "You were saying?"

"Well, apparently, you weren't the only one watching because guess who came a-calling this morning? The evil empire."

His eyebrows shot up. "You're kidding. What did they want? Did you wake up with a big, bloodstained case of diet cola and a threatening note in the fridge?"

Jen wrinkled her nose. "What? No."

"Sorry. Bad *Godfather* reference."

"Okay, well, if we're talking *Godfather*, let me put it this way: They made me an offer I couldn't refuse." She waited for him to play along, but he just looked sort of stunned. "They want to buy Noda. For an obscene amount of money."

He smiled at her conspiratorially. "Right. Like you'd really sell your brainchild to the evil empire."

"That's exactly what I said." She folded the papers in her hand, creasing the documents into smaller and smaller squares. "And then I started thinking."

"About what?"

"About a vacation." She took a short, tentative step toward him. "Do you know how many times we said we should go somewhere and never did?"

"A lot." He opened his hands to indicate infinity.

She risked another tiny step. "So I was thinking, if you added up all the vacations we never took, it'd be like a year's worth of travel."

He shrugged. "Sounds about right."

She sighed and surrendered her last scrap of pride. "What if I sold my company and you quit your job?"

He shook his head and backed away from her. "Jen, come on. Be realistic. You would never sell out to the evil empire."

"But if I did..."

"But you wouldn't! We both know why they want to buy it from you. They'll tear up the formula and Noda will be dead and buried. They didn't make billions of dollars by helping people wean themselves off their soda addictions."

"Indulge me for a minute. Imagine Noda is no more," Jen insisted. "I'm idle and unemployed. You're idle and unemployed. Now what?"

"I'm not following."

"What do we do now that we're idle and unemployed and totally burned out on corporate life?"

"I don't know." He scratched his chin. "Nothing?"

She shook her head. *"Everything."*

They locked gazes.

"I have lots of new ideas. Lots of things I want to do. Travel, learn to sail, plant a garden."

The panic returned to his eyes, but now it was tempered with hope. "Why are you torturing me?"

"I'm not!"

"You are. I'm trying to get out of this with the little shred of self-respect I have left, and you"—he swallowed hard—"are torturing me."

"I'm just proposing that we put our mandatory sixty-day waiting period to good use," she said. "As long as we're still legally married, we should make the most of it."

He retreated farther and raised his forearms to ward

her off. "Take the house. Take the company. Take every last penny in our bank account. I don't care about any of it."

"I don't care about any of it, either. I just want one more chance with you."

"You. Me. Torturing."

"I did some investigating, and word on the street is that baseball season is starting up soon." She smiled. "Turns out, spring training is happening right now."

"I'm aware."

"So I hope you don't mind, but I took the liberty of going a little crazy with the credit card." She raced into her office, grabbed a pile of glossy brochures off her desk, and raced back to the foyer.

"We're going on a baseball junket. First, spring training right here and in Florida. Then, when the regular season starts, we'll hit Wrigley Field, Fenway, Dodger Stadium...wherever. And stay at five-star luxury resorts in every city, because, you know, a girl needs spa treatments and yoga. We can even check out the Hall of Fame in, uh"—she glanced down to consult her brochures—"Cooperstown, New York." She laced her hands together and tilted her face up toward his. "So what do you say? Road trip?"

"Let me get this straight," Eric said. "*You* want to spend weeks at a time watching baseball?"

"I want to spend weeks at a time with you. We have a lot of catching up to do." She winked. "Besides, the baseball junket is only the beginning."

"And we'll just stop working?" He seemed flummoxed at the prospect. "Just like that?"

"We have plenty in savings. Besides, we can always

make more money." She glanced down in a display of false modesty. "I don't mean to brag, but I'm kind of an entrepreneurial genius."

He finally started to smile back.

"Let's blow this town and see the world," she urged. "All those places we talked about." And then, her coup de grâce: "Although, considering all the torrid sex we'll be having, I'm not sure we'll have much time for sightseeing."

He groaned. "Again with the torturing?"

"Baby, you ain't seen nothing yet."

"I should probably say no."

"Hey." She licked her lips. "If you want to turn down all that baseball and torrid sex, I can't stop you."

He watched her licking her lips. "I'll give my two weeks' notice tomorrow."

"Excellent. And when we finally come back home, we'll start a new company. Together. With a support staff and an office not in our house and mandatory weekends off. We can use all the Noda profits for start-up money. Well, all of it except what I already promised I'd invest in an up-and-coming small business."

"What type of business?"

Jen started to laugh. "It's a funny story, actually..."

Ellie

Good news." Alex met Ellie at a coffee shop downtown with a mercenary glint in her eye. "I just talked to our lawyer and she's drawing up all the papers we need to file. Pretty soon, it'll be official."

"I can't believe it." Ellie stepped up to the counter and ordered two lattes. "This is all happening so fast."

"And looky here: I got business cards printed up last night."

"Very nice." Ellie shook out her shaggy new bob. "Hey, notice anything different? I went to Mara's stylist."

"You look about five years younger and eleventy billion times hipper," Alex approved.

"Thank you." Ellie accepted her change from the cashier and dropped the quarter and dimes into the tip jar. Then she turned back to Alex and said, "You know, maybe you should consider booking an appointment with Mara's stylist, too. Not that your current color isn't divine, but..."

"Spare me the Lady Tact routine." Alex twirled a lock

of her red hair between her fingers. "I know exactly how obnoxious this looks. I dyed it myself. Out of a box. Do you need your smelling salts?"

"Please. Haven't you figured out yet that I only *look* sweet and innocent? Speaking of which..." She motioned Alex closer and lowered her voice so the espresso machine nearly drowned her out. "Michael's attorney called mine today and he's had a sudden change of heart."

Alex clapped a hand to her cheek and feigned shock. "What an amazing coincidence."

Ellie shrugged out of her long camel coat and folded it over her arm. "He said he no longer wants to abide by the terms of the pre-nup. In fact, he's offering to buy me out of the house, give me the BMW outright, and fork over a very generous cash settlement. Plus he'll pay all of Hannah's tuition through college."

"It's the least he can do."

"I agree. Oh, and he said I can keep the emerald jewelry his mother gave to me when we got married." Ellie's sense of triumph ebbed for a moment. "But I declined. Every time I wore them, I'd think about Vixen_MD and the night I found out."

"Who cares about Vixen_MD?" Alex was outraged. "Do you know how much we could hock those for?"

"I'm putting them in trust for Hannah," Ellie said firmly. "Along with my engagement ring. He's still her father, and Patrice is still her grandmother, and she'll want the family heirlooms someday."

"I vote we take them all to a pawnshop right now. I saw one a couple blocks back."

"I didn't tell you the best part yet. He's completely

given up on the custody fight. Hannah's primary residence will be with me, and he'll see her on the weekends; no contest. My attorney is stunned. She says she's never seen anyone just roll over like that. This is the easiest settlement she's ever handled. She even went so far as to ask if I'd somehow brought 'undue pressure' to bear."

Alex looked a little alarmed. "And you told her . . . ?"

"I told her that his parents must have intervened for the sake of family harmony and social propriety."

"Good girl." Alex grabbed their lattes as soon as the barista finished foaming the milk. "Now, come on, we told the printers we'd be there at ten. Aren't you dying to see our ad proof?"

"Absolutely. But I'm still trying to figure out where we should be advertising. The newspaper? Local magazines?"

"We'll need a website, for sure," Alex said. "I already have my Vegas connection working on it."

"The casino hacker?"

"Yeah, but don't worry; I told him to make it look classy."

"The problem is, most of our business will be generated through word-of-mouth referrals," Ellie mused. "And the Mayfair Estates crowd is our target demographic. But I can't even set foot in the country club lobby now, thanks to Patrice and the gold-plated Gestapo. I'm blackballed forever."

"Well, then, we'll just have to get creative."

Ellie nibbled her lip. "Hmm. What if you join the country club? I could ask Jen or Mara to sponsor you. Why are you rolling your eyes?"

"You don't see a problem with that plan?" Alex shook her head.

"What? You're not a resident?"

"Do you really think they'd ever vote me in as a member? A few weeks of tweed and cashmere can't erase a decade of sequins and pasties. That's why I'm the muscle and you're the management."

Ellie gave her the side-eye. "You make it sound like we're starting an organized crime ring."

Alex smiled demurely. "Organized crime bosses don't wear twinsets and pearls, now do they?"

"We are going to stay on the right side of the law," Ellie insisted. "Always. Agreed?"

"Now that we're incorporated, I'm a Girl Scout," Alex vowed.

"Do you think I should call the day-care center and make sure Hannah's okay?" Ellie floundered under a fresh wave of doubt and ambivalence. "She didn't cry when I dropped her off this morning, but she's not used to me being gone all day."

"Enough with the mommy guilt. Let's go build our empire." Alex nudged her toward the exit. "Hannah will be fine. She needs to get out and socialize. And *I* need a new haircut. And an apartment. And a car. So let's hustle."

"Okay, okay." Ellie left her phone in her handbag and let Alex lead her outside. "Just let me put my coat on."

The wind picked up, blowing Ellie's hair into her face, so she turned her head to the side and glimpsed a woman in a huge, floppy straw hat peering around the corner of the building. The hat's brim flapped in the breeze, and Ellie was shocked to recognize the pale face beneath.

"Caroline!" It was out of her mouth before she could stop herself.

Caroline Surbaugh took one look at Ellie and lunged back around the corner.

"Who was that?" Alex asked.

"That was the Grand Poo-bah of Mayfair Estates."

"Why is she lurking around downtown Phoenix on a Tuesday morning wearing a ratty old granny hat?"

"I have no idea."

Caroline, apparently resigned to the fact that she'd been made, rounded the corner and approached them with a shaky smile. The seasonally inappropriate hat was the least of her fashion faux pas. She had coordinated her black trousers and driving moccasins with what appeared to be an ivory silk bed jacket. "Ellie Barton! What an unexpected surprise. I hardly recognize you with that fabulous new hairdo."

An obvious lie, but Ellie was too busy trying to ignore the pajamas in public to wonder why Caroline was suddenly acknowledging her existence. "Hello, Caroline. How are you?"

"Very well, thanks." Caroline doffed the hat and fluffed up her flattened black hair. "Lovely morning."

"Lovely," Ellie agreed.

"So!" Caroline straightened the collar of her pajama top. "What brings you to this side of town?"

"Oh, I'm just picking up some proofs from a printer. I'm hoping to start a new career now that..." Ellie cleared her throat and changed topics immediately. "This is my business partner, Alex Ankrum."

"Pleased to meet you." Alex stepped forward, but didn't smile.

"Charmed." Caroline offered her manicured hand for a limp handshake. Ellie couldn't decide who looked more repulsed: the stripper or the socialite.

The conversation dried up after that, but Ellie couldn't leave Caroline alone in an obvious state of distress without at least offering assistance. "Can we drop you off somewhere?"

"No, no, I'm fine." Caroline glanced over Ellie's shoulder and started cursing. "Damn! I've lost him!"

Ellie frowned. "Who?"

"Nobody," Caroline said quickly.

"Her husband," Alex said.

"What?" Caroline gasped. "How dare you suggest that I—"

"The guy at the pay phones." Alex jerked her thumb back over her shoulder toward a bank of phones in the center of an open plaza between office buildings. "Well, he was at the pay phones, anyway."

"Yes, and now he's gotten away, thanks to you!" Caroline glared accusingly at Alex.

Ellie glanced from the pay phones to Caroline and back again. "Am I missing something?"

Alex ignored Caroline's tantrum and took a leisurely slurp of coffee. "She thinks he's cheating."

Caroline choked. "You don't know that!"

"I recently ran into a chick who tracked her fiancé

down at a strip club and caught him in the VIP room," Alex informed her. "I know—total whackjob, right? The expression on her face was the exact one you have right now."

Caroline sputtered half-formed protests for another thirty seconds, then clutched Ellie's forearm and admitted, "I think he's meeting her during the workday. So I decided to follow him. I didn't have much time to get dressed. I've been tailing him all morning. He hasn't even gone into his office yet, and now I've lost him!"

"And he was using a pay phone?"

"Yes! Which is odd, because he always uses his cell. I didn't even know the city still had public pay phones."

Ellie nodded grimly. "Not a good sign. If he uses a pay phone, it means the call doesn't show up on his cell phone records, or even his office line records."

"How long has this been going on?" Alex asked.

Caroline's voice dropped to a hoarse whisper. "I just want to know what's going on. No divorce, no scandal. I just want to know for sure."

"Caroline, if I may..." Ellie offered up one of the freshly minted business cards:

THE OTHER WOMEN
Sympathetic, discreet infidelity investigators
"Why wonder?"

"'Why wonder?'" Caroline read aloud. She looked up at Ellie with a mixture of awe and dread. "This is your new career? Are you accepting new clients?"

Alex nodded. "Always."

"You're hired."

"Excellent," Ellie said. "I think you'll find our fees are quite reasonable."

Alex elbowed her. "Not *that* reasonable."

"Whatever it costs, it'll be worth it." Caroline nodded, recovering her customary composure. "And you'll be discreet?"

"We'll never breathe a word of it to anyone," Ellie promised. "We take confidentiality very seriously."

"In that case, I have some friends who might be interested, too. The men in my neighborhood... well, I don't have to tell *you*."

"No, you do not." Ellie supplied a dozen more cards. "Here, take a few extra."

Caroline slipped the business cards into her handbag. "This is a godsend. You're brilliant."

"Thank you. Now, just give me a phone number where I can reach you—preferably a line your husband doesn't answer—and the best time to contact you."

Caroline scribbled on the coffee shop napkin Alex provided. "If you don't mind my asking, how do you manage to find out the truth? Are you going to follow him and take photos, or what?"

"Every situation is different. We're very resourceful." Ellie glanced over at Alex. "We have what you might call a secret weapon."

"Well, use whatever means may be necessary. I give you carte blanche, so long as it's our little secret." She addressed Ellie with an air of exaggerated casualness. "And of course you'll be at my cocktail party on Saturday. And the charity auction next weekend."

Ellie blinked. "But what about...?"

"Darling, don't be silly. Everyone adores you. You'll sit at my table."

"She'll be there," Alex said.

With that settled, Caroline trilled, "Delightful to see you. Now, I really must be going. Bridge game at noon. Ta-ta."

Ellie and Alex watched Mayfair Estates' queen bee bustle away, then stared at each other in silence for a moment.

"You society chicks are messed up," Alex declared.

"No argument here." Ellie's new cell phone rang. "Oh, that's my work line. I better take this."

She answered the phone in a giddy rush of triumph. "This is The Other Women; how may I help you?"

"Sorry, I'm trying to reach Ellie Barton," said a confused male voice on the other end of the line.

"This is Ellie."

"Oh. Okay. Hi. This is Ben."

Ben? Ben who?

"I got your number from Mara Stroebel."

"Ah." Ellie tried to sleuth out the connection as politely as possible. "And you know Mara from...?"

The voice laughed, deep and dark and sexy, and Ellie felt an unexpected tingle just south of her panty line. "From the emergency room. I'm the guy with the golf clubs and bad aim."

"Oh, *that* guy." Ellie blushed at how breathy she sounded.

"Yeah, that guy." He laughed again.

She did her best to ignore the tingling and steered the

conversation toward the least provocative topic she could think of. "Mara's not pursuing legal action, is she?"

"No, I actually tracked her down. To find out if you were single."

"I guess I am." The breathiness was back. "Well, almost. I'm separated, if you want to get technical about it."

"Does that mean I technically can take you to dinner?"

"I—my divorce isn't final," she stammered. "It won't be for months."

"Okay, then, how about just coffee and dessert?"

"I have a daughter." Ellie knew she sounded curt and defensive, but she couldn't seem to stop herself. "She's three."

"Mara told me." He sounded totally unfazed.

"And I'm starting a business, and I may be enrolling in an accounting class, too." Ellie could see Alex shooting her questioning glances, so she turned her face to the wall.

"You sound like a busy woman," Ben said.

She lifted her chin. "I am."

"Then you'll need to eat to keep up your strength. We'll keep it casual."

All the lousy golfers in the world, and Mara had to get beaned in the head by this one. Ellie took a moment to decide how to answer. He sounded so funny and charming and engaging.

Just like Michael had been in the beginning.

She released the breath she'd been holding. "I appreciate the offer. Truly."

"But you're turning me down," he finished for her.

"It's not you; it's me. Honestly. I'm booked solid for the next six months."

"Fair enough." His tone remained upbeat. "Talk to you in six months." And with that, he clicked off the line and out of her life.

"Who was that?" Alex charged up behind her.

Ellie brushed an imaginary strand of hair off her coat sleeve. "No one you know."

"Bullshit." Alex laughed her loud, throaty laugh, and heads turned all the way down the block. "You should have seen your face."

"Leave me alone and let's get back to business. We have our first client! And she's going to refer us to lots more."

"Don't try to distract me. Who was on the phone?"

"Would you please focus? We have a higher mission here: to track down and bust wayward husbands."

"Yeah, but there's no reason why we can't have a little fun along the way." Alex shook out her wild red hair and challenged, "You *do* remember how to have fun, don't you?"

"Vaguely."

"So call the guy back. Right now."

"But Michael just moved out! What will the neighbors say?"

"Who cares? Do you want to go out with him?

"Yes. Maybe. I don't know anything about him!"

"Let me tell you about this newfangled thing they've invented to get to know more about people. It's called dating. Dial the phone!"

So she did. She bit her thumbnail and punched the

callback button before she lost her nerve, and Ben picked up right away.

"Has it been six months already?"

"You know, I took another look at my schedule, and I may just be able to squeeze you in." Ellie couldn't stop smiling. "Things have suddenly started to open up."

About the Author

BETH KENDRICK is the author of four
previous novels, including *Nearlyweds* and
Fashionably Late. She also writes teen fiction
as Beth Killian. She lives near Phoenix,
Arizona, with her husband, son, and an
assortment of badly behaved dogs. Visit
her website at www.bethkendrick.com.

Captivated by this novel? Enter to win more!

THE BANTAM DISCOVERY
"NEW VOICES, NEW CHOICES"
SUMMER 2008–SPRING 2009 SWEEPSTAKES

GRAND PRIZE: a year of Bantam Discovery books by great new storytellers, a Bantam Discovery Beach Towel, and a Bantam Discovery Blanket. Ten first-prize winners, too!

Enter using the coupon below, or at www.bantamdiscovery.com. See Official Rules on back of the coupon or on the website.

Don't miss these Summer 2008–Spring 2009 Bantam Discovery titles!

Garden Spells
The Wedding Officer
How to Talk to a Widower
Everything Nice

Swim to Me
Thank You for All Things
Good Luck
The Pre-Nup
The Lost Recipe for Happiness

ENTER TO WIN A YEAR OF BANTAM DISCOVERY BOOKS.
The Bantam Discovery "New Voices, New Choices" Summer 2008–Spring 2009 Sweepstakes.

Entries must be postmarked by 1/15/09 and received by 2/2/09 at Bantam Discovery "New Voices, New Choices" Summer 2008–Spring 2009 Sweepstakes, P.O. Box 5018 Bristol, CT 06011-5018. You can also enter online at www.bantamdiscovery.com. No purchase necessary.

Name: _____ Age: _____

Email: _____

Mailing Address: _____

_____

Zip/Postal Code: _____ Phone: _____

Tell us where you purchased this Bantam Discovery title: _____

BANTAM DISCOVERY "NEW VOICES, NEW CHOICES" SUMMER 2008–SPRING 2009 SWEEPSTAKES OFFICIAL RULES—NO PURCHASE NECESSARY

Open to legal residents of the U.S. (excluding Puerto Rico), who are 18 years of age or older as of 4/15/08. Sweepstakes ends 1/15/09.

TO ENTER:
Mail-in Entry:
Enter the sweepstakes by completing this coupon, or handprint your complete name and address, including zip code, and phone number (optional) on an Official Entry Form or 3" x 5" piece of paper. Mail in a hand-addressed (#10) envelope to: Bantam Discovery "New Voices, New Choices" Summer 2008–Spring 2009 Sweepstakes, P.O. Box 5018 Bristol, CT 06011-5018. Entries must be postmarked by 1/15/09 and received by 2/2/09. One entry per person.

Online Entry:
Enter online beginning at 12:00 Midnight, U.S. Eastern Time (ET), 5/10/08, through 11:59 PM, U.S. Eastern Time (ET), 1/15/09, at www.bantamdiscovery.com by following the Bantam Discovery "New Voices, New Choices" Summer 2008–Spring 2009 Sweepstakes directions and providing your complete name, address and email address. Limit one entry per person and/or email address.

Sponsor is not responsible for lost/late/misdirected entries or computer malfunctions.

WINNER SELECTION:
One (1) Grand Prize Winner and ten (10) first-prize winners will be selected in a random drawing from all eligible entries, conducted on or about 2/16/09, by the Bantam Dell Publishing Group, whose decisions are final. Odds of winning depend on the number of eligible entries received.

PRIZES:
One (1) Grand Prize—a full year of Bantam Discovery mass market paperbacks, a Bantam Discovery beach towel, and a Bantam Discovery blanket. The books are THE ADULTERY CLUB, THE YEAR OF FOG, MY BEST FRIEND'S GIRL, GARDEN SPELLS, THE WEDDING OFFICER, HOW TO TALK TO A WIDOWER, EVERYTHING NICE, SWIM TO ME, THANK YOU FOR ALL THINGS, GOOD LUCK, THE PRE-NUP, and THE LOST RECIPE FOR HAPPINESS. Approximate retail value: $85.00. Books will be sent by 3/10/09. Ten (10) First Prizes—a set of Summer 2008–Spring 2009 Bantam Discovery mass market paperbacks. The books are GARDEN SPELLS, THE WEDDING OFFICER, HOW TO TALK TO A WIDOWER, EVERYTHING NICE, SWIM TO ME, THANK YOU FOR ALL THINGS, GOOD LUCK, THE PRE-NUP, and THE LOST RECIPE FOR HAPPINESS. Retail value: $53.91. Books to be shipped by 3/10/09.

WHO CAN PARTICIPATE:
Open to legal residents of the U.S., who are 18 years of age or older as of 4/15/08. Employees of Random House, Inc., its parent, subsidiaries, affiliates, agencies and immediate families and persons living in the same household of such employees are not eligible. Void in Puerto Rico and where prohibited.

GENERAL CONDITIONS:
Taxes will be the responsibility of the Winner. Potential Grand Prize Winner may be required to execute an Affidavit/Publicity/Liability Release within 14 days of attempted notification, or prize will be forfeited and an alternate Winner selected. Non-compliance with any condition will result in disqualification and selection of an alternate Winner. Grand Prize Winner will be notified by mail on or about 2/21/09. No transfer/cash substitution of prize is permitted. Sponsor reserves the right to post, remove and/or modify this sweepstakes on the Internet at any time. Sponsor reserves the right to disqualify entries from anyone tampering with the Internet entry process. If, for any reason, the sweepstakes or any drawing is not capable of running as planned by reason of damage by computer virus, worms, bugs, tampering, unauthorized intervention, technical limitations or failures, or any other causes which, in the sole opinion of the Sponsor, could compromise, undermine or otherwise affect the Official Rules, administration, security, fairness or proper conduct of the sweepstakes, the Sponsor reserves the right and absolute discretion to modify these Official Rules and/or to cancel, terminate, modify or suspend the sweepstakes. In the event of termination or cancellation, the Winners will be selected from all eligible entries received before termination. Sponsor assumes no responsibility for any error, omission, interruption, deletion, defect, delay in operation or transmission, communications line failure, theft, destruction, or unauthorized access to the site. Sponsor is not responsible for injury or damage to any computer, other equipment, or person relating to or resulting from participation in the sweepstakes, or from downloading materials or accessing the site. Sweepstakes is subject to applicable laws and regulations. Participants release the Sponsor, its agencies, and assigns from any liability and/or loss resulting from participation in sweepstakes or acceptance or use of any prize. By their entry, participants agree to these rules. By acceptance of prize, Winners agree to rules and Sponsor's use of their name/likeness for commercial purposes without notification/compensation, except where prohibited by law.

TO OBTAIN THE NAMES OF THE WINNERS:
For the names of the Winners, available after 3/10/09, send a self-addressed, stamped envelope to be received by 2/2/09 to: Bantam Discovery "New Voices, New Choices" Summer 2008–Spring 2009 Winners, Dept. A, P.O. Box 5018, Bristol, CT 06011-5018.

Promotion Sponsor is the Bantam Dell Publishing Group, a division of Random House, Inc., 1745 Broadway, New York, NY 10019.

12-8-08

GAYLORD